unexpected forever

THE CAPE SANDS SERIES
BOOK 2

ELIZA PEAKE

CAFFEINATED WORDS PUBLISHING, LLC

UNEXPECTED FOREVER

By Eliza Peake

Copyright © 2023 Caffeinated Words Publishing, LLC

All Rights Reserved

ISBN #: 978-1-960124-13-5

Cover text: Julianne Fangmann at Heart to Cover

Cover Illustration: Christiana Theocleous at Concepts by Canea

Editing by: Happily Editing Anns

www.elizapeake.com

❀ Created with Vellum

Florida Bull Sharks
National League East
Home: Jacksonville, Florida
Spring Training: Cape Sands, Florida

ROSTER

PLAYER	NO.	POS	B	T	HT	AGE
Owen Kincaid	82	C	R	R	6'2	24
Ian Sterling	63	1B	R	R	6'3	33
Lucas Raines	15	SP	L	L	6'4	38
Steve Washington	29	RP	R	R	6'3	30
Fernando Garcia	59	2B	S	R	5'8	27
Andrew Murphy	12	3B	S	L	6'3	28
Jason Stone	36	SS	R	R	6'0	31
Orlando Hernandez	14	CF	L	L	6'0	25
Kevin Hunter	9	LF	R	R	6'1	26
Jose Munoz	45	RF	L	L	5'11	25
Liam Shea	3	Manager			6'4	42

FLORIDA BULL SHARKS FRONT OFFICE

TITLE	NAME	DEPT	
President & CEO	Derek Emerson	Executive	*Retired player
Executive Assistant, CEO	Ava Clark	Executive	
Director, Baseball Ops	Nate Gentry	Operations	*Retired player
SVP, Marketing & PR	Darcy Emerson	Marketing	
Head of Events	Charley Gentry	Marketing	
Head Physical Therapist	Evelyn Taylor	Medical Staff	

author note

Thank you so much for taking a chance on Unexpected Forever. It's one of my favorite stories so far, but there is some off page content that may be triggering for some.

The following topics are mentioned in the book and may be considered sensitive to some: childhood neglect, death of a parent(s), and drug addiction.

charley

MY MOM always says I'm going to be late to my own funeral.

My mom is rarely wrong.

And if I'm late to the one job I have right now, my brother Aidan will make my funeral a reality.

I have one singular goal.

To get the brother of my best friend—who also happens to be Aidan's girlfriend—to her surprise birthday party I've been planning for weeks.

Her famous, hot as hell brother I might have a teeny-tiny crush on.

A man I've watched play professional baseball for the Florida Bull Sharks on TV for years and had some naughty celebrity fantasies where he is the star.

I ignore my racing pulse and quickly make my way down the hallway of the inn, stopping in front of room seven.

"Tonight, he's just Megan's brother. That's it. Not Nate freaking Gentry. I need this job. And you're on a man sabbatical anyway."

Squaring my shoulders, I rap my knuckles against the door.

When a few seconds tick by without an answer, I lean forward, listening for any sign of life beyond the thick wood.

I check the time on my phone and let out a huff. I'm on time for once. Where is this guy?

Before I can lift my hand to announce my arrival again, the door flies open.

And my jaw drops.

Damn.

Did I say Nate Gentry is hot?

Sinfully, makes-me-want-to-sell-my-soul-to-the-devil hot is more like it.

Especially in nothing but a towel riding low on his hips.

Words and my ability to speak leave my brain as I watch droplets of water cling to his dark hair and tanned skin. My throat is dry as desert sand, and those small beads of water are like a mirage.

The man is large and in charge, all muscle without an ounce of fat. His shoulders look like they could carry the weight of the world.

Black ink in some sort of diamond-like design covers half of one pec. A wide chest tapers down to abs and a sexy V that makes my mouth water.

He clears his throat and my gaze snaps to his. His brows are drawn down, his mouth a flat line.

Busted.

"Can I help you?" he asks.

His deep-voice makes me tingle, but the sharp tone in it could freeze hell over.

I swallow, trying to find words. When was the last time a guy had *me* tongue-tied? Working in a bar over the years taught me how to handle all types of guys. They don't fluster me; just ask anyone in Madison Ridge.

Then again, most guys aren't Nate "Iceman" Gentry, either.

Seriously, get a grip, Reynolds.

I mentally pull myself together and give him my best smile.

"Hey, I'm Charley Reynolds. It's nice to meet you. I'm your escort for the night." I thrust a hand out between us.

As soon as the words leave my mouth, I want the floor to open up and swallow me. His hazel eyes narrow and heat floods my face, but I don't drop my hand.

"I-I mean, I'm here to escort you to Megan's party. I'm Aidan's sister. Didn't he tell you I was coming by?"

He raises a brow and continues to study me for a moment. Warmth floods my body everywhere his gaze lands, which is from the top of my head to the tip of my open-toed heels.

There are a couple of things I notice about Nate Gentry in person that the TV doesn't pick up.

I'm a sucker for beautiful eyes, and Nate's are the most unique shade of hazel I've ever seen. Green with brown swirls and flecks of gold. They remind me of autumn leaves.

He smells amazing. Tendrils of steam fill the room behind him with a woodsy, citrus combination that makes me want to take a deep breath and lounge in it.

My outstretched arm starts to ache, bringing me back to the fact that while he might be really pretty, his reputation for being broody precedes him.

He shifts a step closer and takes my hand in his. My lizard brain is sad to see it wasn't the hand holding up the towel.

"He told me." He clears his throat. "I, uh, just wasn't expect-ing...never mind. Nice to meet you, Charley."

"Same."

Same? That's my response? Great job, Charley.

His large hand wraps around mine, still warm from his shower, completely dwarfing it. A dull buzzing starts in my ears and a current of electricity shoots up my arm.

If I wasn't so stunned, I'd probably be in a puddle at his feet.

Having women fall at his feet is a daily occurrence for him, I'm sure.

"I'm running behind, but I'll be ready in ten."

My lust-induced haze muddles my head like the steam from his bathroom. When my brain finally comes back online, I realize our handshake is now hand holding. I drop my hand and step back.

I check my phone, my gut clenching in panic to see we're cutting it close. "It's a quick walk to the winery from here, but we need to leave in ten unless you want to run. And I'm not running in these heels. Oh, and if we're late, it'll ruin the surprise for your sister."

His gaze drops to my heels, and he tilts his head for a moment, a small smile on his lips.

Wow. Just that small smile makes me lightheaded.

"Right," he says roughly. The muscles in his throat move and those hazel eyes meet mine again. "I can be ready in five."

"If that's true, you'll keep me from being murdered by Aidan."

He runs a hand through his damp hair and gives me a lopsided grin that damn near makes me swoon. "Well, we can't have that. Wanna come in?"

"Sure."

A few minutes alone with him in his suite won't hurt me, right?

I walk past him and try not to inhale too much of the sexiness radiating off him in waves. The click of the door shutting behind me makes goose bumps pop on my skin.

Being among his things feels far more intimate than it should.

"My apologies," he says, heading toward the double doors of the bedroom. "We hit some weather leaving Florida and it delayed my flight. I'll be out in a few."

"I'll be waiting."

He closes the doors between the living and bedroom area. I blow out a breath to steady my racing heart and shaky legs.

I roam around the large suite—willing my body to behave—focusing on my surroundings instead of the man in the next room.

The suite is tastefully done in walnut wood and colors of gray and black, with a pop of burgundy here and there. The midcentury modern vibe feels sleek and expensive, but with a cozy aspect to it.

Just like my cousin Emma, who owns the place with her fiancé, Shane.

I stop at the window and push the sheer curtain aside. This particular suite has the best view of all the rooms at the Gold Mountain Inn. The North Georgia mountains in the distance and the rolling hills of the acreage the inn sits on are spectacular.

Behind the inn, several yards from the main house, a beautiful white gazebo stands, looking regal with the greenery in the background.

Off to the right, piles of lumber sit, ready to be turned into a modernized barn that will hold weddings and other gatherings.

Gold Mountain Winery is on its way to being a premier resort destination in the area and I want to be a part of it.

Last week, I applied for the position of Events Manager. It's a huge leap for me, as my biggest accomplishment thus far has been the ability to carry a tray of twenty tequila shots without spilling a single drop.

But I also have a degree in hospitality management and I've been in the service industry since I was sixteen. In ten years' time, I went from being a waitress in high school to practically running the Silver Moon Cafe, the town's most popular bar.

But event planning is my dream job. Megan's party tonight is a sort of trial by fire for me, to prove I have what it takes to pull off the kind of events that will be held there.

I also want to show my family I'm capable of being more than just the baby of the family and the good-time girl. Which means it's time for me to get my shit together, go after my dreams, and use the degree I've earned.

Hence, the man sabbatical. I need to focus, and men are known to be a distraction for me.

The doors open behind me and I turn. My lips roll inward to keep from drooling.

The man standing in front of me is distraction with a capital D.

Nate Gentry is a weapon of mass panty destruction.

He walks out in a pair of charcoal-gray slacks and navy blue button-down. The sleeves are rolled up, showing off his thick wrists and muscular forearms honed by years of training.

Until this moment I didn't know I had a thing for forearms.

And whatever cologne he's wearing makes me clench my thighs.

My vibrator is going to get a workout tonight when I get home.

He looks like he stepped off the pages of a magazine. In less than ten minutes.

It took me ten times as long just to pick my dress.

He smiles when he sees me. "I'm ready. We okay on time?"

I nod. "If we leave now, we'll be right on time."

The inn is quiet right now, so we manage to make it downstairs and out the door without any fanfare.

We set off down the winding path running from the inn property to the winery where patrons can easily go back and forth. It's scenic, wide, and packed with white pebbles that crunch under our shoes. A slight breeze blows through the tree-lined path decorated with clear lights.

There's a comfortable silence between us, but I can't be quiet for long.

"So, you said you had a flight delay in Florida. Everything else go okay once you got here?"

"Yeah, everything was fine." He pauses, turning his body slightly toward me as we walk, his lips in a slight smile. "How'd you end up being my 'escort'"—he makes air quotes—"for the night?"

I kick a pebble and purse my lips. "I lost at rock, paper, scissors with Aidan."

"Sounds like a story there."

"I planned the party with him. Which worked out well until we got to one point. We couldn't agree on who should bring Megan." I put a hand on my chest. "I said I would be better so I could help her pick her clothes. He had…other ideas. Anyway, we played a round and the winner brought Megan, the loser brought you."

He chuckles and the deep timbre of it sends a shiver down my spine. "I feel so wanted."

I shrug playfully. "That's the breaks, kid."

We walk a little farther before he speaks again. "Listen, I'm sorry if I appeared rude when I first opened the door. It's a defense mechanism. If I open the door to an unfamiliar but beautiful woman, I go into defense mode."

Holy shit. Did Nate Gentry just call me beautiful?

I need a lifeline or my man sabbatical is going to go up in flames.

Much like my underwear.

And the goose bumps rising on my skin? It's just the wind. It has nothing to do with the fact a famous baseball player called this small-town girl beautiful.

"I take it this kind of thing has happened before?"

His lips pull down into a frown. "Yeah. I've lost count of how many times. I like my private life private."

"Well, you don't have to worry about me. I'm on a man sabbatical." I nod firmly, but standing next to him, I wonder who I'm trying to convince.

I speak quickly, hoping he won't bite on my man sabbatical comment.

"Anyway, I do understand the groupie thing. My brother Del ran into that situation when he was on TV regularly. It's better now that he isn't on so often, and most of the time if tourists see him in town, they're cool. But when he first came home, the local deputies had to rescue him and his girlfriend from a line of crazy women."

"It's scary as hell sometimes." He sighs. "And the biggest reason why I've stayed away from visiting Megan for so long. I didn't want to get her wrapped up in all the paparazzi mess."

I smile and punch him lightly in the bicep, which is warm

under his shirt and hard as a rock. "Aw, aren't you the protective big brother?"

He looks down at the ground and rubs a hand over his chin, but a slight smile peeks out. "Maybe."

"Well, from what Megan has told me, you're an amazing brother. Hell, you even bought a bar at the beach for her to run."

"Yeah, until *your* brother came in and swept her off her feet and now she lives here." One corner of his mouth lifts in a half smile.

I laugh. "Yeah, he did. What did you end up doing with the bar?"

"I still own it. Moving forward with renovations. I'll just have to find someone else to run it."

I start to comment but the lights of the winery catch my eye. "We're here. Let's head around back so we won't be seen."

A stepping-stone path leads to the back door. Once inside, we weave around huge stainless steel tanks and other winemaking equipment, making our way up to the main floor.

Inside, the winery is all understated elegance with dark woods, white walls, and wrought iron. The one touch of opulence is the beige marble floors with gray-and-gold veining.

Usually, it's full of people milling around, wine in hand, or standing at the various tasting stations around the room.

But tonight, it's closed to the public, making it dark and quiet, and our footsteps echo on the marble floor.

I'm keenly aware of the man walking beside me. Every so often, I catch a whiff of his cologne, the scent wrapping around me like a hug.

Focus on the task at hand, Charley. In a few minutes, you'll go your separate ways at the party and that will be it.

We follow the signs for the Wine and Vine ballroom, and the murmur of voices grows louder as we approach the room. I slide a glance to him.

"You ready? My family and the people in this town can be a lot, but I'll keep us moving."

Nate stretches his neck from side to side and bounces on his toes like a boxer, making a show of getting amped up. "Born ready."

I can't help but smile. Nate Gentry has a little funny side to him.

Once we walk in, it's just as I figured it would be with my siblings and mother welcoming him with open arms and other guests wanting to shake his hand.

Nate takes it all in stride, smiling politely but continuing to move through the crowd. It's clear he's had practice.

I push through the swinging door, and Nate follows me into the kitchen off the main room. "Thank God, we got here before Aidan and Megan." I wipe fake sweat off my brow. "Okay, my instructions are to keep you in here until Aidan gives me the signal. Then you can come out." I rub my hands together with a grin. "I cannot wait to see her face when she sees you."

Nate gives me a full smile and this time I swear my heart stops. I can see right away this particular smile is one he reserves for his sister.

Breathless from a smile? What is wrong with me?

I lean against the open swinging door so I can see when Aidan and Megan come in. But from the corner of my eye, I study the man roaming the commercial kitchen area.

With those broad shoulders, it's easy to see him as a leader in everything he does. As a catcher, even his position in baseball leans to being the one in charge and taking care of his guys.

"Here they come!" someone whisper shouts, drawing my attention away from Nate.

I wave him over. "They're here."

When he comes up behind me, the heat of his body makes my skin flush. I close my eyes and try my best not to sway into him.

When the group in the room yells "Surprise!" my eyes fly open and I straighten my spine.

And my resolve.

I roll up on my tiptoes, trying to get a glimpse of Aidan and

Megan, but I can't see them for the taller people in front of me. Even in my three-inch heels, I barely skim five-six. "Damn it. I can't see."

"Aidan is looking this way and nodding. Is that our sign?"

"Shit! Yes. You're up."

I follow behind him as he moves through the crowd that parts like the sea parted for Moses. I know the minute Megan sees her brother because she lets out a big squeal followed by an "Oh my God!"

"Hi, Meg-pie," Nate says as he walks faster toward her until they meet in the middle with her jumping into his strong arms. He spins her around before setting her on her feet and kissing the top of her head.

It's a familiar gesture as my three brothers have done it to me and my sisters a million times. I swallow hard against the emotions clogging my throat.

Megan rushes over to me, arms outstretched. "Is this why you couldn't come help me pick out a dress? You little traitor." She hugs me and I squeeze her hard.

"I was sworn to secrecy."

Aidan walks up beside me and drapes his arm over my shoulders. "Hey, you did good. On time and everything."

"Well, if we'd been late, it would have been my fault," Nate says, sliding his hands in the pockets of his slacks, his eyes on mine. "My flight was delayed so I cut it pretty close."

"I still can't believe you're here," Megan says, hugging her brother's side. "It's been four years too long. I've missed you."

"Why don't you guys go get some drinks and food? Catch up?" I ask, going into hostess mode.

When Megan and Nate walk away, Aidan puts an arm around my shoulders. "Thanks for helping me out, Charley. I mean it."

"You know I love Megan too, and I want her to be happy."

"Oh, you don't have to worry. She's plenty happy." Aidan winks and I smack his hard stomach with the back of my hand.

"Ugh. Stop. I don't even want to know about my brother and my best friend in that context. Gross."

He laughs and lifts a hand to ruffle my hair, but I dart away before he can mess it up. He heads toward the table where our mother sits.

I stand along the wall, watching the partygoers eat, chat, and mingle. I've waited tables and bartended for so long it's second nature for me to watch and observe what someone might need.

"You know we have wait staff tonight, right?"

I glance over to see my cousin Emma walking toward me with a smile. "Yeah, but I can't seem to help myself."

"I know what you mean." She stands beside me and gazes around the room. "Tonight, I'm here as a guest, not the owner, and I can't help but go into owner mode and make sure everyone is safe and having fun."

She turns her head and looks down at my dress. "That dress looks amazing on you."

I glance down at the curve-hugging gunmetal gray sequined cocktail dress I decided on after thirty minutes of debating. It's short, leaves part of my back bare, and is not my normal attire.

"Thanks. I've never worn it." I sigh. "Not sure why I bought it anyway. It's wasted on the men here. I just wore it to feel pretty."

That isn't totally true. There is one man that I wouldn't mind if he noticed my dress.

She moves closer and gives me a one-armed hug. "Well, you look gorgeous."

I return the hug then pull back to check out her shimmery black wrap dress. "Now, this dress you got on? I'm surprised Shane doesn't have you in some locked room trying to peel it off you."

"Oh, he tried!"

Her laugh is smooth and cultured. That's Emma. She's kind, beautiful, a badass businesswoman, and engaged to a sexy billionaire.

She's also a recovering alcoholic. Her addiction almost cost her everything, but she managed to climb out of the depths and find a new job, a new life, and a new love.

I want to be like Emma when I grow up.

She pats my shoulder. "Listen, do you have a few minutes? I know this is a party and all, but since I have you here, I'd like to talk business with you. If you're okay with that."

My stomach drops, but I stand straighter, trying to appear cool. Because that's how Emma would do it. "Of course."

I follow her through the crowd, but just before I leave the room, I glance over my shoulder to find Nate staring at me from across the room.

And in a way that tells me he's noticed my dress.

My blood runs hot through my veins and I quickly glance away. Of course, I have to be on a man sabbatical when my celebrity crush rolls into town, looking at me like he wants to devour me.

Good-time Charley would have climbed him like a tree and loved every minute of it.

But I retired her, put her away. I refuse to be the only Reynolds child in town that hasn't made something of herself.

I keep my focus on Emma's back as we leave the noisy room, moving into the quiet lobby, and I hope she can't hear my heart pounding in my chest.

Something in my gut tells me tonight is the beginning of a new adventure.

TWO

nate

THERE ARE several reasons why I shouldn't watch Charley Reynolds from across the room like she's a fucking buffet and I'm a starving man.

Not only is she my sister's best friend but she also has three brothers.

Including Aidan, who carries a gun like it's his job—because it is, being the sheriff of Madison Ridge.

She's at least a decade younger than I am, which is a little younger than the women who usually catch my eye.

Hell, we don't even live in the same place, which would normally be a plus for me. But in this case, it would only complicate things given the fact that our siblings look like they're headed for that forever kind of thing.

Not that I've been to many family functions in the past, but now that I'm retired from baseball and not traveling so much, I plan to visit Megan more often. And I'd probably see Charley.

Hello, awkward.

Lastly, I gave up one-night stands a long time ago. My selective nature means it's been a hot minute since I've had a woman under me. I'm sure that's the only reason why when I watch

Charley talk to guests, I'm thinking of those red lips leaving a ring around my cock.

Good, solid reasons why I shouldn't have watched her for the past couple of hours, enamored by her movements in a form-fitting dress leaving little to my imagination.

I want to pull one of the strings tied at the middle of her back and watch it come undone until all that's left are the fuck-me heels that make her legs look impossibly long.

With her dark wavy hair, deep blue eyes that remind me of the Atlantic Ocean, and curves deserving their own warning label, my head's fuzzy and I can't focus on anything but her.

The feeling reminds me of when I'd taken a ball to the head once.

Not only does she look like a walking wet dream, but in the few minutes I've spent with her, I find she's sassy, funny, and caring.

I don't think she realizes the little unspoken challenge she tossed my way when she said she'd drawn the short straw about having to pick me up.

I have a sneaking suspicion the fact she's on a man sabbatical only makes her that much hotter. I wanted more clarification on that odd piece of information, but she deftly moved the conversation away from that before I could ask.

What really makes me like her is the fact that when we came face to face, she didn't treat me like Nate the famous baseball player but rather Nate, Megan's brother.

I love baseball and it's a dream come true to be paid a ridiculous amount of money to play it. And I love the fans, especially the young kids who still play for the love of the game.

The fame that comes with being a player of my caliber is my least favorite part. These days, I keep my guard up, automatically assuming people will treat me differently, and I'm usually right.

Especially where women are concerned.

At this point in my life, what I don't love are the cleat chasers.

I've had hotel room keys slipped into my hands more times than I can recall.

But as I watch Charley move around the room, being the consummate party host, I must admit, if she slipped me her room key, I'd be at her door in a heartbeat.

I can't remember the last time a woman had me this worked up just by looking at her.

That's something I'm not even going to entertain. My active playing career is over, but I have a new manager career ahead of me next season, once all the negotiations are finalized.

While I avoid one-nighters as a rule, there's something about Charley that makes me want to throw gasoline on that rule and set it on fire.

And to be the guy that gives her all the orgasms coming off her man sabbatical.

My gut tells me Charley would be fun, but risky.

I lean against the bar and sip the double whiskey neat I've been nursing most of the night, pulling my gaze away from the vixen across the room. After three hours, the party is still going strong, everyone enjoying the food, music, and ambiance.

The ballroom is large and open, decorated in casual elegance. White tablecloths cover round tables that dot the room where a few people sit and talk. It's warm and inviting and the perfect atmosphere for my sister. Charley did a great job.

"Hey man, enjoying the party?" A hand claps me on the shoulder.

I turn and smile at Del Reynolds, another one of Charley's brothers. "Yeah. I was just thinking that Charley nailed it. "

Del and I met a few years back when my old team participated in a charity house renovation. The home renovation show he hosted and my team had sponsored the renovation for a family in Florida after a hurricane destroyed their century-old house. Del had been a high school baseball star who hadn't pursued it further, so we'd bonded over our love for the game.

He nods and lifts his hand toward the dance floor. "Looks like it made Megan happy."

I follow his gaze to see Megan and Aidan locked together on the dance floor. My jaw sets as my heart rate increases for a moment before I relax. Those old protective reflexes I have where my sister is concerned still flare up instinctually.

Just because I stayed away physically, doesn't mean I haven't protected Megan in other ways over the years. But now she has someone else to keep her safe.

It pinches my heart to know while we text almost every day, I'm no longer the first person she calls with any news she has.

Aidan is that person now.

But from what I know of the man so far, I couldn't have picked a better guy to take care of the only family I have left in this world.

It gives my heart peace.

I clear my throat. "Yeah. I'll have to thank Aidan later."

"How does it feel to be retired?" he asks, sipping his beer.

"Strange. My body isn't used to not eating five times a day or working out constantly. My knees are thanking me though."

The reality hits me again, but the gut punch isn't as sharp as it had been last month when the first day of spring training came around and I wasn't there.

He nods. "I get it. It took a while for me to remember there wasn't a set to get to every day. But you'll be headed back to the field soon, right? Aren't you managing?"

"Yeah, but not until next season. We're still working through contract negotiations, and the manager I'm replacing doesn't retire until the end of this upcoming season."

I swallow a sip of whiskey. It burns down to my gut, reminding me why I don't drink much. "I was sorry to hear your show came to an end."

He chuckles. "Didn't know you were a fan."

"It's fun to watch. I've learned some things from your show, which is helpful when I talk to the contractor about the bar I'm renovating."

"Well then, sounds like you're ready to come work for Reynolds Construction. Then you can do your own renovations." His mouth widens with his trademark Hollywood grin, and his blue eyes twinkle.

He has the same blue eyes as his sister, only hers captivated me the moment I saw them.

I smile. "Business must be good if you want to hire me."

He lifts a shoulder and sips his beer. "Can't complain."

"Sure you can. And you do." Charley's voice reaches me first, just before the smell of her perfume wraps around me. It's a light and flowery scent that makes me need to adjust my crotch.

That southern lilt in her voice hits my gut like the whiskey I hold in my hand. Every part of my body tightens hearing it.

And I mean every part, including the parts that have no business tightening—or hardening—around her.

She leans against the bar next to me, giving her brother one of those smirks only little sisters needling big brothers can give.

"Hey, squirt." Del lifts his bottle in greeting. "Great job on the party."

"Thank you," she says with a nod in his direction, then looks out over the party. "I'll overlook the nickname since you're paying me a compliment."

"Well, you deserve it, squ—I mean, Charley. Did it help with the job?" Del asks.

Charley bites her crimson-colored lower lip before her mouth curves into a smile so bright it rivals the sun.

"It did. Emma pulled me aside earlier. You're looking at the new Events Manager for Gold Mountain Winery and Resort. Starting in two weeks."

"I knew you could do it, sis. Didn't I tell you?" Del walks around me to give Charley a one-armed hug and a kiss on the top of her head. "Be ready to hear from your future sister-in-law. Once

I tell Addie about this, she's going to want you to arrange the wedding and all."

Charley grins up at her brother. "Bring it on, Ace."

Del nods out toward a table across the room. "And there's my bride-to-be now. I think I'll go ask her to dance and give her the good news."

I look down at Charley once Del walks away. "How about a celebratory drink?"

She glances at her watch. "Sure, why not? Everything's about to wrap up soon. One glass of champagne won't hurt."

I flag down the bartender and within a few moments, a chilled flute of champagne is in Charley's hand. Slim fingers wrap around the glass, and I have a moment of wondering what her hand would look like wrapped around my cock.

Shit, it isn't like me to think with the head below my belt first. I clear my throat and do my best to shift the rod in my pants.

"Cheers," she says, holding up her glass to mine.

"Cheers. Congratulations on your new job. I hope it's all you want and more." I clink my tumbler against her flute, and her eyes soften as they meet mine.

"Thanks. I hope so too."

We drink, her blue-eyed gaze twinkling and holding mine over the rim of her glass. She downs about half of it before licking her lips. "Hmmm, that's good. Glad I chose it."

"You chose the liquor too?"

"Well, I had help from Shane, the winery owner. The man knows his wine. But I know liquor so that part was me."

"Help me out here. Shane is your cousin Emma's fiancé and he owns the place, right?"

She smiles. "Yep. I know, there are a lot of us."

I ignore the momentary churn in my stomach.

"You did a good job. I wanted to thank you and Aidan for putting together such a great party for Megan. I would like to pay you guys back somehow."

She shakes her head. "There's no need for that, Nate."

"It's the least I could do since you guys did the hard part of organizing it."

"Don't worry about it. It was a trial run for me, and since Aidan is family, Emma and Shane gave him a good deal."

From the set of her delicate jaw and raised chin, I know I'm not going to get anywhere with convincing her otherwise. I'll find another way to make my contribution later.

I raise my hands in defeat. "Okay, have it your way."

"I usually do."

Her gaze shifts over to me and a flirty smile plays on her lips. My thumb tingles with the urge to reach out and trace her plump lower lip that's driving me crazy.

She turns toward me and sets her glass on the bar, all traces of humor gone. "I do want to thank you, though."

"For what?"

"For being so kind with all the people here. I know there for a few minutes when we first arrived, it got a little like a photo op session for you."

I shrug a shoulder. "It's not a big deal. I'm happy to do it. This was controlled chaos. And I enjoyed meeting the family that has brought so much happiness to my sister."

I grin and tap a finger against the rim of my glass before continuing. "Especially Stella. I see where you and your sisters get your looks."

Her cheeks turn a sexy, sweet shade of pink. "My mom is a beautiful woman. Modeled a bit back in her day before she met my dad." She tilts her head, a wry grin on her face. "You also met the Poker Posse."

I swirl the whiskey in my glass with a smile, thinking about the little old ladies that surrounded me earlier. "I did. They're sweet, even the grumpy one. But why are they called the Poker Posse?"

She laughs, a throaty but melodic sound. "Those sweet little old ladies are the biggest poker hustlers around."

"You're shitting me." I spy the one in a turquoise dress across the room.

There's no way.

Charley shakes her head, the tip of her finger running along the rim of her flute glass. "Nope, not shitting you, my friend. Those four women wipe the floor with anyone they come across. They go to tournaments every year, and without fail, every one of them comes back with a pocket full of money. Locals know better than to play with them unless they're in the mood to lose."

She glances out into the room and tilts her head. After a moment, laughter shakes her shoulders.

"What's so funny?" I ask.

"They came dressed in their signature colors."

I follow her stare across the room to see the other three ladies —dressed in yellow, purple, and pink—join the one in turquoise. I raise a brow. "Do I even want to know?"

She drains the rest of her champagne and sets the glass on the bar. "Nope. If you're here long enough, you'll run into them in town and see what I mean."

"Leaving me with some mystery, Charley?"

She turns her head and makes eye contact with me. Those eyes are a sucker punch to the gut. "A woman's gotta have some secrets."

"I'm sure you have plenty."

She shakes her head, a smile curving those dark-red lips. "I'll never tell."

My fingers ache with the need to tangle in her dark hair that's swept over one slender shoulder in big waves. I swallow the last of my whiskey in one gulp, a vain attempt to put out the fire she's ignited in me.

When was the last time I'd had such a reaction to a woman? The lust whipping through me is sharp.

If her brothers knew the thoughts I have running through my head as my eyes travel down her body, they'd kill me and make it look like an accident.

The upbeat song fades, and when the opening guitar chords of "Tennessee Whiskey" fill the room, the urge to have this woman in my arms overwhelms me. I set my glass down with a click on the bar and hold out a hand to her.

"Would you like to dance with me?"

She studies my hand for a moment before her eyes meet mine. They're flirty and telling me she wants to say yes. The woman scrambles my brain cells, but damn if it doesn't send a zip of excitement through me.

"Just so you know, your sisters had no problems saying yes," I add. My teasing turns the flirty look in her eyes into something I understand well.

Competition and determination.

My lips twitch when she slides her hand into mine. "Fine, I can't let my sisters have one up on me."

"Of course."

Charley trails behind me as I walk toward the dance floor with her hand in mine. When we reach an open spot, I slide one arm around her petite waist and pull her to me. The feel of her in my arms puts my body on high alert. The pounding of my heart in my ears nearly drowns out the music.

Her bare back is warm against my palm as I clasp her small hand in my larger one.

The top of her head barely reaches my shoulders even in the high heels she wears. But despite our size difference, her body molds to mine like a glove. Her scent wraps around me until I can't take a breath without smelling her shampoo or perfume or whatever the hell it is that makes me want to toss her over my shoulder and take her to my room.

To explore every inch of her for one night.

We don't talk for a few moments, just move our bodies together in time to the music. I try not to think about how well we move together.

It makes me think of other ways we'd move well together.

Fuck. It's been a hot minute since I've felt the sharp, gut-deep pull of pure, physical lust. Although, I can't remember it ever being this intense.

She tilts her head back with a smile. "You made Megan very happy tonight. She's missed you."

Lust takes a temporary backseat to the guilt squeezing my heart. "I've missed her too. I wish I had been able to visit sooner, but between the retirement PR circus, sponsorship obligations, and contract negotiations, life has been on fast forward lately."

Wow, Gentry. Since when do you talk so damn much?

"Well, you're here now and she's thrilled. Are you in town for long?"

"Not this time. But I'll be back more often, at least for a little while."

"Hmmm…she'll like that."

I glance over to where Megan and Aidan dance then lower my head until my mouth nearly brushes Charley's ear. "If the look on your brother's face is any indication, he's ready to take my sister home."

She glances over her shoulder and wrinkles her nose adorably. "Ugh. I mean, don't get me wrong. I love that Aidan finally let someone in. Megan's like another sister to me. I adore her. But"— she shakes her head hard—"I do *not* want to think about them having sex."

I lean my head back and laugh, a light feeling I haven't had in years warming me from the inside out. "I could not agree with you more."

"Does it not piss you off to see a guy hang all over her? You know, the protective brother and all?"

I continue to watch the couple while I answer. "Yes and no. Your brother is a good man."

"The best."

I glance down at her to see a spark in her eye. I smile. "It appears I'm not the only protective one."

She shrugs a bare shoulder. "It's just a fact."

"Anyway, I know he'll take care of her. Love her, make her happy, keep her safe. That's all I've ever wanted for Megan."

"There's no doubt he loves her. It's so obvious."

I look back over at the other couple. "How so?"

"It's in the way he looks at her." She pauses and lowers her gaze. "My dad used to look at my mom the same way."

There's a wistfulness tinged with sadness in her tone. I lower my head again and brush her ear with my lips, and Charley shivers in my arms.

"Cold?"

"Hmm…no."

My grip on her tightens, and my stomach churns as the song draws to a close.

Fuck it.

I want more than four minutes with Charley. I want to get to know her better, in all ways possible. Even if I'm leaving in two days and there won't be—can't be—anything more between us than one night.

She runs a hand over the top of my shoulder before meeting my eyes. "So, what's next for you, Nate Gentry?" she asks with a smile.

I don't know if she means tonight or the future. But for the first time in my life, I don't want to talk about baseball or my career.

"Well, I hope you'll take a walk with me after this."

A slow smile tilts her lips up, and I want to capture them with my own. "Think you'll get lost between here and the inn?"

I chuckle. "No, but I wouldn't mind getting to know you a little better."

Her eyes flutter down before meeting mine again. "I'd be happy to take a walk with you after this."

I raise a brow. "Oh yeah?"

"Meet me in the lobby in thirty minutes." She licks her lips, her fingertips brushing the short hair on the back of my neck. "Then I'm all yours."

THREE
charley

HOLY SHIT. *What am I doing?*

Aidan and Megan say their farewells, and most of the party-goers follow behind them. In the empty ballroom, the gravity of what I'm about to do—or hoping to do—with Nate sinks in.

I mingle among the last of the guests to make sure they all head out and had a good time before checking with the wait staff manager to see they're ready to clean up. Shane will lock the place up for the night, and once I get that all settled, I can leave.

Rushing over to the bar, I grab a bottle of whiskey and two glasses. With my clutch under my arm and balancing my provisions for the walk, I wave to the cleaning crew on my way out to the lobby.

Nate stands with his back to me, looking out the large picture window, and the sight of him makes my stomach flip and my thighs clench.

All those years as a catcher has given him an ass that fills out his slacks all too well.

He turns when the clicking of my heels breaks the silence in the room. The smile on his face makes my blood feel like molten lava. "There you are."

I walk toward him at a slower pace, adding a sway to my hips, until I stand toe to toe with him. "Sorry to keep you waiting."

With one hand in his pocket, he rubs his chin with the other, his gaze sweeping down my body before meeting mine again. "From where I'm standing, it was worth the wait."

Warmth blooms in the pit of my stomach, making my heart pound and heat pool between my thighs.

I need air in a bad way.

Nate licks his lips before holding out his arm for me to take. "Ready?"

I nod and slide my hand around his strong forearm.

He takes the bottle of whiskey and holds it up. "Was this the one I had earlier?"

"Yeah, it was the only brand I picked."

He nods and slides his gaze to me. "Good choice."

As we walk through the unseasonably warm night air, the heat of his skin radiates through the fabric of his dress shirt, and my shoulders relax.

I want this man in a way that borders overwhelming, but there's a part of me interested in *him*. Not the sports celebrity and not the so-hot-he-burns-the-retinas guy. I want the whole man and to know what makes him tick.

But I have to keep in mind my interest in Nate—physical or otherwise—can only go so far. I have a new career to focus on, not to mention we don't even live in the same place.

Even though his sister is my best friend who's dating my brother, the chance of me seeing him again any time soon is remote.

I have one shot, one night to get all this desire for him out of my system.

"Where are we headed to drink this whiskey?" I ask.

He smiles, looking down at the ground as we stroll along. "Ahh, well, I hadn't thought that far ahead. I just really wanted to get away from the people."

"And you wanted me with you?"

"Yeah. Anything wrong with that?"

My pulse races when he lifts his gaze to meet mine. "No, not at all."

"Plus, I figured it wouldn't hurt to get to know each other since our siblings are a thing now."

"Well, there's a beautiful gazebo behind the inn. We could go there."

"Lead the way."

We walk a little farther before I speak again. "Why didn't you invite Grace and Amelia for this sibling get-together?"

"I found out all I wanted to know about them when we danced."

My heart flutters at his words, but I try not to get too caught up in feelings involving that organ.

At the end of the path, I guide us toward a large, dimly lit gazebo. The surrounding darkness makes it feel like it's just the two of us, ratcheting up the tension in me.

The gazebo is empty and we step inside.

"I need to take these shoes off." I set the glasses on the long bench lining one side of the gazebo, grabbing his shoulder with one hand and using the other to slip off my heeled sandals.

I groan when my bare feet hit the cool wood. "Ahh...much better."

Other parts of me need relief too, but it won't be as simple as slipping off my shoes.

Nate picks up the glasses and pours two fingers of whiskey in each before handing one to me. He holds his up for a toast.

"To landing your dream job," he says.

I press my lips together as warmth expands through my chest. The more I'm around him, the more my man sabbatical is becoming a distant memory.

"To new beginnings," I say.

He clinks his glass against mine and we watch each other over the rim while we sip. The liquor burns my throat and lands in a warm pool in my belly.

Or maybe it's the stare he gives me that makes me feel feverish.

His face is partially in shadow from the moonlight slanting into the open-sided structure. With his dark hair and five o'clock shadow covering his strong jawline, he looks a little sinister and a lot intimidating.

I can only imagine what pitchers think when he stares them down right before he hits a home run off their best pitch.

Son of a bitch, he's sexy. I clench my thighs and pray he doesn't notice.

"What's this about a man sabbatical?"

Interesting icebreaker.

"It's to keep me from being distracted while I'm getting my career started."

He makes a noncommittal sound. "When do you start your new job?"

I look down into my glass. "Two weeks."

"Are you nervous?"

"As much as I hate to admit it, yeah. I am. I've been in the same place for ten years and know the job like the back of my hand."

"If Megan's party is any indication, I think you've got what it takes to be successful at event planning."

I smile. "Thanks. What about you?"

"What about me?"

"How does it feel to be retired?" I ask, sipping the dark liquor.

He huffs out a laugh and looks toward the open field bathed in moonlight. "It's just now starting to hit me. This is the first March in many years I haven't been in spring training."

"That's a long time to do one thing."

He sips his drink. "Yeah, but it's all I ever wanted to do."

"Really?"

"Baseball was the only thing I focused on." He swirls his glass.

"I waited until my senior year to go into the draft so it wouldn't take much to finish my degree in business from the University of Tennessee. I guess in some way I knew I couldn't play the game forever. But it still sucks not being there."

"Why *did* you retire? I mean, you're not old."

With a chuckle, he sips his drink before answering. "Thirty-seven is considered getting old in the majors."

"You're thirty-seven?"

"My knees know it. I've been squatting in the catcher position for a long time. I've been a catcher for more than twenty years."

He pauses, searching my face before continuing. "I wanted to go out on top. And the doctors told me my knees would have permanent damage if I went on much longer. Most catchers average about thirteen seasons and I was on my sixteenth. Plus my lower back decided enough was enough."

"Well, you had an amazing career."

He smiles into his glass before taking a sip. "I hit all the goals I had for myself when I entered the league and more. It was the right time."

"Megan's so proud of you, but I know she'll be glad to be able to see you more often. At least until you go into managing."

He doesn't say anything, just raises a brow, with a slight smile on his lips.

I play with the ends of my hair, my stomach fluttering. "Megan told me. I'm not keeping up with you or anything."

A grin curves his lips, making my stomach flip. "You know, she told me a lot about you too."

"Oh? Like what?"

"Things like you're a little firecracker. You're loyal to your family. You took her in like one of your own and helped her get a job, and even though she's only known you a few months, you're the best friend she's ever had. Which is saying something. Megan gets along with everyone, but hasn't always had luck with friends."

Pushing off the column behind him, he sets his glass on the

railing and steps toward me, nearly closing the space between us. "But there is one thing she didn't tell me."

I tip my head back slightly, which makes my chest push out toward him. "What's that?"

Is that breathless voice mine? It's ruining my *play it cool* game. But as I watch his lips while he talks, I want them on my skin so bad I can taste it.

I have no chill where this man is concerned.

"That meeting you would make me feel like I've been hit in the head by a fastball." He licks his bottom lip. "To be honest, I haven't been able to think straight since I opened my door and saw you in that dress."

My breath backs up in my lungs, and he shifts his body, bringing him even closer.

He looks at me from underneath beautifully long lashes and rubs his chin. The look tells me he wants to devour me in two big bites.

I'd die a happy woman.

"What? This old thing?" I run a hand over my hip and bat my eyes, despite the fact my heart races.

His grin widens. I wonder if he even knows the power of his smile. "I shouldn't like your mouth so much, but I can't help myself." He lifts a hand and pushes a lock of hair behind my ear.

With the heat of his body against my front and the cool wood against my back, goose bumps break out over my skin and I tremble.

I swallow hard before I find my voice. "I shouldn't want you to touch me, but I can't help the fact I want your hands all over me."

Lust flares in his eyes and a zing of electricity rushes up my spine when he finally steps close enough to cage me between his big, broad body and the column behind me. Excitement and anticipation fight for top spot in my belly as I look up at him.

"Wouldn't my touching you break that sabbatical of yours?"

"Yeah,"—I lift my eyes up to his and lick my lips—"but this is a special occasion. It doesn't count."

"Oh yeah? What's the occasion?"

"The fact you're here."

In slow, casual movements, he reaches down and takes my glass, setting it on the rail beside me.

His hand slides over my hip, and the weight of it makes my skin burn. His six-foot-two frame towers over me, making me lean my head back to meet his eyes.

"Is that what you want, Charley? My hands on you?"

I nod, unable to speak, his deep voice like a caress when he says my name. Our gazes lock and the sharp bite of lust slicing through me is mirrored in his.

"Is that all you want? Just my hands?" He drops his head and his lips brush against my cheek. "What about my mouth? My tongue?"

His words mesmerize me. "Yes, please."

He hums and rubs his nose down my neck, inhaling. "Fuck, you smell amazing."

"It's just soap."

"Whatever it is, it's driving me crazy."

I close my eyes and try not to moan just from him barely touching me.

It has been a year after all.

"You've monopolized my thoughts all evening long, Charley." He lifts his head and meets my eyes. "That doesn't happen to me."

"What kind of thoughts were you having?"

He growls. "Dirty ones."

"Tell me about them."

"First, I want to kiss that sassy mouth. I want to make you come with my fingers, my tongue, my cock."

I shudder out a breath. "Kiss me, Nate."

As the last syllable passes my lips, his mouth descends on mine.

It isn't a sweet kiss either.

It's greedy and possessive and hot as hell. His tongue is a weapon made to bring me to my knees.

He kisses me like I'm oxygen and he's a drowning man. I curl a hand into his shirt as he tilts his head, taking the kiss impossibly deeper.

When we come up for air, his hips pin me against the column and his hard length presses against my belly. I want to rip off my dress and let him have his way with me.

My eyes flutter open and he looks as dazed as I feel.

"You know, this isn't a good idea," he says, rubbing the pad of his thumb across my bottom lip, his eyes a dark green.

My tongue licks the pad of his thumb. "It's a supremely bad idea."

His lips brush mine. "Yeah. Lots of reasons."

I wrap a leg around his thigh. "You're my best friend's brother."

A hand comes up to the back of my raised knee, and his tongue runs a wet line up my neck. "Your brother is in love with my sister. And he carries a gun."

Our lips meet briefly. "It would just complicate things when we see each other again."

A whisper in my ear. "I hate one-night stands."

My body shivers but I'm on fire. "We have nothing in common."

He drops kisses along my jaw. "I'm too old for you."

"Lucky for you I like to push the envelope sometimes."

His eyes meet mine, and his lips curve into a slow smile that makes my body vibrate with lust. "I like a woman who takes risks."

I raise up a finger. "But let's be clear. It's just a onetime bad idea, right?

"One time only." He tilts his head. "But something tells me it will be the best onetime bad idea I've ever had."

God, this man and the compliments. He doesn't need them to

get me into bed, especially since that kiss alone would make a nun want to burn her habit.

"You bet your ass it will be." I lay my hands on his chest and rise on my tiptoes, bringing our lips within a breath of each other. "Take me to your bed, Nate."

His hands land on my waist and squeeze. "You're sure? Once I get you in that room, it's going to be hard to stop from doing all the dirty things to you."

I narrow my eyes, searching his face and taking in the seriousness of his tone. It dawns on me a guy like Nate has to be careful with girls wanting to sell stories to the tabloids.

My hands cup his cheeks, his facial hair surprisingly soft under my palms. "Nate Gentry, I'm sure. Now, I need you to take me up to room seven and fuck me senseless. Clear enough for you?"

His eyes grow dark and he licks his lips. Yeah, he's going to eat me alive.

I can't wait.

"Crystal clear."

He bends down and picks up one of my shoes. On one knee, he looks up and pats his thigh. I take his cue and lift my foot onto it. The muscles underneath the fabric of his slacks are firm and powerful.

But his large hands are gentle as he maneuvers my foot into the shoe and brings the strap around the back of my ankle. I hold my breath the whole time while he does the same thing for the other foot.

But once the strap is in place, his fingers dance up the back of my calf, caressing my skin. As his hand inches up my thigh, he takes the hem of my dress with it.

He lifts his gaze to mine, holding my stare as he kisses the inside of my thigh, making me gasp.

His other hand moves closer to my core, where there's so much pressure I feel faint.

A fingertip lines the edge of my thong before he drags it along my slit.

My hips buck and I bite my lip to hold back a whimper while he strokes me.

Long before I want him to stop, he stands and licks his finger. With a grin on his face, he says, "Hmmm...you're sweet."

"You're wicked."

"I'm just getting started."

nate

I DON'T KNOW what it is about Charley—the sassy mouth, the banging body, it could be anything really when it comes to her— but the animalistic need to possess her overwhelms me.

My smile widens and before she can respond, I bend down and throw her over my shoulder in a fireman's hold.

Yeah, I'm acting like a damn caveman.

No, this isn't like me.

But I can't recall the last time I wanted a woman as badly as I want Charley. Or the last time I've been so relaxed with a woman that I'm more a man than a commodity.

She squeals and laughs, her small ineffective fists bouncing off my back. "Nate, put me down!"

"Not a chance, babe."

"But I'm flashing the world! And the breeze is…"

"Cold?" I chuckle as I cross the field toward the inn. "Let me help you."

I lay my hand where the hem of her dress barely covers her ass. But I can't resist messing with her a little bit, just like she'd messed with me all night long flitting around in that dress, lighting up my body like a damn Christmas tree.

I shift so my thumb grazes the inside of her thigh. Her skin is like silk, soft and smooth. With each swipe, I inch closer to the promised land. Her breathing changes, coming in small pants.

Lucky for us, we don't run into anyone on the walk to my room, a.k.a. the longest walk of my life.

And let's just say she gets me back for teasing her.

On the way up the stairs, Charley draws figure eights on my back. Each swirl of her finger creeps closer to my ass, making the desire in my gut burn hotter.

"If you want me to find the key and open this door, knock off the doodling, Charley."

Her chuckle is low and throaty and doesn't help keep my hands steady as I fumble in my pocket for the key card.

After two unsuccessful stabs and a string of colorful curse words, I finally line the card up with the slot and swing the door open. Once inside, I close it with my foot, the slam like a starting pistol at the beginning of race.

I lower Charley to her feet, but as soon as those ice pick, sexy-as-fuck heels touch the floor, I have her up against the wall.

Her little purse falls to the floor when her hands end up in my hair, pulling me down to her lips. Anxious to taste her again, I meet her demanding mouth with my own, ready and willing to give her what she wants.

My arms lock around her small waist and I pull her up against me, my aching cock pressing into her belly. My mouth captures her moans as her fists grip my shirt.

Kissing Charley is like holding on to a live wire—electric—and makes me wonder if I'll live through it.

I tear my mouth away from hers and look down at her. Her eyes are closed and her lips are swollen from the assault of my mouth.

God, she's beautiful.

"Why did you stop?" she asks, her eyes fluttering open. Lust thickens her soft, melodic Southern accent I find incredibly sexy.

"I just want to look at you."

When she smiles, my pulse races and my knees threaten to give out.

She cups me through my slacks. "I just want to feel you."

Her hand moves over my cock, reducing me to grunting caveman levels. She gasps when my hands make their way under her dress and caress her clit.

Fuck me. She's warm, wet, and my world is reduced to the way she feels under my hands.

Slowly but surely, this woman is driving me mad.

The need to be inside her is primal.

I shove the flimsy lace panel of her thong aside and sink a finger into her pussy. When a second finger joins the first, she hisses out a yes, clawing at my shoulders and riding my hand like a champ.

"Nate...oh God."

"You like that, baby?"

"Yes, oh yes."

With a slight turn of my wrist, I brush the pad of my thumb against her clit and apply pressure.

"That's right, Charley, come on my fingers. I want to feel you fall apart."

Her hips move faster until the walls of her core clench around my fingers and the panting cries of my name echo in my ears.

With her eyes closed and lips parted, I want nothing more than to see that look with her underneath me, balls deep inside her.

She opens her eyes, her gaze sated but still full of desire. I pull my fingers from her heat and lick them clean.

"I knew you'd be like honey," I say with a grin.

Her cheeks turn a sweet but sexy pink, her blue eyes all fire. With a sinful smile curving her lips, she squeezes my raging hard-on through my boxer briefs. "My turn to taste you."

Moving out of her reach before I end up coming in my pants, I grab her wrist. "Not yet. You'll get your turn, babe. Follow me."

I lead her into the bedroom with my pants unzipped and my cock fighting to break free of its fabric prison.

When we cross the threshold, she turns around, showing me her back. She glances over her shoulder, a sultry smile on her lips and her hands against her chest. "Untie me?"

"Absofuckinglutely."

My pulse pounds in my ears at the thought of doing what I've wanted to do all evening with this little excuse of a dress Charley's wearing.

Pulling the longest string, the bow at the small of her back unravels, loosening the material around her torso.

"Thank you."

"My pleasure."

She faces me and lets her hands drop. The sparkly gray material falls to the floor in a pool around her feet. With her toe, she tosses the dress aside before placing her hands on her hips.

My dick throbs as I lick my lips and rub my chin, taking in the siren standing before me in nothing but a strapless lace bra, a skimpy thong, and fuck-me heels.

With her stare on mine, she reaches up to unhook her bra. Her hands freeze when I shake my head and close the distance between us. "Let me."

She leans her head back and looks me in the eye, dropping her hands. "I'm all yours."

"Oh baby, I know."

"Show me what ya got, hot shot."

I run a fingertip between her breasts, flicking open the clasp. The delicate fabric falls to the floor, and her gorgeous tits are finally bared to me. I cup one, my tanned hand dark against her pale skin.

They're beautiful and fit perfectly in my large hands. It's the one place she isn't as petite as the rest of her.

Her nipples bead up under my teasing thumbs. Her sharp intake of breath hits me in the gut, and whatever blood I have left in the head on my shoulders drains to the one between my legs.

My eyes meet hers. "God, you're perfect."

She gasps as I roll one nipple between my fingers.

Even though she busted my balls earlier, when it comes to sex, she doesn't play coy. Charley's comfortable in her sexuality.

It's a fucking turn-on.

My tongue flicks over a hard nipple, lapping my tongue around it. Her hands run through my hair, long nails scraping my scalp, and her moans make me thankful my pants are already unbuttoned or I'd be in agony.

"Hmmm. That feels good."

The intoxicating scent of her soap and her skin makes me drop to my knees, my mouth skating over the curves and dips of her torso, goose bumps pebbling her skin as I continue my descent down her body.

When I run my hands over her bare ass, my eyes lift to hers. They're dancing with glee as though she knows I have a thing for thongs.

I rub my nose along her panty line, taking in the scent of her arousal and just...her.

The scrap of lace she calls underwear is no match for my greedy hands as I pull them down her legs. When she's completely bare to me, I'm stunned.

If I wasn't already on my knees, she'd take me down.

She's perfect.

Her chest heaves and legs tremble when I run a finger up and down her slit. She tugs on my hair with a moan when I rub her wetness over her clit.

"Lie down and spread those legs."

When she reclines on the large bed, I shuck my underwear and slacks. My cock weeps in relief after being confined for so long.

Grabbing a condom from my wallet, I roll it over my length, tugging hard to keep all the want and need building in my balls at bay.

Charley lifts up on her elbows, her gaze zeroing in on my busy hand, licking her lips with a soft moan.

"See something you want?"

"I want you inside me."

I rub a hand over my chin. "I want my mouth on you. Just one taste."

Famous last words.

She tilts her hips up in invitation as I crawl across the bed toward her.

Between her thighs, I lose all sense of reality when I take one long swipe up her pussy.

Calling on all my years of self-discipline, I stay true to my word.

Just…one…taste.

"Babe, you taste like sin."

Her body is soft and pliant as I kiss my way up and settle in the cradle of her hips.

"Open your eyes, baby."

Her lids blink open, and those stunning blue eyes pull me deeper under her spell.

I smile. "Good girl. I want you to see me when I sink into you."

I rub the head of my dick through her wet folds before sinking completely into her. Our moans mingle together as I hold myself inside her, letting her body adjust to my size.

My forehead drops to hers, both of us panting because she is so fucking tight, I swear I've died and found Nirvana. We fit so well it's like she was made just for me.

I do my best not to pull out and fill her again for fear I'll hurt her.

"You okay, babe?"

"Yes, I'm fantastic. But Nate?"

I lift my head and meet her eyes. "Yeah?"

"You don't need to be gentle."

Heat detonates inside me like a lit match to gasoline.

I reach for her hands, clasping them tight. I lift them over her head and pull out of her, the head of my dick teasing her entrance.

"Then hold on; it's going to be a rough ride," I say just before I slam back into her.

"God, yes," she groans, arching up. "Just like that."

Her tits bounce with the force of my thrusts, her nipples hard peaks jutting up from her flushed skin.

"Fuck, Charley. Your pussy around my cock…you like it hard, don't you?"

"Yes…fuck me, Nate." Her nails dig into my hands as I pin her to the bed, lost in the feeling of her wrapped around me.

I'm reduced to a handful of words as I repeat the thrusts over and over again, the headboard banging against the wall in time with my unintelligible grunts.

Charley half moans, half chants my name, and the slapping sounds of hot sex fill the room.

With every thrust, her pussy grips my shaft, pushing me closer to the edge. I could fuck her all night nonstop, but the way she squeezes me, milks me, fucking *owns* me, I'm not going to last much longer on this first round.

Because if this is a one-night deal, I plan to have multiple rounds until she says mercy.

When she cries my name again—in a sexy, guttural voice I won't soon get out of my head—her walls squeeze me as she comes for a second time.

I can't hold back any longer.

I sink into her one last time and go still, coming so hard my vision dims. The noise I make is a half grunt, half roar, leaving me feeling lightheaded.

We're breathing like we just climbed Everest in record time.

I lower onto my elbows and brush a lock of hair off her forehead. A soft smile curves her kiss-swollen lips and I smile back. "You okay?"

"Oh yeah."

I chuckle and kiss her, then roll off to dispose of the condom.

When I walk back into the bedroom, she's wrapped in a sheet and searching the room for her clothes.

Uh-uh. No way she's leaving now.

I cross the room and wrap my arms around her waist, pulling

her back into me. "Wanna stay?" I ask, nuzzling my nose into her hair, but my stomach feels hollow.

Say yes.

She sighs, burrowing into my chest. "We agreed to a onetime thing, remember?"

"Was it one time? I could swear we said one night."

"It was one time. I think…"

Her voice falters as I pull the sheet away from her body. She lifts an arm up and her hand wraps around my neck, giving me unrestricted access to her body.

Nerves fade away when my cock grows hard against her ass.

"Nope,"—I cup her tit, pinching a nipple—"it was one night."

My other hand finds its way to her clit, the pad of my thumb grazing across it with just enough pressure to make her squirm.

"I'm not nearly done with you, Charley Reynolds," I rasp in her ear as she moves beneath my hands, her body heating up.

"You're not?" The words come out on a gasp when I dip a finger inside her.

"Not in the slightest." I pause, continuing my assault on her nipples and pussy. "I want to make you come again. On my tongue, on my fingers, on my cock."

"Ahhh…" She's writhing against me, on the edge of release.

I pull my hand back, teasing her pussy. "If you leave now, think of all the orgasms you'll miss out on."

She huffs out a laugh. "That would be a tragedy."

"For both of us." I brush my hand over her mound, touching just enough to make her crazy.

"Nate, please…"

"Please what? Tell me what you want."

"I want to come."

"Oh yeah?" I push two fingers inside her, and she arches her back.

"Yes, please," she gasps out.

"I'll make you come, but only if you agree it was one night, not one time."

She nods quickly. "Yes, one night. I want one night. I want orgasms. I want to come."

I chuckle softly. "I'm glad we agree."

I rub my thumb against her clit, my fingers sliding in and out, faster and faster until she detonates, pulling the hair at the nape of my neck.

When the spasms stop, I put my fingers in my mouth and lick them clean. "I can't get enough of you," I say in her ear.

"Jesus, you're killing me," she says on a wheeze.

When she comes down from her post-orgasm high, she turns and wraps her arms around my neck, rolling up on her toes and kissing me.

"There's no place else I'd rather be than here with you," she whispers, her gaze on mine.

I swallow hard against the thickness in my throat.

"Same for me."

Taking her mouth with mine, I lift her off her feet and carry her to the bed.

I roll on a condom and slide into her slowly. This time around, now that we've taken the edge off, I want to savor everything about her.

To see the rosy glow of her skin when she's aroused, to feel every inch of her soft skin beneath my hands, to hear the hitch of her breath when she's about to come.

Later, we settle under the sheets, Charley curling against me, warm and pliant.

I wrap an arm around her, pulling her in closer. Within seconds, her breathing evens out and she snores lightly.

My eyes drift closed to the realization that this is the first time I've ever wanted a woman to sleep next to me.

"ARE YOU SERIOUS?"

"Hell, yeah. I had to do something to get his attention. What better way than to drop an entire tray of shots in his lap? On accident?"

I bob my eyebrows and Nate leans his head back and laughs.

We're lying in bed facing each other after our latest round of earth-shattering sex.

"Okay, so I've told you about some of my shenanigans working in a bar; your turn to share."

He lifts up on his elbow, leaning his head in his hand. "Oh, we did a lot of the typical stuff. The sunflower seed shower when the cameras are pointed at the dugout. Icy Hot in the jock straps. Shaving cream pies."

"Yes!" I point at him laughing. "I remember when Ian Sterling nailed you with one of those a couple of years ago."

He groans and shakes his head. "The bastard got me good. It was menthol and burned like a bitch."

"You looked like you were pissed."

"Oh, I was!" His grin is wicked, and damn, it makes me hot every time. "But I got him back when he least expected it."

"Ooohh, what did you do?"

"I stole his car."

I sit up straight. "You did what?"

He laughs. "I didn't actually steal it. I just moved it. But the best part is we hired a mock camera crew to follow him out to the parking lot. Not only was he pissed off he was being followed, but then he couldn't find his precious Porsche."

"Oh my God! That's so mean. But so good."

"Yeah, not too shabby. He had it coming. He'd been pranking the team all week. So, we all collaborated to get him back."

"Did he learn his lesson?"

"Not another prank the rest of the season."

We chuckle and our eyes meet, tension building between us.

"You know," I say softly, "you're not at all what I expected."

"Oh yeah? What did you expect?"

He reaches up and pushes a lock of hair behind my ear, and it takes everything in me not to press my cheek into his hand.

"I expected you to be a bit more serious. It's the way the media portrays you. You're the cool, collected, broody legendary catcher. The Iceman."

He rolls his eyes. "It's a ridiculous name. But I *am* serious about my work. It's a game and entertainment for people, but it's my livelihood, my job. I'm the captain of the team and I have to keep the rest of the team in line, especially the young bucks."

I pinch the hem of the sheet between my fingers. "Even when Megan has mentioned you, it's how protective you are and how well you take care of her."

He nods solemnly. "Megan is the most important person to me. She's the only family I have left. I'm not big on family but what I do have, I'm taking care of."

It isn't my place to mention that while he does take care of her if she ever needs anything, the one thing Megan wants most from him, he rarely gives.

His time.

But that's not for me to solve for them.

"Makes sense. But you're a funny guy, Nate. I had no idea." I grin and scoot closer to him. "I like it."

"It's you. You bring out the funny side of me."

I bat my eyes playfully, but my heart trips over his words. "I aim to please."

He smiles and trails his fingers down my arm, making me shiver. "Like I said earlier, you aren't what I expected either"—his eyes meet mine—"on any level."

"Care to elaborate?"

"Honestly, I expected more of a party girl, not taking anything too seriously. I was obviously wrong because you're nothing like that."

I frown. "Well, I used to be that way. But I'm twenty-six, and I've had my degree for three years and done nothing with it. I felt stuck in a rut."

"So, you applied for the event planning job?"

"Yeah, and the fact is that I love planning things. I used to plan out theme nights and big holiday events at Silver Moon."

I shrug my shoulders. "It's in my blood, I guess. My mom is president of the Chamber of Commerce, my aunt owns the local inn in town, Amelia runs a bakery...we're all in hospitality professions."

"Well, color me impressed. You did a great job with Megan's party. Obviously, since you got the job."

"I know. I'm so excited to get started. But..."

"But what?"

Would he think I'm ungrateful if I told him that while this job will launch my event planning career, I had other dreams too?

He bumps my knee. "Come on, Firefly. Tell me. Don't leave me hanging."

I sigh. "Well, as excited and grateful as I am for this job, I had other ideas."

"Like what?"

I study his face, looking for judgment, condemnation, something. A scolding look telling me I'm just being reckless, irresponsible Charley.

But all I find is curiosity.

"I've never lived anywhere but Madison Ridge. I always dreamed of getting out of this town and seeing the world. All my siblings—except Grace who is perfectly content to stay here—have left and lived in other places. I wanted to do the same thing."

"Well, I've got a bar in need of a GM now that Megan has bailed on me. If you're interested."

For a moment, I want to jump at the opportunity. It would get me out of Madison Ridge and out on my own.

I'd be around Nate more often. Hell, he'd be my boss.

Though something tells me I wouldn't be able to work with him and not think about the way he makes me feel when he touches me.

It's one night only.

I smile. "That's a generous offer. But I think my days of working the bar are over. I'm ready for something new." I shrug. "Maybe I'll work a few years for Shane and Emma and then do my own thing."

"Well, if you change your mind, let me know. The bar won't be ready for a while anyway."

"That's sweet of you. But it would also make this thing"—I wave a hand between us—"a bit complicated, don't you think?"

He leans his head back and looks at the ceiling. "Yeah, I suppose it would."

We're both quiet for a moment before he turns his head and looks back at me. "Why haven't you left Madison Ridge before now?"

"I don't know. I got comfortable, I guess. I had a job, and I have friends and my family. It was always 'maybe next year' until the dream just faded away."

"And now you have an amazing opportunity here."

I nod. "Yeah. And I feel guilty even saying this to you."

"Don't. I get it. Go with what your gut tells you. My gut has never steered me wrong."

"Never?"

"Nope." He shifts and the sheet falls a little farther down his torso, revealing that V I may have licked a time or two in the past few hours.

"I was cut after my first year with the Angels, so I was a free agent my second year. The Bull Sharks offered me a contract that wasn't the best of the ones I was offered. But after doing some research and visiting the facility, I knew they were the best team to go with."

"How did you know?"

"It was just a feeling I had right here." He pats his rock-hard abs, and it makes me drool just a little. "I've learned to trust that feeling over the years."

"It was definitely the right call. You were their longest-tenured player in the organization's history."

He tilts his head with a grin. *That* grin. "You do know a lot about me, don't you?"

Heat floods my cheeks and I try to duck my head, but he's quick. Laughing, he sits up and snags the back of my neck, pulling me close, our foreheads touching.

"Since I know you're not a stalker, I like that you know my stats and you know about the game I love so much."

His lips brush mine lightly once, twice, and he pulls back slightly so I can see his face.

"But you know what I like most?"

"What?" My voice is barely a whisper.

"I like that you treat me like I'm a normal guy. It's been a long time since a woman I've gone to bed with has done that."

I grin. "Well, it was my pleasure."

His smile fades, his expression serious. "You're going to be great at whatever you decide to do, Charley. You've got a fire in you that makes you a force to be reckoned with."

I study his face. "You barely know me."

His lips curve in a smile. "I'd say I know you pretty well at this point."

I roll my eyes. "You know what I mean."

"Yeah, I do. But I stand by what I said. I have faith in you."

Those words are a balm to my heart. As much as I love and admire my mom, even she hasn't said those words to me.

For this man—who I just met but feel like I've known for years —to say he has faith in me is overwhelming.

He cups my face and kisses me, soft and slow. But before long, it turns heated, almost primal as he lays me back and settles his broad body between my legs.

"Charley." My name is a reverent plea from his lips as he kisses my neck. "What are you doing to me?"

I arch against him, gripping his shoulders. "Nate…"

"You want me to make you come again, Firefly?"

"Yes, yes, yes."

His eyes on mine, he moves down my body until his face is between my thighs.

"Hold still." He clasps my hands to my sides as his tongue does an erotic dance on my clit.

I moan, bucking my hips against his mouth.

"Tell me what you want, Charley."

"I want to come."

"Yeah? I'm going to make you come so fucking hard with my mouth, Firefly. I love sucking your clit, hearing you moan."

And the man delivers in spades.

When he rolls on a condom and slides into me, swift and deep, the feeling of pleasure is almost too much to bear.

His thrusts are long and slow, but soon the tempo picks up and I can tell the orgasm building in me will be one for the record books.

When I finally explode, I see stars and my limbs go numb. He's right behind me, slamming into me one last time before stilling against me, my name on his lips, pouring his release into me.

When we finally catch our breath, he brings me a washcloth and cleans me up before getting in bed and pulling me against him.

"Nate, before I forget."

"Yeah?"

"Thank you for all the orgasms."

His chest rumbles with laughter under my ear. I smile, liking the fact I can make this serious man laugh.

As I drift off, listening to his deep breathing, curled into his side, my chest tightens and I know I'm in deep shit.

Even though I was mindless with lust, I caught the nickname Nate used.

Firefly.

I want to ask him why he called me that. But that feels far more intimate than trading funny stories, so I won't ask.

I don't want to hear something that will make it easier for Nate Gentry to burrow his way into my heart.

This night with Nate is sex only. The best sex I've ever had, but that's beside the point.

I know I have to let him go in the morning, and all I'll have are the memories we made.

And that will have to be enough.

nate

WHAT SEEMS LIKE MINUTES LATER, I roll over to find an empty, rumpled bed beside me.

I run a hand over the sheets that are still warm from her tight little body and smell like her hair.

Adrenaline courses through me and my chest tingles.

It's a reaction I don't understand.

Most of the women I sleep with are women I've known for a while and we have a mutual friends-with-benefits arrangement.

They know the deal. No strings, just sex.

I'm relieved to find them gone in the morning.

The few times back in the early days when I would stupidly pick a woman up in a bar, they were harder to get rid of, wanting to hang for breakfast the next morning like it meant they were my girlfriend or something.

I wasn't a girlfriend type of guy.

But inexplicably, I have the urge to cook Charley breakfast, get to know her better, listen to her tell me funny stories.

Even more odd, I want to tell her things about me. Watch her listen—really listen, not listen with starry eyes—when I talk.

I rub my eyes with the heels of my hands. None of that can be a reality. I know me and that's never going to happen with a woman.

I threw away the key to that Pandora's box a long time ago.

I have my sister and my teammates, who are the closest thing to family. That's more than enough for me.

But if Charley's still here and game, we can finish what we started before the sun comes up.

I kick off the sheets and pull on my discarded slacks. I don't bother with underwear because once I find the blue-eyed vixen, our clothes won't last long.

The tension in my body releases when I find her in the kitchenette, wrapped in one of the robes provided by the inn. She turns and stops when she sees me, two bottles of water in her hands. A shy smile curves her lips. "Hey. I was thirsty. Thought you might be too."

The robe covers her from head to toe, but the top gapes open, gifting me with a view of her glorious tits.

I clench my jaw, wishing I could keep from wanting her again, but like a predator after its prey, I'm unable to stop myself from stalking toward her.

With her eyes on mine, she lifts her chin but backs up until she hits the wall. There's no fear in those blue depths, only need and a desire matching mine.

My mouth waters for another taste of her skin, her mouth, her pussy. "Actually, I'm hungry."

"Oh. Well, since it's so late, I don't think room service—"

I cage her between my body and the wall. "I don't need food, Charley." I run my finger over her exposed collarbone, her throat moving as she swallows. "I just need you."

With my stare on hers, I pull on the loosely tied knot around her waist. My hands run over her shoulders under the robe, making it fall and pool at her feet.

The water bottles fall to the floor as our mouths crash together, and her hands unbutton my pants, shoving them down to my thighs.

I hoist her up against the wall, and she wraps her legs around my waist, locking her ankles at my lower back.

Her arms come around my neck, and with our faces inches apart, her eyes flutter closed when I tease her clit with the tip of my cock. I line up with her hot opening, ready to push into all that heat.

And then I freeze, my stomach dipping.

Fuck, we need a condom.

Her eyes widen as though she realizes the same thing. A second later, her face softens and she cups my cheek with a hand. "I'm on the pill. I've never been with anyone without a condom before. And I just had a physical a couple of weeks ago. I'm good if you are."

My mouth goes dry and I lean into her hand. "I've never been without protection either. And honestly, I haven't been with anyone other than you since my physical six months ago. I'm all clear."

Her eyes flare at my words, and something passes between us I can't put my finger on. I kiss her palm. "I'm more than okay with it."

Her smile slays me, and I have the overwhelming urge to claim her as mine.

"Hold on, babe. It's gonna be a rough ride." I adjust my hold on her, gripping her ass firmly in my hands.

"Promise?" She grabs my shoulders as I snap my hips, filling her to the hilt.

I've lost count how many times I've been inside this woman tonight, but each time feels like the first time.

Correction. This is better than the first time.

There are no barriers between us, and the feel of her silky walls contracting around my hard length makes me think my head might actually explode.

Claiming her mouth with mine, I pull out and slam back into her, pinning her to the wall. I swallow her moans as our tongues tangle and we find our rhythm.

"Fuck, Charley. You feel phenomenal," I murmur against her neck, inhaling her intoxicating scent and unable to form any more words.

"Oh, God, yes, Nate." Her eyes open, and the blue of her irises is as dark as the night sky. "Harder."

I reach between us and, with my thumb, circle her clit, applying just the right amount of pressure she loves. She heaves out a breath and her pussy clenches. "Oh, God, yes."

My name falls from her sweet lips over and over, and with each thrust, I'm one step closer to losing my mind. I've lost myself in the feel of everything about her.

Her tits bounce against my chest, her nails scrape against the short hair at the nape of my neck, and her thighs tighten around my waist.

I want to hold back, but the way her pussy constricts around my cock when she comes again has my balls tight and sends a tingle up my spine. With one last thrust, my world implodes.

I slap my hand against the wall over her head and try to catch my breath. Our pants mingle when I lower my forehead to hers.

Only years of training my leg muscles keep me standing upright, but they're shaky.

Before I drop her, I step back, and her legs unlock their vise grip around my waist as I lower her to the floor.

Her arms stay around my neck and my hands still cup her ass. It's as though we can't let the other go.

Maybe I don't want to let her go.

I rub my thumb along her pillowy-soft bottom lip. Her tongue darts out and licks the tip of my finger. The sensation shoots straight to my chest, making it ache.

There are no words. Just our eyes saying things that are best left unsaid.

Bending at the knees, I pick her up and carry her back to our bed. She may not be mine, but for tonight, this room, this bed, this night is ours.

She doesn't protest, doesn't try to leave, when I gather her close to my side again. Goose bumps slide along my skin as her fingertip lightly traces the outline of the tattoo on my pec.

"Nate?"

I look down to find her eyes on me, a solemn weight to them. "Yeah?"

"I just wanted to let you know I had an amazing time tonight. And you'll always be special to me."

I smile as my heart beats hard against my ribs. I line her jaw with my forefinger. "You'll always be special to me too."

I want to memorize her soft skin so I can remember what it feels like when I have to fall asleep without her. "My gut didn't steer me wrong."

Her brows furrow. "About what?"

"That being with you would be the best one night I've ever had."

Her eyes are shiny, and I know by the time I wake up in the morning, she'll be gone.

And I'll let her go.

She reaches up and draws my lips down to hers. The kiss is soft and sweet and feels like what I know it is.

Goodbye.

SEVEN

charley

Two Months Later

"HEY, YOU FEEL OKAY?"

I lift my head from the desk to find Shane Kavanaugh, my boss, staring at me, his brow furrowed.

Picking up my pen, I try to appear productive. "Um, yeah. I'm good."

Shane pushes off the doorjamb and walks into my office, sitting down across from me. His cerulean-blue eyes narrow on me, making me shift in my chair.

The man is intimidating as hell.

Not only does he look like he stepped off the pages of a high-end cologne ad, but he's also a bona fide billionaire. Gold Mountain is just one of many wineries and vineyards his family has owned around the world for the last century or so.

Despite his looks and prestige, he's a down-to-earth guy who'd rather play in the dirt of the vineyards than be in a boardroom.

He and Emma have taught me more since I started this job than I learned in any of my leadership classes.

Each day I work for them, I'm glad I took the job. I may still be in Madison Ridge instead of exploring a life somewhere else, but what I'm learning with them is invaluable.

"Don't take this the wrong way, but you look worn out, Charley."

I drop the pen onto the desk pad and lean back in my chair, rubbing my temples. "Whatever the hell this crud is invading my body for the last few weeks is killing my energy. I thought I had it kicked but it came back."

"Have you seen Doc?"

"Not yet. I'll make an appointment at some point." I need to do it sooner than later because this shit is ridiculous and making my life miserable.

I face Shane with a smile, giving him my full attention. "I know that's not why you came in here to see me. What can I do for ya, boss?"

"Actually, it was my primary reason for stopping by. I've noticed you seem a little off lately."

Panic grips my belly, and I almost lose what little breakfast I ate this morning.

"I'm sorry, Shane. I'll—"

He holds up a hand and gives me a warm smile.

And let me just say, I know why my cousin fell so hard, because wow, the man's got a killer smile.

"Charley, stop. You're doing an amazing job. I have no complaints. I just wanted to check on you as someone who loves you, not as your boss." He wrinkles his nose. "And we've had this discussion before—you know I think boss is an archaic term."

"I know. Call you Shane."

"Exactly. Now that we've gotten that out of the way, I do have another reason for stopping by."

I pick up my pen and open my notebook. "Yay, what ya got?"

"Think you're ready to handle your first wedding here?"

I sit up straight. The lethargy that's my constant companion disappears. "Absolutely. Who's the happy couple?"

"Emma and I are."

My eyes widen. "Hold on. You want *me* to handle your wedding?" I lay a hand over my pounding heart. "Does Emma know about this?"

He chuckles and kicks his long legs out in front of him, crossing them at the ankle. He's cool as a cucumber while I'm having a complete meltdown.

"Of course she knows. She wanted to tell you herself but she had an appointment."

My insides go gooey seeing Shane's smile, so full of love for my cousin.

Oddly, it makes me think of Nate and the last smile he gave me before we fell asleep late into the night.

I'm not proud of the fact I snuck out of Nate's room just as the sun came up. But I knew in my soul if I didn't get out of there, I'd be in trouble. Mentally, emotionally, and sexually.

I'd left him a note thanking him for the unforgettable night and wishing him well.

I haven't seen or talked to him since.

It's what we had agreed on. One night, no strings.

But the weight in my chest tells me I miss him. I miss his touch, his smile, his laugh, and the funny side he doesn't show many people.

He isn't what I expected when I met him—the guy I'd watched on TV for so many years.

He's more.

I have no idea what to do with all these feelings, other than ignore them.

I shove aside all thoughts of Nate and the one glorious night we had together, along with the knotted feeling in my stomach every time I think of him.

Focusing back on Shane, I clear my throat. "Okay, what are we looking at as far as timing goes?"

Shane and I spend the next half hour talking about the timing of when the barn will be completed and how it'll line up with what he and Emma want.

"I think Emma will handle everything from here," Shane says as he stands, indicating our meeting is over. His lips curve in a wry smile. "She is the bride, after all."

"You know, we could have Megan take some photos of the barn being built. Put it up on the website. Plus, we can include photos of how we decorate it for your wedding."

My mind whirls with all the possibilities.

He nods with a smile. "Great idea."

"Thanks." If I didn't think it would be unprofessional, I'd jump up and down and clap my hands with glee.

"We've decided to hire a web designer in-house. I'd like you to work with them on that once we get them in here."

"I can do that. And I'll email you and Emma the package I put together."

"That works." At the doorway, he turns back and studies me. "You still look pale. Why don't you take the rest of the day off? Get some rest."

I wave a hand and scoff, even though the overwhelming urge to lay my aching head down and sleep sounds way too appealing to me. "I'm fine. I need to get back to work on these cost reports. Especially since now I have a wedding to oversee!"

"You can take it home, if you'd be more comfortable."

"I'm good. Promise."

But an hour later, I'm not good. I can hardly keep my eyes open, my head's pounding, and my stomach heaves like I'm on a raft in stormy seas.

Whatever I have needs to be gone by the weekend. The Memorial Day festivities start in a few days, and I'll be busy helping Mom with Chamber of Commerce activities.

At the moment, it sounds exhausting.

I send Shane and Emma an email letting them know I'm leaving early and head home.

I change clothes, turn on the TV, and face plant onto my bed. I must have fallen asleep at some point because the next thing I hear is a man's voice.

And not just any man's voice.

I raise my head and blink my eyes to find Nate's stupidly handsome face on my TV screen.

It's a well-made, slick, black-and-white commercial for a well-known athletic brand. His deep voice narrates as shots show him in the company's clothing working out in a gym, then running down a deserted road.

The camera pans in for a close-up of his muscles and at one point shows him using the bottom of his shirt to wipe his face, giving the millions of viewers a glimpse of those abs and sex lines that haunt my dirty dreams.

God, he's gorgeous.

The last scene is an action shot of him in midswing at home plate. His sexy voice recites the company tagline before it ends.

The ad makes the ache in my gut to touch him again nearly unbearable.

I sigh and roll over, staring at the ceiling.

I have zero regrets about spending one night with Nate. His body is a work of art like a carving of Roman gods or something.

And the way he moved it? Strong and graceful like the elite athlete he is. It was hands down the best sex I've ever had. He's a magic man between the sheets, and I know without a doubt he's ruined me for all other men.

At least I have the memory to keep me going. With our siblings engaged—Aidan popped the question after Megan's party—we'll no doubt run into each other again.

Even more reason to stick to the one time only rule to keep things from being too complicated.

So why does this thing with Nate feel so unfinished?

The peal of the doorbell brings me out of my musings. I roll up out of bed, but apparently too fast because my stomach lurches.

"Oh, shit."

Breathing in through my nose and out my mouth, the riot happening in my belly settles down.

"What are you doing to me, body?" I mutter, clutching my stomach as I trudge to the door.

"Hey!" Megan says when I open the door. "Aidan's working tonight so I thought I'd come by to see if you wanted to get dinner."

My mouth waters but not for food. I run for my bathroom, barely making it in time.

I flush the toilet and shift from my knees onto my butt, leaning against the wall, my chest heaving.

A few seconds later, Megan rushes in, her eyes wide, and crouches down next to me. "Are you okay?"

"I don't know."

She brushes back the stray hairs escaping my ponytail. The tips of her fingers are soft and cool against my skin. "Did you eat something bad?"

I swallow. "No, I've hardly eaten today."

Megan finds a washcloth and wets it before laying it on my forehead.

"Thank you," I whisper, closing my eyes. "That feels good."

"Let me go get you some water. Don't move."

"Trust me, I won't."

I sigh and lean my head against the wall.

I hate being sick. It does nothing but get in the way of all my plans.

When I open my eyes, my gaze lands on the box of tampons sitting in a basket next to the toilet.

A cold snake of fear runs through me, making me shiver. I think back to when I had my last cycle.

Oh my God...I can't remember when it was.

When Megan comes back in, she hands me the glass and sits down next to me. "Thanks."

I sip the water to help my parched throat, but it does nothing to help the unease in my belly.

"Megan, I need a favor."

"Anything, girl."

"First, can you help me up?"

"Sure." She helps me stand—my stomach protests but the water stays down—and I open the medicine cabinet, taking out my pill pack.

Everything looks like it should; all the days up to today are gone.

So why can't I remember when I last had my period?

I put the pill pack in the cabinet and close the door. The mirror reflects the two of us in it.

Megan looks as fresh as a daisy with her bright red shirt showing off her dark hair, reminding me of another Gentry.

Next to her I look like death warmed over with my ratty T-shirt and bird's nest hair.

Her reflection frowns. "Charley? What's up?"

"I'm trying to think of when I had my last cycle. It should have been a couple of weeks ago and yet, I don't remember having it."

"What was going on at the time? Anything to help you remember?"

I blow out a breath and think back. "I've been stressed trying to learn my new job. I helped at the Silver Moon when they were down a person over one of the spring break weekends. I worked and slept and that's about it."

She leans against the doorjamb. "You have been busy lately. We missed our last queso and 'ritas night."

"I know." I rub my forehead with the back of my hand. "I think that's why I feel so worn out."

"Maybe the stress and work threw your cycle off?"

"Maybe."

But the unease in the pit of my stomach yawns louder as I realize I really don't remember when my last one was. There's only one way to know for sure.

"I hate to ask this, but could you drive me to that drugstore outside of town?"

She raises a brow and stares at my reflection in the mirror for a beat. "You need a pregnancy test."

I turn to face her and lean against the sink. "I need a pregnancy test. And I don't want the whole town knowing about it. I don't need this to get back to my mom when I'm sure it's just a false alarm."

It had to be.

I can't be pregnant; I'm on the pill. Nate and I were careful. We used condoms.

Well, except for that one time, but I'm on the pill. They were almost 100% effective, right?

Almost doesn't count in this case, my conscience so kindly reminds me.

Shit.

"I have so many questions," Megan says, "but I'll refrain from asking until you know for sure."

"Thanks."

We head out of Madison Ridge to the one chain drugstore nearby, and much to my relief, I don't see a soul I know.

"I didn't know there were so many kinds of tests," Megan says, standing next to me in front of multiple shelves with all sorts of pregnancy and ovulation tests.

"Me either. It's overwhelming. I've never done this before."

"Neither have I." She grabs a blue-and-pink box from the shelf. "This one looks good. It says the words 'pregnant' or 'not pregnant' in the window. Says it only takes three minutes. And there are two tests in the box."

"Buying." I take the box from her hand and drop it in the basket. My eyes scan over the shelves.

"I'm buying these too. Just in case." I drop in two other brands, one with pink lines and one with blue lines that say rapid response.

"How many tests do you plan to take?"

"All of them." I drop a few more in and my stomach churns. "Let's get the hell out of here."

Half an hour later, I pee on one of the sticks and, with a shaky hand, set the timer on my phone for three minutes.

I pace my small bathroom, willing my mind to go blank until the timer goes off. I pick up the stick, and my mind goes numb when I read the word in the pane.

Pregnant.

EIGHT

charley

"I GUESS THAT EXPLAINS IT."

Megan stands next to me, arm around my shoulder, looking at the seven pregnancy tests I took. All of them are positive, leaving no doubt I'm truly pregnant.

With Nate Gentry's baby.

"I guess so." I sniff, trying to hold back more tears. I've done nothing but cry for the last ten minutes.

I walk into my bedroom and lie down on my bed.

I stare at the ceiling, trying to figure out who I've pissed off in the universe to earn this twist of fate.

I've finally managed to get my shit together and start my career. I put the partying and good-time girl reputation behind me in an effort for my family and this town to take me seriously.

Hell, I'd even refrained from sex for a freaking year!

In one night, I managed to decimate all that hard work and permanently alter my life.

The bed dips when Megan lies down next to me.

"I know you have questions, so ask away," I say.

"Nah. If you want to talk about it though, I'm here. I've got all night."

I turn my head to see her hazel eyes watching me.

Would my baby have those same hazel eyes?

My head spins as it dawns on me that my best friend will be my baby's aunt.

I can't decide if I'm thrilled or scared.

I can't decide if Megan will be happy or hate me for sleeping with her brother.

I look back at the ceiling. "You know what's crazy? I wasn't a slut or anything, but I'd had my fun with the guys. And never had a false alarm. I'm still trying to figure out how this happened. I mean, we used condoms. And I'm on the pill. We should have been double covered."

I don't tell her about the one time we didn't use a condom. It feels like a private moment between Nate and me. It isn't something I want to share with my best friend, even if she is his sister.

We also thought we'd be okay since I'm on the pill.

"Weren't you on some antibiotics a while back?"

I frown. "Yeah, for a sinus infection. Why?"

Megan sighs. "Charley, antibiotics can make the pill quit working."

I sit straight up. "Are you fucking kidding me?! Why didn't anyone tell me?"

She sits up next to me, her eyes wide. "Didn't Doc tell you?"

I think back to my appointment with Doc, the town's primary physician and my uncle.

"I vaguely recall him mentioning it. But I didn't pay much attention. I was on my man sabbatical so I didn't worry about it. There was no one around here I was going to break that for."

"Yeah, what about that anyway? You'd been man free—dating and otherwise—for a while."

"Right at a year."

"That's a long time."

Truthfully, it hadn't been hard not having sex or dating.

Until Nate.

The spark between us was more like an explosion. The intimacy I'd felt with him was unexpected and rattled me more than I care to admit.

"What are you going to do? Are you keeping it?" Megan asks gently.

I swipe at the tears falling on my cheeks. I'm not a crier, but ever since those seven sticks told me my life has taken a major detour, the hormones started raging in the form of my eyes leaking constantly.

"Yeah. I mean, this isn't how I'd pictured myself having a family. I thought I'd be older, married, and have an established career." I rub a hand over my still-flat belly. "But there's no doubt I'm keeping it."

Megan's smile lights up the room and she grabs my hand. "Oh, I'm so glad. That baby is going to be so loved." She pauses, her lips pursed. "So, the million-dollar question. Who's the daddy?"

A sharp pain hits my chest. It feels wrong to tell anyone but Nate first. Even if he doesn't want anything to do with the baby, he's the father and should know first.

"Um, well. I kinda want to tell him first. So please, don't say anything to Aidan yet either, okay?"

She nods her head side to side. "I understand. I'd be the same with Aidan." She shifts on the bed, leaning closer. "Can you give me a hint?"

I laugh. "Well, it's a guy."

She rolls her eyes. "Smartass. Do I know him?"

Better than I do and I'm carrying his baby. "Uh, yeah."

"Hmmm...someone I know." She taps a finger to her lips. "And you just said you wouldn't break your sabbatical for a guy here."

Damn, I had said that, hadn't I?

"So, he doesn't live here?"

I avert my eyes from her stare. "No."

She frowns. "Who would I know that doesn't live here but..."

I meet her wide eyes and watch as realization dawns on her. Her jaw drops. "You slept with my brother?"

Shit, this is what I was afraid of, her hating me.

I bite my lip and tears blur my vision. All I can do is nod.

Her mouth opens and closes a couple of times before she finally forms words. "When he was here for my party?"

I twist my fingers in my lap. "Yeah."

"Wow." Megan sits a moment, staring out into space before sliding her gaze to me, tilting her head.

"I saw you guys talking at the bar and then dancing later. But I didn't think it would go anywhere. You'd sworn off men and Nate doesn't date much, but he also doesn't do one-night stands very often." She pauses. "I assume this was a onetime thing?"

"Yeah." I rub my hand on my legging-clad thigh. "Are you mad I didn't tell you?"

She shakes her head. "No. I'm stunned, though. I mean, I don't regale you with stories of having sex with your brother, so I appreciate you not telling me the deets on having sex with mine."

She shudders a little, then squeezes my hand. "But I need you to listen to me. There's something you need to know."

The way she says it, along with the earnestness in her eyes, makes my chest tingle. I have a feeling I'm not going to like what she has to say. "I'm listening."

She rolls her lips inward and stares at our hands, then looks back into my eyes.

"I love my brother. I adore him. He's been my hero my whole life. He protected me from our parents when we were little. But by protecting me, he took the brunt of a lot of shit from our parents and, after they died, from my aunt and uncle. They never laid a hand on us, but the emotional abuse and neglect were there for Nate. Because I had him, I didn't suffer like he did."

In my mind's eye, I see a dark-haired boy holding a younger girl, keeping her safe from the people whose only job is to bring security to their lives. It makes my chest heavy with sadness for those little babies.

Megan blows out a sigh. "Because of our childhood, Nate has always said he never wanted kids. With his career being like it is —baseball being his life—he never wanted to neglect his kids the way our parents did us. I'm telling you this to prepare you. You may not get the reception you're looking for when you tell him."

I don't know how to respond so I stay quiet.

She continues. "I love you like a sister so I'm warning you, don't let your emotions get too involved when it comes to him, Charley. I don't want him to hurt you. And he will."

She shakes her head sadly. "As much as I hate it for him, it's just how he's built. And I don't see him changing."

I nod, my stomach turning and what feels like an anvil weighing me down. "I just want to tell him and be done with it. Then I can tell my family and start planning how I'm going to handle all of this. Whether he's on board or not."

"He's coming to visit later this week. He'll be here Wednesday. Want me to tell him to stop by?"

My stomach drops. I can't help but wonder if he would have called to tell me he was here? Would we have hooked up again or avoided each other?

Not that it matters now. I can't avoid him, and I definitely can't hook up with him.

"No, I'll get in touch with him." I swipe at my eyes. "I think I've had enough for tonight. I'm just going to get some sleep."

"Want me to stay?"

"No, but thanks. I'll be fine." I walk her to the door where we hug and say our goodbyes.

My body's exhausted, but my mind races, processing how my life has been altered.

I have a million questions and zero answers. While I'd love to think there could be more between Nate and me, what Megan said only solidifies the fact we barely know each other.

I'm an event planner from small-town Georgia, and he's a future contender for the National Baseball Hall of Fame.

While my family is considered wealthy, I have to work for my money.

Nate is a millionaire many times over who never has to work again.

He's a sports celebrity, the Tom Brady of baseball, and known all over the world.

No one outside of the Madison Ridge city limits knows me.

He's thirty-seven and has seen the world.

At twenty-six, I've never been out of the United States.

I love my big family. He apparently doesn't even want a family.

We couldn't be more different if we tried.

But there is one thing I do know. We made a life together and he deserves to know about it.

What he does with that information is up to him.

"MR. GENTRY, we're making our descent in about five minutes."

I open my eyes to find the blonde flight attendant leaning over me. Sitting up straighter in my seat, I nod. "Thank you."

She shifts closer, her cleavage pressed close to my face. "Do you need help with your seat belt?"

"No, thanks. I can handle it."

Her smile falters a bit as she stands upright and stalks to the back of the jet I chartered.

She's obviously new. The other attendants learned long ago I'm not one to help them join the mile high club.

The pilot comes over the intercom with instructions for the crew. I half listen and look out the side window, my mind wandering to the texts Charley sent me yesterday.

> Charley: Hey you. I heard you're coming to town for a few days.

> Me: Hey gorgeous. Yeah. I planned to stop by and see you while I was in town.

Charley: Yeah, yeah. Likely story. *smile emoji*
But seriously, I would like to see you. What time
do you arrive tomorrow?

Me: 3:30

Charley: Why don't you stop by after you get
here?

Me: I'll be there.

A CURL of lust shoots through me at the thought of seeing her
again. Two months later and she's still the star of my dirty
fantasies. I shift in my seat because every time I think about her, I
get a hard-on.

While my body is ruled by the head south of the border, the
head on my shoulders wants to know more about her.

With her, my worries about contract negotiations, sponsorships, or other business dealings fade away. With her, I'm
simply a man enjoying life, not a celebrity burdened by
obligations.

The plane comes to a stop, and I grab my bag. Outside, I slide
on my aviators against the sun shining bright in a clear blue sky.
The warm air is cooled by a slight breeze, making it the perfect
temperature.

It's beautiful here, and my idea of hanging around Madison
Ridge for the summer sounds perfect. I can't wait to get started
looking at the rental properties I've lined up.

As for Charley and me? I'm not sure where we stand. We
made a deal, one time only. Would she want to amend our deal?

I'll find out soon enough.

Twenty minutes later, I've picked up my rental car and I find
myself standing in front of Charley's door.

The sound of chirping birds fills the air, and her small bungalow-style home has a neatly trimmed yard and colorful flowers along the walkway.

I ring the doorbell and blow out a breath, my heart pounding in my ears. Why are my palms sweating?

The door opens and there she stands in front of me.

And it's like the world around me goes quiet.

I lift my shades to get an unfiltered look at her.

Her snug T-shirt with the local university's name on it displays all her curves, and the tiny denim shorts showcase her shapely legs. Her silky dark hair is piled up on top of her head in a messy knot, a few tendrils of hair escaping to frame her face.

Her mouth curves in a shy smile. It's uncharacteristic of the woman I spent the night with and shifts something in my chest.

She shoves her hands into her back pockets and shuffles her feet. "Hey."

"Hey."

We stare at each other for a few moments. Her denim-blue eyes shine as bright as the sun despite the dark circles under them and the paleness of her skin. It looks like someone pulled the plug on the light inside her.

My chest tightens. Is she sick? She looks like she needs to be in bed.

In spite of the fact she looks like she could fall asleep standing up, she's still gorgeous as fuck.

My first instinct is to gather her up in my arms and hold her close. But I push the feeling aside.

We spent one night together. We have nothing in common, and with her brother marrying my sister, I don't see how we can be anything more than friends.

Fuck, this is complicated.

She clears her throat. "It's good to see you."

"It's good to see you too, Firefly."

The nickname I inadvertently gave her slips out before I can stop it, and her shy smile turns into a grin that punches me in the gut.

One halting step at a time, she moves toward me, and before I think about what I'm doing, I raise my arms and she steps into them.

The lavender scent of her shampoo wafts to my nose, and our night together immediately replays in my mind.

After a moment, she untangles herself and steps aside. "Come in."

I step inside Charley's domain where the house is cozy and with a ton of natural light.

A blanket sits in a pile in the middle of the sofa and an e-reader lies on the coffee table, the screen dark.

As a reader myself, I'm curious as to what kind of books capture her attention.

It's a dangerous line of thinking, wanting to know those small details.

She moves to the sofa, putting the throw pillows back in their place and folding the blanket over the back. "Want to sit down? Or want something to drink?"

"Water will be fine."

I sit down and look at the framed photos on the mantel. Pictures of her family in various stages along with photos of her with friends vie for space. I smile when my gaze lands on a photo of Charley and Megan. They wear huge smiles, with Charley's arm wrapped around Megan's neck.

"Here you go."

She hands me a bottle of water before taking a seat in the chair perpendicular to the sofa.

I smile, in spite of the dread that's slick in my stomach. "So, what's up?"

She bounces her leg, taking a sip from her bottle of water as though working up courage. My gaze lingers over her from the top of her messy knot to her flip-flop covered feet. Her toes are tipped in a bright pink I find sexy.

I focus back on her face and narrow my eyes.

"You look pale."

She laces her fingers together in her lap and looks away. "I'm fine, but I have been sick recently."

Fear slithers into my veins, making me sit up straighter. "Are you okay? Can I do anything for you?"

Her stare slides to mine, and her eyes are shiny with tears, which immediately puts me on alert.

I want to take her hand, but I'm not sure if it's appropriate. I spent hours inside this woman and yet I don't know if I should hold her hand.

Shit, this is confusing.

"Charley, whatever it is, you can tell me."

She blows out a breath, then looks me in the eye.

"I'm pregnant."

My heart stops and my ears ring.

Pregnant?

The word plays over and over in my head until it doesn't seem like a word at all.

Pregnant?

I'm not sure how long I sit there, but at some point, Charley waves a hand in front of my face and the motion of it snaps me back to reality. "Nate? Hello? Did you just die on me sitting up?"

I blink and swallow some water before I can speak. "Pregnant? Are you sure?"

She nods. "I peed on seven sticks. All positive. I've had all the symptoms. I see the doctor the day after tomorrow to confirm."

"But...I don't..." I can't form a fucking sentence. "We used protection."

Hello, Captain Obvious.

Maybe I did better when I couldn't form a full sentence.

She rubs her eyes with the heel of her hands. "Apparently the antibiotics I took for my sinus infection rendered the pill ineffective."

When I shoot to my feet too quickly, I'm left momentarily lightheaded. "I need a minute."

Without waiting for her response, I barrel out the front door and pace the length of her front yard like an agitated tiger in a cage, my hands tunneling through my hair.

How the fuck wings around in my head. A light sheen of sweat pops on my skin as denial fights for a place amidst my thoughts of *how* and *what now.*

I'm not the playboy type the media likes to portray me as, but I've had my share of women over the years. And outside of one lying, money-grabbing groupie, I've never even had a close call.

The one time I take a risk, it backfires on me. In a life-altering, permanent way.

I've never been one to do anything half-assed, but this is the one time my competitive streak could have taken the night off.

I stop pacing and blow out a breath, pinching the bridge of my nose.

As much as I want to rage at the situation, I know I can't.

It was a mutual decision to go without the condom. And while I don't know Charley well, I know by the look on her face and her posture that she's not lying or trying to trap me.

It makes me like her even more than I already do.

Now it's time for me to man up and face the music.

When I get back inside, she's standing on the other side of the coffee table, wringing her hands, and watching me like a wary, wounded animal.

"Sorry, I just need some time to process this."

She nods. "I understand. I cried for ten minutes straight when I found out."

It's a gut punch to hear that. I clear my throat. "How far along are you?"

"About ten weeks. I figure my due date is some time in late December."

"And you're okay?"

"Other than morning sickness and fatigue, I'm fine."

"Good." I rub the back of my neck, my mind racing of what to do now. "I'm going to go."

Her eyes widen. "You're leaving? Right now? Are you serious?"

Fuck me. This isn't going well. "I'll be back, but I need to think."

"Think about what?"

"There's a ton of things to think about, Charley. You've had days to process and think about all the ramifications of this, but I've had five minutes."

She crosses her arms over her chest and blows out a breath, studying me. "You'll be back?"

"Yes. I promise."

The frown marring her lips deepens but she nods. "Fine."

Her tone tells me it's anything but fine.

TEN

Me: Good morning. Are you still speaking to me?

Charley: ...

Charley: Of course, Nate.

Me: Well, I wouldn't blame you if you weren't. I shouldn't have left. I feel like shit about it.

Charley: You needed time to process. I get it.

Me: Yeah, but I should have stayed with you. Instead I ran like a fucking coward. I'm sorry.

Charley: Don't beat yourself up, Nate.

Me: Can I come over? We have things to talk about.

Charley: Yes. You're right. We have a lot to figure out.

Me: I'll be there in fifteen.

Charley: See you soon.

. . .

A SENSE of déjà vu runs through me as I stand on Charley's porch, but before I can ring the doorbell, she opens the door.

And my heart drops to the floor.

She's pale and her hair is a disheveled mess. A weak smile touches her lips. "Hey."

I don't wait for her to invite me in. Crossing the threshold, I pick her up in a bridal hold, carrying her to the couch. "You should be lying down."

"I don't need to lie down. I need to get dressed."

Stopping, I gaze down to see she's hardly wearing anything. The white T-shirt is hanging off one shoulder, giving me a glimpse of the soft curve of her tits.

And does she call those tiny excuse for shorts actual clothing?

As I hold her, all I can feel is the soft skin of her legs. My fingertips tingle with the need to touch her. My gaze travels up to her lips, where her breath hitches slightly when I let one finger run along her thigh.

Get your head out of the gutter, Gentry. You're here to talk baby stuff.

I clear my throat and shift my stare to her shorts, but judging by the tightening of my crotch, I'm not sure that's any better. "Why the hell did you answer the door wearing that?"

Those blue eyes roll at me. "Honestly? I just threw up and was rinsing my mouth out when I heard you pull up. I didn't even think about what I was wearing."

"What if I'd been a random stranger?"

"I looked out the window and saw it was you!" She tosses a hand in the air with a huff. "Could you please put me down? I'm fine."

"You look anything but fine, babe."

"I swear, I'm fine. It's just part of this whole deal." She gestures to her stomach.

We stare each other down for a few moments until I reluctantly set her on her feet.

"Thank you. Give me a few minutes to get dressed and then we can talk. Help yourself to coffee."

I sit on the sofa, and a few moments later, she reappears, dressed for work in high-waisted black slacks and a green sleeveless top. Her hair is pulled into a tight ponytail high on her head.

It's a side of Charley I haven't seen before. Professional Charley is hot as fuck.

She sits in the chair across from me and lets out a sigh. "Before you say anything, I want to make it clear with you that I don't expect anything from you. I told you because you have the right to know as the father. But I also understand the deal."

I raise a brow, not liking where this train of thought is going. "The deal?"

"It was a onetime thing. We made no promises and that's fine."

My blood pressure rises with the thought that she'd think I want nothing to do with my child.

Well, it isn't like you know each other very well, my conscience helpfully points out.

Before I can respond, the doorbell rings.

She growls under her breath and stomps over to open the door, where her brothers Noah and Del stand on the threshold.

Just fucking perfect.

I run a shaky hand through my hair, reining in my temper.

"What are y'all doing here?" she asks, her frown deepening.

"Is that any way to talk to your landlord?" Del walks in first, grinning at his sister.

His gaze falls on me and his head pops back. "Oh, hey, Nate. You must be the one driving the monster SUV out front. Didn't know you were in town."

Setting aside my nerves, I put on my game face and meet him halfway across the room, where we shake hands. "Just got in yesterday. Good to see you again."

I nod to Noah, sliding my hands in the front pocket of my jeans. "Hey, Noah. How's it going?"

He nods back, a slight smile on his lips, but his eyes are watchful. I know the look of a protective brother. "Good, thanks."

The front door slams. "Seriously, why are y'all here?" Charley asks, standing between me and her brothers.

The two of them look at each with wary expressions before looking back at Charley. "Got some bad news, squirt," Noah says.

"Don't call me…" Charley rubs her temples. "Never mind. What's the bad news? Are you raising my rent?"

"No, but remember how we had that inspector come out to check all of our units?"

Charley crosses her arms. "Yeah, so?"

Del sighs. "He found mold here. The kind where you shouldn't be living here and we'll need to make repairs before you move back in."

Hell no, she's not staying here while she's pregnant with my baby.

Her arms fall to her sides. "H-how long is that going to take?"

Noah shrugs. "We don't know yet. We need to get a mold remediation company out here and see what we're dealing with. Could be a few days. Could be several weeks."

The answer hangs in the air when the doorbell peals again.

"What is this, Grand Central fucking Station?" Charley says, throwing up her hands.

The thoughts I've had about finding a place in Madison Ridge are solidifying by the minute. I need to pick one of the rentals and—

I tune back in just in time to find Aidan stalking over to me, in uniform, a murderous look in his eyes.

Oh shit. He knows.

"Aidan, what the hell is wrong with you?" Noah asks, pushing back on his brother's shoulder. It doesn't deter the sheriff in the least.

Del holds his arms out to his side. "Can someone please tell me what's going on?"

Aidan gets right up in my face. "Where do you get off taking advantage of my sister, asshole?" His lips barely move and his voice is tight.

Anger pounds in my blood as I straighten, staring him straight in the eye. It takes all my discipline not to knock him on his ass.

Not only is the man packing, but I don't need an assault charge showing up in the media, especially right now.

Plus, after what I just learned, I'm tied to this guy in more ways than one.

"How long did you take advantage"—I make air quotes around the words—"of Megan before I finally met you? Of all people, you have no room to talk, Sheriff." I practically spit the last word.

His eyes spark with anger but also resignation. "It's different. We're in love and I didn't get her pregnant and then leave."

"I'm going to kill her," Charley mutters darkly before slamming the door again.

She stalks over and stands between me and her three brothers. Aidan looks like he wants to skin me alive, Noah looks like he's in the twilight zone, and Del looks like he's ready to bolt.

"Nate just found out yesterday, okay? Back off." She pokes a finger into Aidan's wide chest. "And you're not supposed to know, anyway! Megan is dead to me."

Aidan jams his hands on his hips, still glaring at me, but his stance has lost some aggression.

"Don't be mad at Megan. She swore me to secrecy, and I let my temper get the better of me."

"Yeah, where did that come from, bro?" Del asks.

"You told Megan already?" My tone comes out sharper than I intend.

She turns to face me, biting her lip. "Well, sort of. She came over and I got sick and then she took me to the drugstore. I wasn't going to tell her before I told you but"—her eyes fill with tears as she stares up at me—"she figured it out. I'm sorry, Nate."

All the anger and frustration with the whole situation since I stepped foot in this house yesterday slips away seeing a single tear roll down her face.

I swipe it away with my thumb, then cup her cheek. "You don't need to be sorry, babe. You just caught me off guard."

She smiles through her tears. "Much like this whole situation between us, huh?"

I chuckle, my thumb stroking her cheek. "Yeah. Something like that."

A throat clears, and I sigh when I find her brothers standing shoulder to shoulder, arms crossed over their chests.

Yeah, now they all look ready to fillet me.

Charley turns and mimics their stance with a smaller, but no less formidable version of her own.

"Yes, I'm pregnant. And yes, I'm having it. And no, you guys don't get a say on anything. Nor do you need to go run your mouths to Mom."

"When are you telling her?" Noah asks.

She raises her chin. "Soon. So y'all keep your traps shut."

"Fine," Noah says before leveling his blue gaze at me. "Do you guys have a plan?"

"Yeah, we do." I lay my hands on Charley's shoulders, giving them a light squeeze.

She looks over her shoulder with eyes so earnest, it makes my chest ache and my protective streak roar to life. "We do?"

"Yes, Charley. We do."

I never wanted a family, knowing what my career involved. But a child deserves to have a father who does more than supply the sperm and support check. Charley deserves a better man than me.

Money and fame don't erase your past.

But I won't deny what I know deep down is mine.

Sometimes you have to lean into the curveball and make the best of what's coming at you.

I look each of her brothers in the eye before looking back down at her. "Charley's going to live with me."

charley

I WHIP AROUND, dislodging his hands from my shoulders. "Move in with you? What the hell are you talking about? I have a place." I gesture around me.

Nate crosses his arms and narrows his eyes. "A place with mold that needs to be fixed."

I scoff and cross my arms. "I can stay at the inn down the street. It's fine."

It isn't fine. It's going to put a dent in my checking account. My aunt owns the inn in town, but it isn't going to be free. Even with the family discount, it's going to hurt.

But I'm not sure I can live with Nate. Just being around him sends my emotions into a tailspin.

Noah sighs. "Come on, Charley. You know everything here in town is booked solid, especially this weekend. What if the project goes on for weeks?"

I turn to my oldest brother. "What if I stayed with you?"

"You don't want to do that," Aidan says, shaking his head.

I sigh. "True. He's weird about his space."

Noah frowns. "What? I'm not that bad. I just like my space. But whatever you decide, you can't stay here tonight."

"You could stay with Mom," Del says, with a grin.

I shake my head. "No way. I love her to death but we drive each other crazy."

"Sounds like I'm not the only one weird about my space," Noah mutters.

"You know what, guys? Why don't we let Nate and Charley work this out?" Del asks.

He uses the same tone when he's trying to convince homeowners to decide on his TV show.

They all file out and I close the door behind them, leaning back against it. "Nate, I can't move in with you."

"Why not?"

"Well, first of all, you don't live here."

"Already working on it."

"You are?"

"Yep. What else?"

My mind blanks, but I know there's a reason. Or a hundred.

I shake my head, trying to clear it. "Look, we're just two people thrown into a situation we have to work through. And we hardly know each other."

He raises a brow. "We're a little more than that now, don't you think? Besides, living together would give us more opportunities to get friendly with one another."

"We could do that without living together."

He drops his hands to his hips, jaw tight. "What's the real problem here? So far, we seem to get along. You need a place to stay, and I'll have a place you can stay, rent free."

I hold up a finger. "No way. I'm not going to live there for free."

He throws up a hand. "Fine, you can pay rent. I'll even have my lawyer draw up papers. Would that suit you?"

I tilt my head with a smirk. "What makes you think you'll find a place so fast?"

He rubs the back of his neck. "I mentioned to Megan a few weeks ago that I might spend some time here this summer, and she gave me Addison's number. Addison sent some listings to my assistant last week. I've narrowed it down to two."

My belly flutters and I tap a finger against my throat. "Oh. Well. I didn't know that. I guess you are working on it."

He moves closer to me, making my pulse scramble, and slides his hands into the back pockets of his jeans. "I planned to call you once I knew. I hadn't made any decisions yet. At least, not until now."

His T-shirt stretches across his pec muscles and I lose track of what we're talking about for a moment. He sighs and gives me a smile.

"What do you say, Charley? We're having a baby together. The least we can be is friends. Get to know each other."

I didn't want to tell him that in our one night together, I'd managed to do more than get pregnant. I have the feeling if I get too close to Nate, I'm going to get burned.

Regardless of the tiny human growing inside me.

"If you don't move in with me, where are you going to live while they fix your place?"

I rub my forehead, not ready to deal with moving. Hell, I've just barely finished processing that I'm pregnant. "I don't know. I mean, I just found out I can't live here. I'll probably end up with one of my sisters."

My nose wrinkles, thinking there's no way I can live with Amelia. Her kitchen is pristine and she's always put together, but her one-bedroom apartment is a hot mess.

"Well, I want to know you and my baby are safe, Charley."

I can't help the shiver running over me when my gaze meets his. The protective gleam in his eye is hot as hell.

"Nate," I sigh, "I know what you're saying. And it makes sense on some level. But I just don't think it's a good idea."

He looks at the floor and blows out a breath. "You're probably right. It's already a complicated situation; living together might make it worse."

"Exactly. Glad we're on the same page."

Why don't I feel better that he agrees with me?

"I still plan on staying in town though, so the door is always open for you, Charley. That's not going to change." He glances around. "Where are you staying tonight?"

I shrug, trying to calm the nerves twisting my gut. "I don't know. Maybe Grace will let me crash on her sofa."

Nate raises a brow. "You sure? Have you told anyone else about the baby yet?"

"No."

The more I think about it, the less staying with any family seems ideal. It's bad enough all my brothers know and I haven't told Mom yet.

He runs a hand through his hair. "Look, I know this isn't ideal, given what we just discussed, but you could stay with me in my suite at the Gold Mountain Inn tonight. Then you can figure out your next move tomorrow."

"Uh, no way. There's only one bed in those suites. Remember?"

Our eyes meet and memories of our night together hang in the air between us.

"Yeah, I remember."

His voice is deep and reminds me of all the things I shouldn't think about.

He clears his throat before he says, "I'll sleep on the pullout. Hell, I'll even get another room if it makes you feel comfortable."

I shake my head. "No, I'm not going to kick you out of your suite, and I'm not letting you pay for my room."

Nate sighs heavily and lifts his arms out to his sides. "Charley, I'm trying here. You tell me you're pregnant with my baby. I offer you a place to stay. I want to help and you won't let me."

I pace away from him and stand in front of the window, my arms crossed.

What's wrong with me? Most women would be thrilled with his reaction if they found themselves in my predicament.

How many men would leave tracks when they found out they were about to be an unexpected daddy?

That should give him some sort of brownie points, right?

I turn to him and nod. "Okay, I'll stay with you tonight. But just for tonight. And I'll take the pullout."

He shakes his head. "Hell no, Charley. You get the bed; I'll take the sofa."

I sigh, fatigue settling into my bones. "Fine. I'll come by this afternoon after work. Let me go pack a bag."

LATER THAT AFTERNOON, I'm standing in front of the door to the suite.

Room seven, of course.

Because the other suites were occupied.

Just perfect.

Somewhere along the line I must have pissed the universe off, because my resolve is really being tested.

I knock on the door, memories of the night I met him flooding my brain.

But this time when Nate opens the door, he's fully clothed with no towel in sight.

It's a shame now that I know what's underneath those clothes.

"Hey," I say and point to the number on the door. "Oh, the irony."

Nate chuckles softly and shakes his head, stepping back for me to walk in. "No kidding."

Inside, a glance around the room shows the room looks the same as it did the night we stayed here. Butterflies take flight in my belly, like they did that night.

But these nerves aren't ones of excited anticipation but anxiety.

Nate moves past me, my suitcase in tow, and heads toward the master bedroom. "I'm just going to put your bag in here."

"Okay, thanks."

I follow him into the room, going straight for the bathroom.

It's the one room we didn't have sex in that night.

There's no way I can be in the same room with Nate for long. Not when he looks hotter than I remember in his jeans and T-shirt.

And where the large bed we had our one night together sits between us.

I close the door behind me and drop my toiletry bag onto the counter before peering into the mirror.

A week ago, I was a twenty-six-year-old, single gal living the dream.

Now, I'm a twenty-six-year-old walking cautionary tale.

I point at my reflection. "Don't even think about doing something stupid. Again."

I take a few minutes to use the facilities and wash my face. When I come out, Nate's standing in the middle of the living room space, scrolling through his phone.

He looks up when I walk in and smiles. "Hey, do you want something to eat? We could order room service or go down to the restaurant if you want."

I cover my face with my hands and promptly burst into tears.

"Oh, shit. Charley, what's wrong?"

Strong arms come around me, and I bury my face in his shirt. He holds me, one hand rubbing my back, while I cry like a baby for what seems like forever.

When the tears finally run dry, I pull away and look up at him.

He's so handsome it hurts to look at him. And he's being so nice to me when the truth is, Nate Gentry could have his people take care of me.

Of course, his sister is my best friend and that would have made for an awkward family dynamic.

But the man is a celebrity with millions to his name. He didn't even question if the baby is his, which is odd now that I think about it.

The fact he didn't makes me like him more. And I can't like him like that.

We're forever tied together, but that doesn't mean we'll ever be a thing.

He swipes at a tear with his thumb, his eyes shadowed with concern. "Are you okay?"

I nod, giving him a weak smile. "Yeah, it's just hormones. I'll be fine."

He raises a brow. "You sure?"

I take a step back and his arms fall away, letting me go. I miss the warmth and safety of them immediately.

"Yeah. I'm going to go lie down for a little while. If you're hungry, go ahead and eat. Don't wait on me."

Before he can respond, I turn and flee to the bedroom and shut the door.

He doesn't follow me, thankfully. I'm mortified I soaked the front of his shirt with my tears.

On the other hand, I miss his touch.

And I'm really hating these fucking mood swings.

Changing out of my work clothes and into a tank top and leggings is a relief. But once I lie down, it feels like hours of tossing and turning pass before sleep finally overtakes me.

Dreams of a little baby girl with my dark hair and Nate's hazel eyes fill my head. Her tiny hand wraps around his finger and he smiles a heartbreakingly beautiful smile at her.

I wake up with a start, my chest heaving. I glance over at the nightstand to find a bottle of water and my cell phone sitting on it.

The clock on my phone reads 9:45 pm.

Holy shit. I slept away the whole evening.

Grabbing the water bottle, I take a long drink of it before I head out to find Nate.

This time, I find him sitting at the bar, typing on a laptop. He once again greets me with a smile, but it's guarded this time.

"Hey."

"Hey." I run a hand over my hair, trying to tame the wayward strands. "Sorry for sleeping so long. And for crying on your shirt."

He snaps the laptop shut and leans back in the chair. "It's okay. I got some work done. Besides, you're pregnant. I hear the mood swings are normal."

"Have you been around a lot of pregnant women?"

A smile touches his lips. "No. But I heard all kinds of stories from a teammate when his wife was pregnant a few years ago."

"Hmmm…"

"You hungry? I ordered a few things off the menu earlier."

"Yeah, I'm starving actually. What ya got?"

He smiles and pushes back, standing. "I know there's a cheeseburger and fries. There's also—"

I hold up a hand. "Enough said, I'll take it."

"Go ahead and sit down. I'll warm it up."

I drop my chin into my hand, watching him move around the small kitchen. He's dressed casually, in dark gray sweatpants and a black T-shirt with the Florida Bull Sharks logo on the back. And he's barefoot.

Why does the sight of his bare feet feel strangely intimate?

For such a large guy, he moves with a grace only elite athletes of his caliber can pull off.

"You seem to know your way around the kitchen."

"When you're on the road as much as I used to be, you learn how to cook."

He warms the food and makes a plate for each of us.

We settle into a comfortable silence for a few minutes as we eat.

"This is a good burger," I say before stuffing my face with fries. "I think Nugget and I were hungrier than I thought."

"Nugget?"

"Yep. It's my nickname for the baby."

He chews, but his gaze drops to my belly, where my tank top is stretched across the still-flat expanse, before it drifts up, lingering on my boobs, and then back to my eyes.

There go those damn butterflies again, and this time I have the added torture of tingling nipples.

The man didn't even need to touch me for my body to respond.

He nods. "I like it."

"Can I ask you a question?"

"Shoot."

I swallow and set down my burger, unsure if I even want to hear the answer, but I can't help but ask the question.

"When I told you I was pregnant, you believed me. I mean, you had a little freak-out session, which is totally understandable. But why didn't you ask me for proof or something?"

He narrows his eyes. "Because you don't strike me as the type of woman to lie about something like this."

His words warm my soul and make me feel special. It's almost as though he knows me.

"Well." I run a finger along the edge of my plate. "Didn't you have a problem with a woman a few years back? Claiming she was carrying your child?"

His jaw tightens and he pushes his empty plate away. "Yes. But that situation was different. She knew the score upfront, and when I chose not to see her again, she retaliated."

He glances away and runs a hand through his hair. "She thought she could make some cash and get a quick dose of fame to help her acting career."

"But you..." His eyes meet mine. "I knew the moment I met you that you'd never use me for money or fame. Just like I know even if we aren't together, we'll at least be friends for the sake of the baby."

My stomach dips at his words. I'm touched but also a little sad he knows we could never be anything to each other.

It's complicated doesn't begin to cover it.

"I'll never keep your child from you, Nate. I promise."

"I know."

We stare at each other for a long moment before he blows out a breath and nods to my plate. "Are you finished?"

My stomach turns when I look down at the half-eaten plate of food. "Yeah, I'm good. But I can take care of it."

Before I rise out of the chair, he swipes both plates and heads to the sink.

I should know better than to underestimate the catcher with the fastest pop time in the majors.

The man moves quickly and precisely.

I stand there, once again watching him, and come to a decision. One that might bite me in the ass later but, in the long run, I think will be the best thing for Nate, me, and the baby.

"Okay, you win."

He finishes loading and closes the dishwasher, a bemused look on his face. "What did I win?"

"I'll move in with you, but only until they get rid of the mold at my place. And,"—I hold up a finger—"there will be rules."

He walks toward me, closing the gap between us, his hazel eyes focused on me. "What kind of rules?"

"One, I *will* be paying rent, so draw up those papers. Two,"—a second finger joins the first—"I will have my own room. I'm not sharing with you."

His lips quirk in a smile.

I hold up a third finger. "Which should make rule number three easy-peasy. No sex. Got it?"

"Is that it?"

I think about it for a moment, tapping a finger on my chin. "For now."

His eyes study my face for a moment before he holds out a hand in the small space between us. "Deal."

When his hand closes around mine and desire flares in his golden-green eyes, heat pools between my legs.

I lift my chin, sliding my hand from his, and step away. "Glad that's settled."

There's something about Nate Gentry that makes me want to give in way too fast.

I did it once and the consequences have been life-altering.

In a few months, I'll be a single mom, juggling life with a baby in tow.

I know Nate won't abandon his kid, but the truth is he won't be a present parent.

Still, he's here now and I meant it when I said I wouldn't cut him out of his child's life.

"Hey, do you want to go to the doctor with me tomorrow?"

The slow smile he gives me makes my insides melt. "Absolutely. What time's the appointment?"

"Nine o'clock."

"Okay, what time do we need to leave?"

"8:45 will be fine."

"I'll be ready. Thank you for inviting me."

After a moment, he reaches out and runs his thumb over my bottom lip. I hold his gaze while the pad of his thumb passes over my bottom lip once, twice, before he drops his hand.

Memories of our night together slam into me, making it hard for me to breathe.

"Good night, Firefly."

Rule number three is going to be the death of me.

AT 8:45 SHARP, Nate knocks on my bedroom door.

I open the door to find him holding two cups of coffee and looking so good in jeans and a T-shirt, I want to rip my clothes off and beg him to have his way with me.

Of course, I refrain.

"Good morning. Coffee? It's decaf."

He grins at me, heat pooling in my lower belly. Damn him and that grin. It's how I ended up here in the first place.

"Another fact you learned from your teammate?" I ask, taking the cup from him. Our fingers brush and I concentrate on the rich aroma in an effort to ignore the tingle running up my arm.

"Yep." He shrugs. "It stuck with me since I'm an advocate for caffeinated coffee."

"Me too, usually." I sip, and the perfect amount of sugar and cream flavor the brew. "Hmmm…"

"Did I get it right?"

"Oh, yeah. I like a little coffee with my cream and sugar."

"Why doesn't that surprise me?"

And why didn't it surprise *me* the man knows exactly how I like…well, most anything? "It's perfect. Thank you."

"You're welcome. Ready?"

I nod and we head out.

Once in the cabin of his oversized SUV, the scent of his cologne —which thank God doesn't make me sick—plus the scent of coffee wafts around me. It's oddly comforting.

Must be the pregnancy hormones.

"What's on your agenda today?" he asks, maneuvering the large SUV through the town square traffic, which is busier than usual.

"After my appointment, I'm going to work. I don't work this weekend, but the winery will be busy, so I'll make sure there's enough inventory set up and ready to go."

"Think you'll have some time to come see a house with me?"

I glance over at him, mesmerized by the way his muscular arms ripple as he grips the wheel. He looks relaxed and yet perfectly in control.

It does funny things to my lady parts.

"Uh, yeah. What time?"

"Four o'clock? Addison said she could meet me there."

"Addison will be there?" Unease is slick in my stomach.

"Why…oh, yeah. She's your sister-in-law, isn't she?"

"Yep." I look out the side window and sigh. "I'm sure she knows by now since Del knows. But I don't like that my mom doesn't know yet."

Mom and I butt heads but there isn't a woman in the world I respect more than Stella Reynolds.

"Well, what's stopping you from telling her?"

"Well, I wanted you to know before anyone else found out."

"And now I know." He glances over at me. "What else?"

"I want the doctor to verify it for sure. Even though seven tests can't be wrong."

He parks and shuts off the engine before turning to me. "I have an idea."

I settle back into the seat and meet his eyes. "I'm listening."

"What if I go with you to tell your mom after work? And then we can look at the house tomorrow?"

I shake my head. "That's sweet, but you don't have to do that."

He tilts his head. "Why not? Stella seemed to like me pretty well when we danced that night."

"Yeah, well, you hadn't impregnated her daughter yet."

"Fair point. But don't you think this will be easier if she sees we're going to work together on this?"

I peer out the windshield, thinking over his words. Were we really going to do this together? It's a nice thought and I'm sure his intentions are good, but what happens when the baby is here and it's time for him to head back to Florida?

Rumor has it he's first in line to manage his old team next year. At some point, he would head back home.

Still, if Mom sees we're doing this together, it might soften the blow of good ol' Charley screwing up once again.

And just when she was getting her life together.

I can hear the town grapevine now. And there's no way I can let this news get farther before Mom knows.

"Let me think about it."

A few minutes later we're checking in at doctor's office, which is blissfully empty.

"How have you been, hon?" Wilma, the longtime front desk manager asks me.

"Good. How about you? Did your grandson get into the art program up here?"

She grins and pops her gum. "He sure did, and he's going to stay with me for the first year."

"Well, congrats to him. I know you're happy to have him around."

"I can't wait for it, sugar." She leans forward as I scribble my name and new insurance info down on the form. "Who is the handsome man you brought with you?" she asks, her voice low, her eyes narrowed. "He looks awfully familiar."

Well, shit. I hadn't thought this through. "Um, it's—"

The phone rings, relieving me of having to answer. I quickly take a seat next to Nate so Wilma can't grill me on any more details.

"Did you know the baby is the size of a strawberry right now?" Nate asks, scrolling on his phone.

I turn my head to him, my lips parted. "How do you know that?"

He shrugs a shoulder. "I looked it up. And yes, it's a reputable medical website."

My heart turns over in my chest. "You looked up pregnancy facts?"

"Yeah, sure." His gaze slides to mine. "Why not?"

"I-It's not something I'd thought you would do is all."

The look in his eyes is stormy. There's tenderness, hurt, and frustration. My eyes start to burn, and I draw in a deep breath to keep the waterworks at bay.

He leans closer, our knees touching, and lowers his voice. "Charley, I'm all in on this. I want to know how our…"

"Little Nugget?"

"Yeah, how our little Nugget is doing." He lifts a hand and pushes a strand of wayward hair behind my ear. "I'll take care of you and our baby. In whatever way you need."

For someone who doesn't know me very well, the man seems to get me. It's disconcerting. *He* is disconcerting.

Wilma opens the door to the waiting room. "Charley, you can come on back."

We follow Wilma down the hallway to an exam room. Nate sits in a chair and Wilma hands me a specimen cup. "We need a urine sample, hon. Val will be in shortly."

When I come back a few minutes later, my uncle Doc and my cousin Val—also a doctor—are in the room, chatting with Nate.

"I've never seen a ball travel so far before. It should've had its own flight crew!"

How did I forget my uncle is a huge baseball fan?

Dad had been as well, a fact that pinches my heart, even though I'd only been seven when he died. After Dad passed, my uncle still came over to watch games with me and my brothers.

Nate's deep chuckle fills the room and it's like a warm blanket wraps around me. When Val sees me, her eyes widen slightly, a million questions on her face.

Yeah, this is going to be fun.

I smile and kiss my uncle's cool cheek. He smells like peppermint and Old Spice, and a wave of nostalgia washes over me. "Hey, Doc."

"Hey, sweetie. Well, I'm going to get on out of here and let Val do her thing." He shakes Nate's hand. "Good to meet you, Nate."

Once he leaves, Val smiles at me, shifting into doctor mode. "Okay, Charley, climb up on the table and let's get your vitals."

I sit quietly while she takes my temperature, blood pressure, and pulse, asks me a few other questions, then enters the information on her tablet.

"When did y'all go all fancy?" I ask.

She taps the screen. "A few weeks ago. I told Doc we might be small but it doesn't mean we can't have technology. We also hired a new nurse. She starts next week."

"That's great. I can't believe he's retiring."

"I know. I thought the man would die in that old chair in his office." She shrugs. "But Aunt Lindsey said she wants to travel, and she's got someone watching the inn for her now. And now that I'm here, he has no excuses."

It'd been a shock to us all when Doc had announced his retirement over the holidays and brought on another doctor full-time. We always figured he'd sell the practice or work until he dropped.

Val had been an ER doctor until last fall when she'd moved back to Madison Ridge after falling in love with her best friend, Brian, a deputy in town.

"Your vitals are good, Charley. What brings you in?"

I blow out a breath. "I think I'm pregnant. Actually, I *know* I'm pregnant. I took seven tests. All positive." My hands fidget in my lap, even though Val's gaze is professional.

She's quiet for a moment, glancing between Nate and me. My cousin has an amazing poker face.

I wonder if she's ever played with the Poker Posse.

I also wonder if random thoughts are part of the pregnancy brain I've read about.

"Okay," Val says, "sounds like you've got the test front covered, but we'll just do one more for confirmation and to add to your file." She taps the screen again. "When was your last cycle?"

"Mid-March."

She nods, making a note, and then sets aside the tablet with a smile. "Let me go run the test real quick." She pats my knee. "Sit tight."

Nate and I sit quietly. There are so many things I want to say. Yet I don't know what to say to the man who I'm now tied to for the rest of my life.

A few moments later, Val comes in, a smile on her pretty face.

"Well, test number eight confirms it. You are indeed pregnant."

"I didn't think seven tests could be wrong."

Val chuckles. "Why don't you lie back and let's see if we can hear the heartbeat."

Butterflies take flight in my belly and I look at Nate. He leans forward, his forearms on his thighs, hands clasped between them, his stare intent on mine.

Val helps me lean back, then grabs a small handheld machine and squirts blue gel on my stomach.

She moves the wand on my belly for a few moments until she finds the spot.

A rhythmic sound fills the room that sounds like a heartbeat underwater. "There it is," she says, smiling.

Nate appears by my side, his hand in mine. I look up at him. His throat moves as he swallows, his golden-green gaze on mine. "Our baby," I whisper.

"Yeah…" His voice is low and husky. He leans forward and kisses my forehead then the back of my hand.

Val raises a brow but doesn't say a word.

She's going to be after me like a dog with a bone sooner than later.

Listening to the sound of my baby's heartbeat makes tears clog my throat, and inexplicably, I want to see my mom and hug her.

"Nate?"

I wait until his eyes meet mine.

"Let's go see my mom."

His lips curve into a soft smile. "Whatever you want, Firefly."

"Judging by your last cycle, I'd estimate your due date to be mid-December," she says.

We wrap up the appointment, with Val giving me some prenatal vitamins and contact information for an OB for future checkups. "We can do regular pelvic exams here, but we don't have an OB on staff. But Dr. Miller is great. You'll love her."

We wave goodbye to Wilma, who's ensuring someone on the phone their foot isn't going to rot off, and head out the door.

Once we're settled in the SUV, I turn to Nate. "Would you mind if we went by my mom's house now?"

He turns his head and I feel the full force of those eyes. "Not at all."

I let out a breath and smile. "Good. Let me text Emma and let her know I'm taking the day off."

I direct him toward her house and lean back in the seat.

There's a comfortable silence between us as I figure out how the hell I'm going to tell my mother she's going to be a grandmother.

I also try to figure out how the hell Nate and I are going to handle this living like roommates thing. Roommates having a baby together.

It's weird.

Because we aren't a couple. We never will be.

Our lives and careers are on two different, far apart paths. The most I can ever hope for is friends.

It will have to be enough.

All I want now is to take care of my baby, give it the best home I can.

It isn't all about me anymore.

THE RIDE IS quiet between us.

I'm still in awe of hearing my baby's heartbeat.

My baby.

My body is energized as the news sinks in for real.

Holy shit. I'm going to be a dad.

It isn't like I didn't realize it when Charley told me. But hearing the actual heartbeat made it even more real.

I also need to call my publicist, my assistant, and Derek Emerson, the GM of the Bull Sharks.

Someone will need to handle the press because while I may not be an active player anymore, my name still ends up in the media. Especially right now since I'm in contract negotiations for the manager position next year.

I don't care what they say about me, but I won't subject Charley to the vultures. The longer I can protect Charley and my baby from the part of my life I hate most, the better.

I glance over at Charley, who's looking out the window as we drive farther out of town. The sunlight slants over her dark hair, bringing out some red strands, reminding me of fire.

It's beautiful and a feature of Charley's I hope our child inherits.

The possibilities are endless, and my chest expands, a mix of feelings running through me as the magnitude of what's happening continues to sink in.

I'm not sure how we're going to handle the future, but one thing I do know is I'm going to be as involved as I can be in my kid's life.

It won't be easy, but I'll have to make it work because I won't be like my parents.

I glance back over at her again, and she meets my eyes, giving me a soft smile before looking away.

In spite of it all, that smile sends a shot of pure desire straight to my crotch.

I want to pull over and relive our night together in the backseat.

I'd give up all my Gold Glove awards to feel her under me and hear my name fall from those lips one more time.

Get your shit together, Gentry.

Wanting her is how we found ourselves in this situation, but my dick hasn't gotten the memo yet.

I shift in my seat and discreetly adjust my jeans.

"Take a left at this next road," she says, breaking the silence.

The houses on this road are farther apart, with wider expanses of land between them.

"It's the red mailbox on the right."

I turn onto a long driveway. "It's pretty out here."

She smiles. "Yeah, it is."

As we get closer, she groans. "Shit. What the hell are my sisters and your sister doing here?"

Within moments, we pull up, and I park behind a couple of vehicles sitting in the driveway.

I shut off the engine and peer out the front windshield at the large two-story farmhouse-style home with a front door matching the red mailbox.

"Is this the house you grew up in?"

"Yep."

"It's beautiful."

There's an empty feeling in my gut looking at her childhood home. What would that have been like?

"My dad built it. It's way too much house for Mom, but she says she can't bear to leave it."

There's a wistful tone in her voice and her hands twist in her lap.

I reach over the console and take a hand in mine. It's warm and soft, and the light floral scent of her skin fills the cabin. "What's going on in that head of yours, Firefly?"

She looks out the side window. "I'm thinking about what my mom's going to say. What my dad would think if he were here. I'm missing him right now."

I want to wrap her in my arms, to comfort her. My chest tightens, thinking of how she misses her dad. Another feeling I know nothing about.

I haven't missed mine a single day since he died. He didn't deserve to be missed.

With a heavy sigh, she turns to me. Her blue eyes are bright and anxious. "The press is going to have a field day with this. And I don't know what to do with that."

I clench my jaw and look away. I hate the fact a part of my life I never wanted and only tolerate gives her any kind of anxiety.

Shifting in my seat, I lean close to her, lightly pinching her chin between my thumb and forefinger to make sure her eyes meet mine. "Listen to me, Charley."

The storm of emotions swirling in her eyes awakens a primal feeling in my gut. It's a protective streak in me I've never felt for a woman before.

"I don't give two shits what the press says about this. They make up all kinds of shit anyway to sell a story. It'll last two days and be forgotten. Okay?"

"Okay."

"And I'm going to take care of you and little Nugget."

She smiles. "Okay."

We stare at each other for a moment, and I move my hand to the back of her neck, her skin soft under my palm, her silky hair brushing the back of my fingers.

I want to pull her to me and kiss the hell out of her.

But I don't.

Instead, I kiss her forehead, allowing myself to breathe her in for just a moment. My racing heart settles down.

I release her and get out of the truck, coming around to open her door. "Ready to do this?"

"As ready as I'll ever be."

I follow her to the front door, and my gaze falls to her ass in those snug jeans.

Without warning, she turns around, drawing me up short. "I—wait, are you checking out my ass?"

My eyes snap to hers.

Busted.

I grin. "What can I say? Those jeans"—I gesture up and down—"skim your curves perfectly. And can I just say they make your ass look exceptional?"

Her cheeks flush a pretty pink and she bites her lip, but one side of her mouth curves.

I want to cover her mouth with mine so bad I salivate.

"Nate, you can't say things like that to me. Especially here."

I huff out a laugh. "I'm well aware, Charley."

"You know it only complicates an already complicated situation."

I look down at the ground and rock back on my heels before meeting her gaze.

"You're right. I'll behave. We're just friends."

Friends who barely know each other and are having a baby together. Not fucked-up at all, right?

She hesitates, a shadow crossing her eyes before she nods quickly. "Right. Just friends."

"What were you going to say? When you turned around?"

"Oh." Her brow furrows. "I don't remember now."

We stare at each for a few moments, the spark between us alive and well.

She finally turns away and starts up the sidewalk. This time I keep my gaze on the ground and far away from the sway of her hips.

She walks in, calling out for her mom.

"In the kitchen!" Stella calls back.

Charley sends me a hesitant smile before she leads us to the back of the house.

It's a large home with gleaming hardwoods and warm, muted earth tones. Despite its high ceilings and large rooms, it's homey.

Nothing like the house I grew up in, which was never a home.

I shove the thought away as we draw closer to the kitchen where feminine voices fill the room.

"Hey, guys," Charley says when we enter the room.

Stella, Amelia, Grace, and Megan sit at a large island in the middle of a massive state-of-the-art kitchen. A couple of note-books, photos, and a laptop sit on the counter in front of them.

They turn to face us, and when they see me, there's a mixture of surprise and curiosity on their faces.

Except for Megan. A knowing smile plays on her lips.

Time to put the game face on in spite of the fact I feel physically ill.

As I look at the Reynolds women, I'm momentarily stunned at how much they look alike. They all have dark hair and blue eyes. They're all beautiful in different ways.

But there's something about Charley that pulls at me in a way her sisters don't.

"Hey, big brother," Megan says, sliding off her stool and giving me a hug.

"Hey, Meg-Pie."

She steps back and looks from Charley to me, her gaze questioning. *Did she tell you?* "When did you get here?"

I nod at her unspoken question. "Day before yesterday."

"Hey, there," Stella says, a smile on her face. Her brows lift slightly when she greets me, but she quickly recovers. "Nate, what a nice surprise."

She comes around the island, greeting us with hugs and cheek kisses.

"Mrs. Reynolds, it's good to see you again."

I nod to Amelia and Grace. "Ladies, how are you?"

"Good," they say in unison, still eyeing us.

Charley points to her sisters. "What are y'all doing here in the middle of the day?"

Grace shrugs. "School's out, so I'm free as a bird for the next two months."

"Maddie's covering the bakery for me while I'm here," Amelia says, then gives Charley a pointed look. "What about you?"

Charley glances at me briefly. "I'm off today."

"Y'all need a drink?" Stella asks, shifting into hostess mode.

Like you wouldn't believe.

"I'll take some water, please," Charley says.

"Nate?"

"I'm good, thanks."

Charley's right when she says hospitality runs in her blood. Her mother is the consummate host as she offers snacks and tells us to take a seat.

But the slick, uneasy feeling in my gut is persistent.

"We're just working on some final touches for the Memorial Day festival next weekend," Stella says, sliding back on her stool, looking between me and Charley. "What are y'all up to?"

Charley shifts her feet and knots her fingers together at her waist. "I have some news."

Stella's smile stays in place, but it's a practiced smile. "Good news, I hope."

Charley tilts her head and looks over at me. "Yes. I think it is."

There's a twist in my chest and I want to pull her in next to me.

The ladies lean forward, waiting for her to continue. Charley licks her lips and blows out a breath.

"Nate and I…" She pauses. I take her hand in mine and squeeze. She sends me a grateful smile. "Well, we're having a baby. I'm due in December."

Shocked silence fills the sunny kitchen.

I give in to my urge and put an arm around Charley's shoulders, pulling her close to me. I don't think I need to protect her from her own family, but I want them to see that Charley and I—while complicated—are a team.

"We know it's unexpected, seeing as we haven't known each other for very long." I meet Stella's eyes, so much like her daughter's. "But we're going to work out this coparenting thing together."

I look down at Charley and hold her stare as I say, "I don't know what the future holds for us. But I promise I'll take care of you."

She blinks and I realize too late we're still standing in front of other people. "Um…also, Charley's moving in with me. I don't want to miss anything while I can."

"It's just temporary," Charley counters.

I try to keep my muscles from tensing up and the irritation at bay when I hear her comment.

"Mom?" Charley's voice wavers as she steps away from me and toward her mom, taking her hand. "What are you thinking?"

I glance over to Grace and Amelia, who are watching their mom take a moment to process the bombshell.

I know how she feels.

Stella blinks and looks between us. Then her eyes water and she smiles. "I just have one thing to ask you," Stella says, her stare intense as she looks at Charley. "Are you happy?"

Charley looks up at me before looking back at her mom. "Like Nate said, it's unexpected and we have a lot to figure out. But yes, I'm happy. I can only hope I'm as good a mom as you." Her eyes widen. "Oh no! I'm going to miss the family Thanksgiving trip! I'm so sorry, Mom."

"Oh baby, don't worry about that."

"I want you guys to go, okay? Don't cancel it because of me."

"Are you sure?" Stella's brow rises.

Charley nods quickly. "I'm positive." She glances over her shoulder at me. "Nate will be with me."

"Oh sweetie, I'm so happy for you!" Stella's tears fall unchecked down her face. She wraps Charley in a hug that lasts several moments. When she releases her, she turns to me, opening her arms.

"Welcome to the family, Nate. We're crazy, but we'll always have your back."

My heart pounds at the thought of having family backing me. People other than Megan. Why would they do that? They don't even know me.

Still, I smile and hug Stella, while the girls gather around Charley, hugging her and asking questions.

Megan comes up to me and hugs my waist. "It's going to be okay, big brother."

I kiss the top of her head. "I know."

She joins the other ladies, and happy, feminine chatter fills the room.

I keep a smile on my face, but the icy fingers of fear claw at my throat.

Family.

The very word sends shivers down my spine.

Deep down, I want nothing more than to fit into the Reynolds clan like Megan managed to do. But family is one area of my life I prefer to watch from the sidelines.

I'm simply not built for all the things that come with having a family. Getting close to them, being vulnerable.

But as I watch Charley with her mom, sisters, and best friend, I can't deny the mix of feelings running through my veins.

It's a heavy dose of fear mixed with longing.

I will always be there for my child. I'll make sure they never felt what I did growing up.

But for anyone else, I'm too far gone and broken to fit into that kind of world.

No matter how bad I want it.

charley

"GOOD MORNING, FIREFLY."

I raise my eyes from my laptop and swallow the bite I'm chewing. One brow lifts at his sweaty workout attire. "Where did you come from? I thought you were upstairs."

He smiles and shakes his head, getting water from the fridge. "I went for a run."

I make a face. "Running, ugh."

"You don't run?"

"Only if someone's chasing me with a knife or my ass is on fire."

"It's good for you. You should come with me sometime."

"How far do you go?"

"Today I did almost five miles."

"I'll just stick to walking, thanks."

I eye him over my coffee mug from my place at the kitchen island. I must admit I don't mind seeing the results of his running habit.

The man looks downright sinful, all hot and sweaty. The white sleeveless T-shirt plasters to his skin in places, his black shorts riding low on his hips.

I want to see his happy trail again.

"Charley?"

"Yeah?" I sit up straight, snapping out of my daydream. "Sorry. What did you say?"

He's standing on the other side of the island, smirking like he knows exactly what I'm thinking. "I said, I'm glad to see you're eating."

"Oh, yeah. Peanut butter burritos."

His eyes light up. "I've been eating those since I was a kid. I used to eat those a lot on the road as a quick snack."

I nod. "Megan told me. No wonder it's all the kid seems to want. It's the one thing I've been able to keep down so far."

His brow furrows. "Are you still feeling sick?"

I shrug my shoulders. "Sometimes, but it's a million times better than it was at first. It gets better the further along I get."

"I'll be happy to make you one of mine next time. They're top-notch."

"And he's so modest, ladies and gentlemen."

"Why be modest when you know you're good at something?"

I shake my head and chuckle, admiring the movement of his throat when he takes a drink of water.

After he swallows, he narrows his eyes at my plate.

"Hold on, what else is going on there?" He gestures to the half-eaten burrito.

"Oh, I added an egg, bacon, and sweet relish."

"Relish?"

"Yep, and it has to be sweet."

He grimaces. "That's disgusting. Why would you ruin it with sweet relish of all things?"

I shrug and rub my stomach. "Nugget likes what Nugget likes. Who am I to judge?"

He makes a gagging sound and I laugh, picking up the food and taunting him with it. "Aw, come on now. This little thing is going to make you gag?"

"Get that away from me, Charley. I hate sweet relish. Pickles aren't supposed to be sweet."

I slide off the stool, coming around to his side, waving it toward him. "Come on, just try it. You'll love it."

He steps back with a hand out. "That's nasty."

I start laughing as I get closer to him. "Try it. For me?"

"No way." Laughter fills his voice as he turns his head when I put the food up toward his face.

"But Nugget wants you to try it."

He side-eyes me and then looks at the food in my hand. "Fine. But you don't play fair."

He grips my wrist and lowers his head, taking a bite. My breath hitches at the contact of his skin on mine.

I watch as he chews and I know when he's hit the relish. His nose wrinkles and he swallows fast. "Fuck, that's disgusting."

We laugh, and it takes a moment for me to realize he still has his fingers wrapped around my wrist. His smile fades when his eyes meet mine, and he tugs me closer.

My insides light up like a Christmas tree being so close to him.

The man is like a furnace. With the heat radiating from his body, even my sleep shorts and tank top are too much.

I bite my bottom lip and his eyes follow the movement. With something that sounds like a soft growl, he lets go and takes a step away from me.

"I need a shower." He turns and leaves the room.

Like his fine ass is on fire.

I sigh and toss the rest of my food in the garbage.

I try to read more of the *What To Expect* baby book, but my mind keeps wandering back to the man upstairs.

This is why I made rule number three. It's to save me from myself. I knew if I made it, Nate would respect it.

We've lived together for a month in this too-big-for-two-people modern house with gorgeous mountain views.

Right after we moved in, he'd been gone for two weeks, taking some broadcasting gigs and calling the games for his former team.

But when he's here, we get along well, like friendly roommates. We've managed to follow all the rules I made, including sleeping in separate rooms and me paying rent.

And because Nate is the consummate gentleman, my vibrator has seen more action than ever.

My body knows what it wants.

It wants the six-foot-two sex on a stick package walking back into the kitchen.

His hair is damp and slicked back, his jeans and T-shirt fitting his athletic body to perfection.

The words I'm looking at may as well be in Latin, so I shut the book and try to focus on my laptop screen in front of me. But I couldn't tell you what I was looking at if you held a gun to my head.

"What's that?"

My attention snaps to focus on the screen. "Oh, cribs."

"You like that one?" He gestures to the screen.

"Yeah, it's gorgeous."

It's a beautiful gray sleigh bed crib I just added to my baby nursery Pinterest board. It's also way out of my price range. And even though I know I could ask Nate to buy it, my pride just won't let me.

He scratches his head. "I guess we need to start thinking about those things, huh?"

"Yeah."

"The baby website hasn't said anything about it yet."

I smile and shake my head. "It's so adorable you're following along."

He shrugs, his cheeks turning pink. "I want to know what's going on so I can be supportive."

"Well, thank you. I appreciate it."

"Hey, what are you doing today?" he asks, sitting on the stool next to me and biting into an apple.

The way his jaw moves when he chews makes my skin flush. I've got it bad if I think he's sexy eating an apple.

"I've got a call with a client in an hour. But that's all I've got planned so far. Why, what's up?"

"I need your expertise."

"Mine?"

"Yeah, you know bars, and I need help with mine."

"Okay. What kind of help do you need?"

He chews, his face thoughtful. "Where the best place would be to put the main bar, table placement for best traffic flow, things like that."

His eyes meet mine, and a smile lifts one side of his mouth. "My contractor asked me questions the other day and I had no idea what to tell him."

"You don't have a consultant?"

"I tried a couple but they weren't right." He glances at my computer. "But if you've got plans or work to do, don't worry about it."

"No, I don't mind helping."

He smiles and my insides melt. "Great. Just come to my office when you're ready. I can show you the blueprints."

"Okay."

I head upstairs to dress, prep for my call, and—much to my dismay—count the minutes until I get to spend time with Nate again.

AFTER MY CALL WRAPS, I type up notes before heading to Nate's office.

"I like that smile on your face. Your call went well?"

I walk into his lair and take a seat.

The room's refined, but not stuffy, cozy with a fireplace in the corner, and screams man with its dark-brown woods and blue-gray painted built-ins.

It suits the man behind the desk well.

"Yeah, it was. The couple is throwing a surprise wedding.

Telling everyone they're having an engagement party, but it will actually be a wedding."

He smiles. "If anyone can knock someone off their feet, it's you, Firefly."

Our eyes hold and I don't think we're talking about surprise weddings anymore.

He clears his throat and looks at the sleek monitor in front of him. "Did you know at fourteen weeks, Nugget is the size of a peach right now?"

"Do you look up baby facts all the time?"

"Of course."

As though it's a foregone conclusion.

My heart flutters in my chest, and I swear my ovaries want to explode. Something about this man looking up baby facts gives me all the feels.

And I don't need to have those feelings.

"Of course, silly me. What else does it tell you?"

"Nugget should have all its major organs now and be developing reflexes. It also says you should be getting more energy soon so you should exercise, and your clothes may be getting tight."

I run a hand over my still mostly flat belly. "Yeah, pretty soon these jeans aren't going to fit."

"Sounds like we need to go shopping. My treat."

"Believe it or not, that sounds like torture. And you're not paying for my clothes."

"I can call my assistant and have her send you some things. And I want to pay for your clothes."

I stiffen my spine. "I can take care of myself, Nate. I don't need your money."

He sighs, leaning back in his chair, pinning me with a stare. "Charley, I'm well aware you can take care of yourself. I'm not trying to imply you can't. I mean, you pay me rent when you don't need to, for God's sake. But I'd like to do this for you. Please?"

Well, hell.

"I'm sorry. I just…" I look out the picture window, the mountains in the distance. "I'm just trying to prove to my family I'm not a screwup. And prove to you I'm not here because I want your money."

I want him. Just him. But I am not telling him that part.

He leans forward and holds out a hand, offering his palm. When I settle my hand in it, he clasps his fingers around mine.

"I have never once thought you trapped me into this if that's what you're thinking."

His thumb runs over my knuckles with the lightest touch I feel all the way down to my toes and makes warmth pool between my legs.

"I take responsibility for my actions, okay?"

He raises a brow, waiting for me to answer. But I can't form a word around the ball of emotion in my throat, so I nod.

"Good." He releases my hand and sits back in his chair. "Your next appointment is in a month, right?"

My lips part in surprise. "Uh, yeah. July 25th. How do you know?"

"Well, it says here, you go about once a month. And you told me about the last one while I was out of town. I did some calendar adding." He taps his temple with a grin.

"Ah yes, baby math."

"Yep. I wanted to know so I could be there this time."

"There's not much to it, Nate. I know you're a busy guy."

He levels me with an exasperated stare. "I told you I'm in this thing. When are you going to stop fighting me every step of the way?"

I hold up both hands. "You're right. I'm sorry. I'm used to being on my own and I—"

"Don't want favors. I get it. So, the 25th you said?"

"Yeah." My body softens and it begins to sink in that maybe Nate is for real.

I know, the guy moved me into his house. But just because he's a good man and doesn't want to see me sleeping in my car, doesn't mean he has to be into all the other things like doctor appointments and baby facts.

Yet he is. And I should stop fighting him. But I'm afraid if I do, I'll end up letting my guard down more than I should.

It's a slippery slope.

He clears his throat. "Before we get to the bar blueprints, I wanted to get your opinion on something."

"Sure."

"What do you think about me buying this house?"

I blink. "You want to buy this house?"

He looks out the window. "When I retired, I thought I would find some property up here near Megan. I'm always looking to grow my real estate portfolio." He brings his gaze back to me. "I have even more reason to buy a house here now."

His eyes cling to mine, analyzing my reaction.

There's a lightness in my chest as I smooth a hand down my thigh, keeping my eyes averted from him. It takes all my control to tamp down the glee I feel.

"Well, if that's what you want, I think buying this house would be a great investment."

"Good." I find it impossible not to return his infectious grin.

The man will be the death of me with his smiles and grins.

"Ready to talk bars?" he asks.

"Ready."

For the next hour or so, we look over the blueprints of the old oceanside restaurant he purchased last year. The layout is already pretty good, but I give him some additional ideas of where he could do things without compromising the integrity of the building.

"See, it would be better to open this up over here," I say, pointing to a side of the drawing. "but this column right here is probably load-bearing so you can't remove it without replacing it with a structural beam."

"Hmmm…" Nate stands next to me, looking down at plans on

his desk. One hand rubs his chin, while the other crosses his broad chest, his face contemplative. "Yeah, my contractor mentioned that."

He taps his finger on his jaw before sliding his gaze to me. "But you think it would flow better without it there?"

"Yes."

His brow furrows as though not convinced. A thought hits me and I hold up a finger.

"Okay, how about this then? You could add a support beam here,"—I point to a place on the blueprint—"and then have some structural columns but in different places that won't hinder the flow but will keep the integrity."

He tilts his head, staring at the drawing. Then he nods, that smile I love slowly forming on his lips. "Yeah, it could work." His eyes meet mine. "How do you know so much about this?"

"You're forgetting who my family is, Gentry."

"No, I just didn't realize you'd been exposed to so much of the business."

"When I was little, my dad would take me to job sites sometimes. I was only five or six at the time so I didn't really understand what was going on, but it seemed so exciting whenever he took me."

My mind wanders back to being held in my dad's arms, feeling so safe and protected, wearing a yellow hard hat way too big for my head. I blink back tears.

"Anyway, I also worked with Noah when he needed help in the office. And then of course, Del's *Property Ace* show ran for ten years. I guess I picked up a few things along the way."

"I'd say you did. Thanks for your help."

"Anytime. I'm here to help you bring your inner Sam Malone to life."

He turns to face me and blinks. "Did you just reference *Cheers*?"

"Where everybody knows your name? Of course," I say, scoffing.

Shaking his head, he laughs. "You never fail to surprise me, Charlotte Reynolds."

I shrug, ignoring the thrill running through me at him using my full name. Something no one else does unless I'm in trouble.

"Marcus, the owner of the Silver Moon, used to have it on at the bar. Not sure I've ever caught an entire episode at one time, but I've seen enough to know what's going on."

He nods. "On the rare occasion my uncle and I sat down to watch TV, he would watch classic 80's television. *Cheers* was one of his favorites."

"Norm!" we both say at the same time before laughing.

"Okay, who did you crush on? Diane or Rebecca?" I ask him, leaning against the desk.

He pauses, gathering up the blueprints. "Rebecca. All the way." He snaps a rubber band around the rolled papers. "I guess I've always had a thing for beautiful, feisty, independent brunettes."

The look he gives me is downright sinful. When did the room get so hot?

We share a heated stare that's only broken when his phone rings. He gives me a wicked smile as he moves closer and reaches around me to pick up the ringing interruption.

I should be happy to be saved by the bell, but as his arm brushes against mine, I only feel an impotent frustration.

He slides a finger across the screen to answer. "Hey, Darcy. What's up?"

"Hey, handsome. Just checking in with one of my favorite players." The voice is feminine with a hint of sultriness.

Who the fuck is Darcy and why is she talking to him like that?

A feeling I'm not familiar with whips through me. If memory serves, it feels a lot like jealousy.

I don't like it.

And if the smirk on Nate's face is any indication, my face is conveying my displeasure.

"I'm not one of your players anymore, Darce."

"I'm aware of this sad fact. When are you headed back this way? We have a birthday to celebrate."

The more this woman talks, the more my blood boils. Nate stands there, leaning against the desk, talking to her in front of me like it's no big deal.

Judging by the conversation and her flirty tone, they're familiar with each other, and it doesn't sit well with me. I need to get out of here before I make a fool of myself.

I get his attention and nod to the door with my head, mouthing *talk later,* before turning away, not waiting for his response.

But a hand snags my wrist and I'm spun back around. Nate's hazel eyes hold mine while he talks.

"Listen, I've got something to take care of. I'll be there next week and we can talk more then."

He ends the call while she's still talking and tosses the phone on the desk.

"Something you want to ask me, Charley?"

I raise my chin and look him in the eye. "Whose birthday is it?"

A smile plays on his lips. "Mine. It's the 15th. Is that the only thing you want to know?"

I file that little tidbit away but avert my gaze. "No. What you do and who you talk to aren't my business."

He tugs me closer until I'm standing between his muscular thighs. His fingers graze my cheek before tilting my chin up so I have to look at him. "You sure?"

"Yes." Despite my best efforts, the whispered word is full of uncertainty.

"I'm going to tell you anyway, and you can do what you want with the information."

I don't say anything because I really don't care who she is to him. Not...at...all.

"Darcy Emerson is the head of marketing and communications

for the team. I had called her earlier so I could go over my press release with her."

Some of the tension coiled in my belly loosens.

"She's also the daughter of the owner. I've known her and her brother, Derek, a long time. She's like a sister to me. I've never dated her and have never wanted to date her." His eyes roam my face. "Especially now."

My chest flutters, hoping I know what he's saying. But I've been wrong about men before.

"Well, just because I'm preg—"

He lays a finger over my lips, his eyes flaring. "Don't you dare say that. It's not because you're pregnant, Charley. I haven't thought about another woman since I met you."

His hands tunnel into my hair and he lowers his mouth, almost touching mine, while he stares into my eyes.

I'm frozen in place. My fingers ache to touch him and my stomach somersaults. All thoughts of rules and the reasons for them fly right out the window.

Before I take my next breath, his mouth's on mine, claiming me.

I don't hesitate. I open my mouth and welcome him in. My hands curl into his shirt, pulling him closer to me, and I rise up on my toes.

I've missed this with him.

His kiss, his touch, the way his cock felt inside me. The connection that's been there from the start.

It's a passionate but slow kiss, designed to seduce. He's chipping away at my resistance until my world consists of nothing but the two of us.

I whimper against those lips slanted over mine, wanting more from the kiss, wanting everything from him.

A loud chiming sound fills the air and we jump apart. He looks around to see where the sound is coming from.

"Shit," he says, picking up his phone. "I need to take this."

"Of course." I walk backward, away from him and his brain-melting kisses. "I'll see you later."

I hightail it out of the room, hearing him curse before he answers the call that saved me.

When I made rule number three, I should have been clearer. At the time, I feared it would be his cock that would take me down if I had the pleasure to experience it again.

I should have added his mouth and his hands. Those things have their own brand of weaponry to slay my heart.

With his words and his kisses, it would be easy for me to fall. Easy for me to think we actually have a shot at being a family.

But I know the score.

Nate and I are forever tied together because of the baby I'm carrying and nothing more.

FIFTEEN

UNDER THE EARLY July Florida sun, the baseball diamond is pristine in a way only a major league field can be.

At my first game in the show, I'd never seen greener grass, redder clay, or whiter, straighter lines on a field.

I spent sixteen years looking at the field from the bench of the dugout. As I sit here now, alone, the quiet stadium surrounding me, I realize just how much I miss it all.

The energy of the crowd, practice, the ice baths, and the grueling schedule I both loved and hated.

Retiring from active play was the right choice, but I'm not ready to let go of being part of the game.

"I thought I'd find you here." A deep voice fills the space around me, making me smile.

Lucas Raines, veteran star pitcher of the Bull Sharks, and the closest thing I have to a best friend, strolls into the dugout grinning.

Lucas and I practically came up through the organization together, with him being traded to the Bull Sharks the year after me. He's the only other player on the team that's been with them almost as long as I have.

And he's still going. At thirty-nine, he shows no sign of slowing down.

The man has a multimillion dollar arm built by the gods. We were a solid team, anticipating each other's moves and signals.

He's dressed in his uniform, ready to take the field for practice starting soon. A pang of longing flashes through me.

"Hey, man." We bump fists as he sits down next to me.

Baseball is a game heavy on superstitions, so it doesn't escape my notice we sit in the same places we did every home game.

"How's it going, Gentry?"

"Not bad. How's your new catcher?"

He shrugs. "He's young, but coming along."

"He's got some good stats behind him." Though I know for Lucas, it is more about how well he connects with his catcher than any stat.

"Yeah. He's good for the team. For me? Jury's still out." He bumps my shoulder. "Still hoping they can talk you into changing that manager contract into a player contract."

I chuckle. "Not likely."

Especially now.

"Hey, I gotta try. Haven't heard much out of you lately."

"Yeah, I've been busy."

"How's the bar coming along?"

"Well, I just found out the contractor I hired ended up landing a huge job in North Carolina he couldn't turn down. So, it's on pause for now."

"I know someone who can help you. You remember Theo Thomas?"

I furrow a brow at his random question. "Former NFL quarterback?"

"Yeah. He started a renovation business after he retired last year. Went up to New York for a while but moved back here recently. I bet he could help you."

"That'd be great. Text me his number when you have a

chance." I smile. "Didn't know you knew any of the pigskin players."

"He's a fraternity brother and we've kept in touch." Lucas pulls out his phone and his fingers fly across the screen, and a moment later my back pocket pings. "Give him a call. Hopefully he can get you going."

"Thanks, man."

"Hey, Cape Sands needs some place to get a good drink that doesn't require a reservation or a dress code like the beach club."

I chuckle. "I'm happy to oblige."

"Grapevine says you've been doing some commentating. You headed to Seattle for the All-Star game?"

"Yeah, fly out tomorrow morning."

He looks over at me. "You like that gig?"

I shrug. "I like it enough. I'm at least involved with the game."

"Yeah, but not enough for you."

Lucas doesn't know too much about my past, but he knows me well enough I can't deny it without him calling bullshit.

"No, it isn't enough."

"You sign your contract today?"

"No."

He turns his head and I feel the weight of his stare on me. "What do you mean? I thought it was a done deal."

"It is. Mostly."

"So, what's the problem? We need you leading the team, Nate. Hollister's doing great this year, but the man's ready to retire."

I blow out a breath, guilt weighing on my chest. "I know."

"But you didn't sign?"

I cross my arms over my chest and slouch back against the bench, letting out a long sigh. "There's a new development making me hesitate."

"I'm listening."

I drop my head for a moment before meeting his gaze. "I'm going to be a father."

His brown eyes bug out of his head. "Say what?"

"I'm going to—"

He holds up a hand. "I heard what you said. I just can't believe it." He stares out at the field. "Holy shit. How did that happen?"

"Raines, I'm not giving you a birds and bees lesson."

"Fuck you, man. I know that lesson inside out."

With his girl in every port reputation, I know he isn't lying.

He continues. "I mean, after the stunt that one girl pulled a few years back, it's unexpected coming from you."

I rub the back of my neck. "Yeah, I know."

"So...who is she? Do you like this woman? Are you sure it's yours?"

I cut my eyes to him and my spine stiffens at the last question, but I keep my temper at bay because I know he's not wrong in asking.

"Her name's Charley, yes, I like her, and I'm sure it's mine."

"What's so different about her?"

I look out to the field, thinking about Charley. We're getting to know each other slowly, but surely. "For starters, she's not a cleat chaser. She treats me like I'm just a regular guy. She's smart, funny, sassy as hell."

The grin I've seen make women swoon spreads across his face. "Aw, shit. You *do* like this girl. As in like her, like her."

"What the hell does that mean? Of course, I like her. What are we, in junior high?"

"Man, you didn't once say anything about what she looks like."

I pause. I hadn't, had I? Shit.

"So, what does she look like?"

I pull out my phone and flip to a picture Megan sent me. She'd sent several photos of the party, but this was the only one with Charley in it.

It's a full body shot of her in that hot as fuck dress I peeled her out of, and she's looking at the photographer with a smile. It's a sexy, mysterious smile. The one that turns me inside out.

Lucas whistles low. "Holy hell. She's hot. I don't blame you for wanting to hook up with her." He looks over at me, a teasing glint in his eye. "If you decide she's not for you, you know I'm a sucker for curvy brunettes."

"Don't get any fucking ideas, Raines," I growl, shoving the phone back in my pocket.

He holds his hands up, laughing. "Kidding." He claps my shoulder. "You've got it bad."

I scoff. "I don't got it bad."

Yes, I do. But I don't want to.

"Whatever you say, Gentry. Where'd you meet her?"

"At Megan's birthday party back in March. Charley's her best friend. And her brother is my future brother-in-law."

He blinks, then shakes his head. "That's not complicated at all."

I stand to pace. "Tell me about it."

"And where does Charley live?"

"In the same town north of Atlanta where Megan lives—Madison Ridge."

"Are you guys a thing now?"

"I mean, we live together. But we're just friends."

"Jesus, Nate. You live with her? Retirement didn't slow you down, did it?"

I sigh and lean over the rail, wanting the field to bring me the peaceful, easy feeling it always does.

But it doesn't.

I haven't felt peace since I left Madison Ridge—and the curvy brunette who's having my baby—over a week ago.

I sigh. "It was a one-night thing. We hooked up after the party."

I still replay that night in my head. It might be my permanent spank bank visual.

I turn to face Lucas, laying it all out there. "The truth is I couldn't get her out of my head. But I didn't even try to call her because we had a deal. One night only."

Lucas chuckles. "That turned out well."

"Yeah, right? But we didn't talk again until the end of May when I went back and she told me she was pregnant."

I pin him with a look. "And I believe her because she has no reason to lie to me. It was as much of a shock to her as it was to me."

"Well, then. I'd be hesitant too in your shoes." Lucas lifts the ball cap off his head and runs a hand through his dark hair. "I wish I had some advice for you."

"The truth is I can't see how it would work anyway. I mean, it has to now that a child is in the picture. But as a couple? No way."

"Why?"

"First of all, she's too young for me. She's only twenty-six and just starting out with her career. I just retired from one. And then there's the fact that…"

I trail off, not wanting to voice my next thoughts out loud.

I'd spent the last couple of decades avoiding getting too close to a woman so I couldn't hurt her. Getting close eventually led to a relationship, which led to marriage and a family.

With my fucked-up childhood, I don't know how to be a dad or a husband, and I've never met a woman I wanted to try with.

Until now.

I want to be different with Charley and my child she's carrying, but can I?

The fact I can't answer without hesitation scares the shit out of me.

Lucas joins me at the rail and claps a hand on my shoulder. "Wow. A woman finally took down Iceman Gentry."

I scoff and roll my eyes, but my heart races. "Whatever, man."

"You know, the media is going to have a field day with this."

Worry and resentment fight for top spot in my gut. "Yeah, I know. My publicist sent me a release to look over this afternoon. And I'm going over it with Darcy this afternoon before we release it."

"You sure nothing's been leaked?"

"Yeah, Sharon's been keeping her eyes peeled for any stories or pictures," I say, referring to my assistant.

"Thank fuck for Sharon."

"No kidding. But Madison Ridge is like Cape Sands. It has tourism, but they're no strangers to celebrities. Her brother is Del Reynolds and her boss is a billionaire winery owner from California."

"No shit, Del's her brother?"

"You know him?"

Lucas nods. "Was paired up with him at a celebrity golf tournament a few years ago." He looks out to the field. "Huh. Small world."

"Yeah. Well, it doesn't change the fact that once this shit breaks, I've put her in the line of fire to be harassed."

I might have been able to protect Megan from it all, but Charley's another story.

He claps me on the shoulder. "You're one of the hardest-working guys I know, Gentry." The smile keeping his bed warm at night curves his lips. "You keep my ass in line, that's for sure."

I scoff. "Well, you need it."

"I'm trying to pay you a compliment here."

"Carry on."

"You're also a great guy. A true gentleman. I know you'll do the right thing for Charley, the baby, and you."

"Thanks, Raines."

He holds up a finger. "Wait, I actually do have a piece of advice. I know how you are with relationships. You don't get too close. But if you want this woman in your life as more than a baby mama, don't hesitate. You'll regret it."

I raise a brow. "Speaking from experience?"

He looks out to the diamond for a moment, a shadow crossing his normally carefree expression before looking back at me with a smile that doesn't reach his eyes. "A story for another day, Gentry."

He smacks me on the back. "Now, suit up. I need to practice

and since you're here, you may as well be my catcher again for a little while."

———

AFTER SPENDING time with the team while they practiced, meeting with Darcy, and grabbing dinner with Lucas and Derek Emerson, the Bull Sharks GM, I'm glad to be home.

I told Derek about Charley and the press release. He was grateful not to hear the news from the media, especially since we're near the end of contract negotiations.

With the news going out tomorrow, I need to warn Charley.

I change into a pair of sweats and grab my phone before heading out to the back deck. A glance at the clock tells me it's nearly nine p.m. I hope she's still awake.

Me: Hey, Firefly. You awake?

Charley: Yeah, just shut down work for the night. About to read my baby book.

Me: Working? Are you by yourself at the winery? Is someone there to walk you to your car?

Charley: Slow your roll, dad. I'm at home. *eye roll emoji**

Me: Okay, good. Why are you working so late? Are you getting enough rest?

My phone rings and her face fills the screen when I answer.

"Figured I'd show you proof of life," she says by way of greeting, a smirk on her pink lips.

If I were with her I know what I'd be doing to those lips.

I chuckle and adjust my crotch. "Thank you."

She leans back on a pile of pillows. "As you can see, I'm in bed. Have been for a while. I'm getting plenty of rest."

God, she looks so damn good.

Her dark hair is piled into a messy bun on top of her head, and a couple of loose strands frame her face. Her tank top hugs her tits in a way that makes me wish I were a fucking piece of fabric.

She's got that pregnancy glow about her, and my fingers ache to touch her.

Maybe I do have it bad.

I clear my throat of the desire strangling me. "How are you feeling?"

She rubs an eye with her knuckle. The move is adorable as hell. "Pretty good. I've got more energy, less nausea. But I'm wiped out after a full day of work." She smiles a contented smile. "But I love my job and wouldn't change a thing."

"I looked it up. Nugget's the size of an avocado this week."

Her smile grows, lighting up her face, her free hand rubbing the slight swell of her belly. My chest expands with an ache to be with her.

"I'm starting to show a little bit. Seems like she should be bigger than an avocado."

"She?"

Charley nods. "Yep. I think it's going to be a girl."

"What makes you say that?"

She shrugs. "Just a feeling."

I grin. Her eyes darken slightly and she licks her lips.

Yeah, that's another thing I read on the baby website. Increased sex drive.

Since we aren't having sex, it's probably a good idea I'm not going to be there for another week.

When I get home and in the same space, smelling her light, floral perfume, feeling the pull I always feel when I'm near her?

It's going to be fucking hell.

I try to think of something else to talk about. "What's got you working so late?"

"Some last-minute things on a wedding shower we have in a few days." She moves her laptop onto the nightstand and settles back. "What about you? How are you? How was your day? How's Florida?"

I miss the shit out of you. "Hot, humid. Like Florida in July. And

I'm exhausted, but in a good way. I hung out with the team for a while during practice."

"I bet you loved that."

"I did. I've missed it."

"It's understandable. That was your whole life for years."

I love how she understands me. I love how easy it is to talk to her. It also terrifies the shit out of me.

"Yeah, it was."

"How did the contract negotiations go?"

I rub the back of my neck. I didn't want to tell her I'm stalling in the form of some bullshit nitpicky contract changes. It's a sticky situation.

I want to be there with her and the baby. All the time. But there are problems.

If I do what I really want to do with my career, it keeps me in Florida and traveling a lot.

Then there's the issue of my inability to let anyone get close. My former teammates are the closest thing I have to family other than Megan, and I like it that way.

Or at least I did.

Now, I'm just confused.

Finally, there's the fact we aren't together as a couple. And yet, there's an intimacy between us I can't deny. An attraction between us so strong we had to make fucking rules to keep things from getting complicated.

It's making me crazy. Traveling is my only saving grace right now, even though she's always on my mind.

But I'm not the one for her. And as gorgeous and sensuous as she is, there's no way she'll stay single forever.

The very thought of her with another man makes me want to punch the wall.

Charley tilts her head. "That bad?"

Her voice snaps me back. "Uh, it was fine, why?

"Your face looks like you want to murder someone."

I run a hand down my face, trying to erase the emotions I

don't need to have from my face and brain. "Sorry. We hit a couple of snags Lou will negotiate."

"That's good." She nods before breaking into a smile. "Oh, I almost forgot! Thank you for the chocolate." Pink tints her cheeks. "I've already eaten half the box."

She slaps a hand over her mouth, her eyes wide, making me laugh. "Hey, babe. They're made to be eaten."

"But they were so colorful and glossy. They almost looked too pretty to eat." She lifts a shoulder with a grin. "Almost."

I chuckle. "I'm glad you enjoyed them."

"And I will continue to enjoy them tomorrow."

Which reminds me as to why I texted her in the first place. "Hey, listen. I wanted to let you know my publicist is going to send out the news about us tomorrow. I wanted to let you know to be vigilant."

"Do I need to worry?"

I don't miss the fear that flitted across her face. I clench my jaw, hating the fact she's worried about this and I'm not there.

"No. We kept it vague. We only mentioned your first name and from Atlanta. Nothing specific. But these days, people can find all kinds of info. And I just want you to be prepared."

"I talked to Del last week about how to deal with anyone that may approach me. He gave me some pointers. Plus, you know Aidan. He'll make sure nothing happens."

Relief floods through me knowing Aidan is there not only for Charley but also Megan.

"Good, that makes me feel better."

"I got this. You go do your big shot broadcasting stuff."

She squares her shoulders with a little shimmy of her chest. I keep my eyes on her face.

Mostly. I didn't notice her nipples through her tank top at all.

I don't have a case of raging blue balls and an ache in my chest either.

"Yes, ma'am," I say with a smile. "I'll be home next week."

"I'll be watching the game so don't be one of those cheesy commentators, okay?"

I laugh. "I would never."

She smiles. "Good night, Nate."

"Night, Charley."

We disconnect and a few seconds later, my phone pings.

Charley: I miss you.

My eyes slide closed and I rub my hand over my chest where my heart pounds. With those three words, it solidifies the one thing I know.

I am so fucked.

Me: I've made a decision. And Nate will just have to deal.

Megan: Okay...sounds serious. What did you decide?

Me: This baby is staying in my belly for the rest of my life.

Megan: *thinking emoji*

Megan: I don't think that's how it works.

Me: That's just too bad. It's staying up in this oven.

Megan: What brought this on?

Me: I'm reading this baby book and it's talking about the ways to deliver.

Megan: Okay...*shrugging emoji*

Me: MEGAN, THERE ARE ONLY TWO WAYS THIS BABY CAN COME OUT!!

Megan: I need more info.

Me: *eyeroll emoji*

Me: The baby either comes out of my hooha or they fillet me like a fish.

Me: Neither one of those is an option. So, in she stays.

Megan: Awww! You think it's a girl??

Megan: *gif of little girl jumping up and down*

Me: MEGAN! PAY ATTENTION! What am I going to do???

Megan: Ummmm...have the baby?!

Me: I curse the day I ever saw your brother's grin.

Megan: Stop or I'll give you a play by play of how Aidan and I made use of his handcuffs again.

Me: *Vomit emoji*

Me: Fine. I won't talk about it.

Me: Wait...again?! No, no. I don't want to know anything about my brother's junk. Ew.

Megan: Can't they give you drugs or something that will make you not feel it?

Me: Yeah, but I also read that sometimes they can't give the epidural. Like if the baby comes too fast or something.

Megan: I'm sure they can give you something to help.

Me: OMG

Megan: What now?

Me: It says here that I have to figure out if I want an enema or not before delivery.

Megan: Why would you need a...oh.

Me: Is this saying I could shit myself?! Oh my God! As if it isn't bad enough for my vagina to be out there for the world to see, I could shit myself during delivery?!

Megan:...

Me: That's it. Yep, she's definitely staying in there.

Me: Seriously, Megan, I'm scared. What if I suck at being a mom? I just want to do right by this baby. It wasn't expected, but now that it's happened, I just want to be as good of a mom as mine was.

Megan: Girl, you're not going to suck at being a mom. You're going to kick ass!! I mean, you had some amazing role models. Your mom, your aunts. They're all badasses. And so are you. And I think it's normal for a first time mom to be scared.

Me: I haven't been around a lot of kids in my life. Especially babies. What if I don't know how to hold it? What if I drop it on its head??

Me: I'll traumatize the kid for life. She'll end up a goofball like Del.

Megan: It wouldn't be so bad for your kid to end up like Uncle Del.

Me: OMG. It just hit me that he's going to be an Uncle. And so are Noah and Aidan.

Me: And Grace and Amelia are going to be aunts!

Me: Oh crap. I better keep this girl away from Ame. She'll have her flirting from the stroller inside a month if I'm not careful.

Me: *Crying emoji*

Megan: I can't wait to be an aunt!

Megan: *gif of man throwing glitter in the air*

Megan: But seriously. We're all here for you. I don't know what's going on with you and my brother, but he seems to be...happy. It's unexpected, but I'm ecstatic for him. He's a great man, especially if lets himself be happy.

Me: I don't exactly know where we are either. But things are good between us. And he is a great man.

Me: I'm just overwhelmed. There's so much to do and so little time to do it.

Me: Every week when Nate tells me how big the baby is, I can't help but wonder what he or she will look like. I'm DYING to know!!!

Megan: ME TOO!!!!

Me: There's a hospital tour I read about that I'd like us to take. Think Nate will go with me?

Megan: You won't know unless you ask him.

Me: You're right. I love you, Megan. Thanks for being here for me. You're going to be an amazing aunt! *heart eyes emoji*

Megan: You made me cry, bitch. I love you too. You're the sister I never had.

Megan: It's getting late. Go rest before you make my brother crazy.

Me: See you Saturday! Night! *sleeping emoji*

Me: Night! *heart emoji*

charley

THE FOLLOWING SATURDAY, I'm in the office, finishing up paperwork on the bridal shower I just wrapped up.

But my mind is elsewhere.

In Seattle, Washington to be precise.

I miss the hell out of Nate. Work has kept me occupied, but he's never far from my mind.

We talk or text every day and the first thing he asks is how I'm feeling. We've become friends, though our conversations do tend to have a flirty tone to them.

I would have never expected Iceman Gentry to be a flirt, but the man knows how to make a girl swoon.

Every night, I'm glued to the TV, watching any bit of All-Star game coverage I can find just so I can hear his voice.

The announcement of his impending fatherhood makes its way through the mainstream media outlets. As promised, his official release called me by name and that I was from Atlanta, but that was it. They didn't even have a picture of me.

I'm thankful for that.

Though, I thought I saw a guy the other day with a camera aimed at me, but when I looked again, he was gone.

I think I'm a bit paranoid.

There's all sorts of speculation about me. Some are harmless, like I'm an old high school flame—funny given our age difference —but some of it is disgusting, calling me a money-hungry call girl he met at an orgy.

After that, I stopped looking at social media and the Internet.

"Hey, you hungry?" Megan is standing at the door, holding up two bags of food.

"Yes," I groan. "Starving."

We sit and talk about how the shower went. She photographed the whole thing, and judging by the first glance the bride-to-be had of the photos, Megan worked her magic as always.

"Hey, you have that wedding planner's number, right?" she asks, popping a fry in her mouth.

"Yeah, wh—" My eyes widen. "Y'all picked a date?"

She grins, her hazel eyes so much like Nate's sparkling. We both jump up and hug.

I have two sisters, but being the "oops" baby means the closest sister in age to me is eight years older. I love them dearly, but we've never been super close.

I've never been super close to any female until Megan. We hit it off like we'd known each other for years.

The fact she's going to be my sister-in-law and the aunt to my baby is just icing on the cake.

"What celebration did I miss?" Emma asks from the doorway.

"Aidan and I set a date." Megan turns to her with a grin.

Emma claps and rushes in to hug Megan. "That's terrific! I'm so happy for you. Finally got the stubborn man nailed down."

"Yep." Megan shrugs a shoulder. "It was surprisingly easy. I gave him some options and he said he just wanted to be married to me. Tell him when and where to show up."

We all swoon over that comment. I love that my brother has found a woman that brings out the best in him and sees through his wounds.

Emma glances over at my desk before bringing her gaze to me. "I didn't mean to interrupt your lunch, but I wanted to let Charley know I had a talk with the mother of the bride before she left today."

My mouth goes dry and my eyes dart toward Megan, whose eyes are wide.

I cannot fuck up this job. Before the stick displayed *pregnant*, my goal was not only to find a job I could make a career out of, but to prove to everyone I'd grown up.

But now, I need this job to support Nugget too. I fully believe Nate will help financially, but my independent nature won't let me completely depend on him.

I swallow hard. "W-what did she say?"

Emma smiles and pats my shoulder. "Don't look so terrified. It was a glowing review. Said the facility was stunning, the food and wine pairings were top-notch, and you handled her daughter like a pro even though she's something of a bridezilla." She winks. "Sounds like the mom knows what's up."

I let out a shaky breath and put my hands to my cheeks. "Oh, thank God. You had me worried there for a minute."

Emma laughs and puts an arm around my shoulder. "Charley, relax. You're doing a great job. I promise, if you start to screw up, I'll let you know. Okay?"

Megan's eyes widen. "Are you crying?"

I nod and wipe at the corner of my eye. "Stupid pregnancy hormones. These are happy tears, I promise."

Emma hugs me. "Go home and rest. You kicked ass today."

"I will."

Once she's gone, Megan and I get back to our lunch and talk about wedding plans, where she makes me cry like a baby asking me to be her maid of honor.

A half an hour later, an unfamiliar ping comes from my phone.

I swipe at the screen and frown.

"What is it?" Megan asks.

"It's a notification from the doorbell system. Nate insisted on having it, especially once the pregnancy news broke."

"Has anyone been lurking around?"

"So far, no paparazzi have landed on my doorstep, thankfully, but many of the townspeople of Madison Ridge have managed to give me their opinion."

I pull up the app and tilt my head, zooming in on the picture. "What is that?"

Megan comes around and looks over my shoulder. "A big-ass box."

"I see that, Einstein."

A large, rectangular box, wrapped in sage-green paper and a white bow, sits on the front porch.

"We need to go see what it is."

"We?"

"Well, yeah. I'm no doctor, but you can't get that box inside by yourself."

Twenty minutes later, the pretty wrapped box sits in the middle of the foyer.

I'm breathless as I slam the front door. "I need to exercise more."

"Give yourself a break. You're baking a human."

She's not even the slightest bit winded, damn her.

"What did you order?"

"Nothing. But it's addressed to me, so let's open it."

I untie the bow and we tear at the paper until what's in the box is revealed.

I gasp and my eyes fill with tears.

It's a crib. But not just any crib.

It's *the* crib. The one I'd been looking at a couple of weeks ago. I didn't think he'd paid any attention.

"Oh, Charley. It's beautiful."

The wood is a soft gray with gorgeous sloping curves and drawers built in the bottom. My mind conjures up an image of a dark-haired baby girl sleeping, tucked in with pink blankets.

"Here, this came with it." Megan hands me an envelope.

I tear it open, my vision blurry with tears.

This looks like the perfect spot for little Nugget to get some ZZZ's.

Call me when you get this.

- Nate

P.S. I always pay attention when it comes to you.

I stare at his words, my stomach on a roller-coaster ride.

It's like he's in my brain, knowing what I want before I do. He makes it hard to keep him in the friend zone.

Megan wraps me in a hug. "You okay?"

Not in the least.

I nod, tears spilling down my cheeks. "Again,"—I wave at my face—"they're happy tears."

For the most part.

"Good. Listen, I'm going to head out. Aidan should be home soon and you've got to call my brother. Tell him I said hi and he did good."

Before she walks out the door, she turns back to me. Her eyes are almost pleading. "Be patient with him, Charley."

She gives a little finger wave and is out the door before I form a response.

I lock up behind her and sit on the floor in front of the box. I don't know how long I sit there staring at it, but a few minutes later, the doorbell starts to ring incessantly at the same time a notification from the camera app pings on my phone.

"Charley, open the door!"

"Megan?"

When I open the door, she rushes inside and shuts the door quickly behind her. "Call Aidan. There are reporters blocking the end of your driveway, and they tried to chase me!"

"W-what?" A tremor runs through my body when my blood runs cold.

"Reporters, Charley. Somehow they figured out where you live."

With a shaky hand, I open the app. Sure enough, at the end of the driveway, cars are lined along the street.

Some of them are careful not to walk onto the property, but others are a little more brazen. I even see one in a tree.

"Oh my God…"

My stomach churns, and it takes all my gag reflex skills to keep my lunch down.

Nate is going to lose his shit.

Aidan picks up on the first ring when I call him.

"Hey, what's up?"

"Aidan…" My voice wobbles and I hate it. I mean it isn't like these people are coming to kill me, but the idea of them invading my privacy this way is terrifying.

I now know what Del and Nate meant when they said scary.

"What's wrong, Charley?" Panic along with his commanding tone laces through Aidan's voice.

"There are reporters at my—I mean, Nate's—house. They're blocking the driveway and Megan can't get out."

"I'll be there in five." My brother's voice is cold and hard as the sirens go off in the background.

True to his word, five minutes later, my phone pings again when the Sheriff's SUV stops at the end of the driveway and Aidan steps out.

My brother's a formidable looking dude at six-foot-three and built like a linebacker. He's also former military and sees everything.

His superpower is being able to take people down with just a stare.

The reporters and photographers start to scurry away, and while I can't see it, I know he used "the look" on them. Including the guy in the tree, who jumps down, landing on his ass before he runs to his car.

Aidan walks in a few minutes later, his face a thunderous mask. It isn't until he sees Megan and takes her in his arms that it softens into concern instead of anger.

"Y'all okay?"

"Yeah," I say, blowing out a breath. "It was just tense there for a minute."

"I'll have Landon come out here tonight, and I'll keep a deputy on it until this blows over."

"That isn't necessary, Aidan."

He gives me a hard look. "You're my pregnant baby sister and you're alone out here right now. It's more than necessary. And you need to let Nate know about this so he can take security precautions."

I nod absently, thinking about how I do *not* want to tell Nate, but knowing I can't get around it.

Megan and Aidan wait around until my cousin and deputy, Landon, shows up to play watch dog until tomorrow morning.

When I'm finally alone, I stare at the crib for a little while longer, images of the future running through my mind.

A future I want with Nate, in spite of the issues with the press. But I know it will never be mine.

LATER THAT NIGHT, I decide I've put off calling Nate long enough. I waited, wanting to make sure I didn't break down in sobs when I talked to him.

I also torture myself a bit by watching the recording of the home run derby, where he commentated.

With a sigh, I lean back against the pillows. It never fails; when I see Nate Gentry on the screen, lust curls in my gut and my heart aches.

Truth is, I've watched him for years, thinking lustful thoughts.

But now that I've gotten to know him, he's more than one of my top five fantasy fucks.

He's flesh and blood to me now.

I miss the man as much as I miss the sex.

The charcoal-gray of his suit and the blood-red tie fit him perfectly. His dark hair is combed back, but one errant lock falls over his forehead.

My fingers flex with the need to run them through the thick mane like I did the night he kissed his way down my body.

And when the other commentators talk the reigning Home Run Derby king into hitting one last ball, drool pools in my mouth.

Even in his dress shirt, the camera picks up the play of his muscles when he swings.

And hits the ball into the stands.

When he grins and looks at the camera, I swear he looks into my soul. Add the deep timbre of his voice, and the throb between my legs is unbearable.

I turn off the TV and, before I can change my mind, pull up his number and hit the green button.

"Hey, Charley. How are you?"

"I'm good." I blow out a quiet breath, trying to sound like I've been relaxing with a book.

Not watching his latest segment on ESPN and debating another vibrator session. "How about you? How was your sponsor dinner?"

Rustling comes through the speaker, and images of his long, sculpted, muscular body flash through my mind and make me clench my thighs together.

Is he wearing a shirt? Is he shirtless? It occurs to me that outside of our one night we spent in the same bed—where he was deliciously naked—I don't know Nate's sleeping habits at all.

"Long. But it was productive. They want to continue our partnership."

"That's good."

"Yeah," he says on a sigh, "but I'm just ready to get home."

My heart flips in my chest. "To Florida?"

"No. To Madison Ridge."

The roller coaster in my belly is in free fall. I cover my mouth to hide the wide grin he can't see anyway. I school my voice to tame my giddiness. "Oh."

Good answer, Charley.

"When I say home, I mean the place where we live."

"Alright then."

"Didn't you have your wedding shower event today?"

"I did. And it went better than I expected."

"She was a bit of a pain in the ass, wasn't she?"

I laugh. "Yes, and she's the queen of passive aggression. Oh hey! Speaking of weddings…"

"Were we speaking of weddings?"

"Well, yeah. Sort of. Doesn't matter. What does matter is Megan and Aidan set a date."

"Oh yeah?"

"Yep, next October. She and Emma are nailing down dates since they're going to have it at the winery."

"She called me earlier but I missed it.."

Pain shoots through my head, and there's a churning in my gut I can do without.

I really don't want to tell him this and have him worry on the other side of the country.

"Yeah, so it might have been that. Or it might have been about the incident we had today."

Silence greets me from the other end for several beats. "What incident?"

I wince at his words that are colder than arctic air.

"Some reporters blocked the driveway and we had to call Aidan."

All I can hear from the other end is Nate breathing. And not in a sexy kind of way, but in *the bull has seen the red flag* kind of way.

"Nate, everything is fine now. All Aidan had to do was show up and they all took off."

"Did any of them talk to you?"

"No. They didn't even yell or anything. But they all had cameras, so I guess they just wanted photo proof of me."

"I'll take care of it," he says, his words clipped.

I know that I have to let him do what he needs to do, so I don't fight him. "Okay."

"Are you okay? No one hurt you?"

All of the iciness in his tone is gone and my Nate is back. "I'm fine. They didn't even get up close to the house."

I decide not to tell him about the guy hanging from the tree. His head might explode.

He blows out a breath, and the relief in his voice is tangible.

"Good, that's good." He clears his throat. "So, did you receive a package today by any chance?"

If my grin gets any bigger, I'm going to look like I have a coat hanger in my mouth.

"Yes, the crib came. How did you know that's the one I wanted?"

"I have my ways. I can't tell you all my super-secret powers."

I play with the drawstring of my shorts. "It's beautiful. I'm surprised you didn't have it sent put together already."

"I'm glad you like it. And I wanted to put it together myself."

I close my eyes against the warmth blooming in my chest. One by one, he snips those razor-thin threads keeping him in the friend zone.

"Hang on a second," he says.

His name pops up for a FaceTime call. I answer, laughing. "What are you doing?"

"I want to see your face."

His handsome, grinning face fills my screen and I want to kiss the glass.

From the angle of the phone, I find the answer to my shirt question.

His broad tanned shoulders stand out against the stark white of the pillow he leans against. The light around him is dim, giving him a shadowy, almost dangerous look.

God, he's spectacular.

While he sits there looking like a freaking underwear model, the tiny picture in the corner of my screen shows me looking like I put my finger in a socket. I run my fingers through my hair, trying to tame the worst of the flyaways.

"Stop fidgeting. You're beautiful, Charley. I mean it."

My cheeks heat and I drop my hand. "Thank you."

"How are you feeling? Still eating that nasty burrito concoction?"

"Listen, eggs and bacon already go together. What's a little peanut butter and relish added to the mix?"

"That's so disgusting."

"That's so delicious."

"I'm just happy you have your appetite back. My girl needs to be healthy carrying our precious cargo."

Emotions swirl in my chest like they always do when he mentions anything about us and our baby. It seems so intimate for two people who are just becoming friends.

But the lines are blurring for me and I'm not sure what the hell we are anymore.

"Hey," he says, "did you know Nugget is the size of a pomegranate right about now?"

I laugh, loving the weekly report he gives me. "A pomegranate from an avocado?"

"Yep, growing like a weed already."

"She'll be here before we know it."

"Still thinking it's a girl, huh?"

"Yep. I just feel it in my bones."

He smiles. "Well, you are carrying the baby, so I trust you."

It seems like a good time to talk about the hospital tour I want to take. But my stomach is in knots and my heart pounds. Why am I so nervous to ask him?

"Hey, so the hospital has a tour for expectant parents where they show you around the maternity wing and stuff. I was wondering if you'd want to go with me when the time comes."

I hold my breath waiting for his response.

"Of course, I'll take the tour with you. Just let me know when so I can get Sharon to put it on my calendar. I also had her put the ultrasound on my schedule so we're all set there."

Who the hell is Sharon?

"Who's Sharon?" I ask, trying for nonchalance but failing.

"My assistant."

"You have an assistant?"

"Well, yeah."

A vision of a hot blonde with big boobs wearing a tight dress enters my mind.

Stereotypical and totally unfair, I know, but I can't help it. On the heels of that vision, something hot and snarly snaps inside me.

A slow smile spreads across his face. "Are you jealous, Firefly?"

"What? No. I don't get jealous."

Liar.

He taps on his screen a couple of times and my phone pings with a text. "I just sent you a photo of Sharon."

I switch over to messages and open the picture. He has his arm around an attractive brunette with a great smile. He looks happy and relaxed standing next to her in his baseball uniform.

She's also old enough to be his mother. "Well, she's...pretty."

"She's worked for me for over a decade and has been more of a mother to me than my mother ever was. She and Archie have been married for forty-eight years, have four kids, and eight grandkids."

"Oh. Well. That's nice."

And I'm an utter fool.

He grins. "Feel better?"

I smile. "I blame the hormones. I blame them for everything these days."

He laughs, and it sends shivers down my spine. "You've got nothing to worry about, Charley. Since I met you, you're the only woman I think about."

I bite my lip and look away, heat warming my cheeks. Emotions are caught in my throat, leaving me unable to speak.

When I look back at the screen, his smile is soft, making my heart actually swoon.

"Did you know your whole body takes on a blush color when you're aroused?"

I close my eyes against the onslaught of feelings his words evoke. "Nate, I told you. You can't say things like that to me."

When I open them, he stares at me through the screen, all playfulness gone from his face. His eyes take on the dark green-gold color that twists me inside out.

"This rule number three we have. No sex. You meant like physically, right?"

"Well, yeah." What's he getting at?

"What about phone sex? Does that count?"

"Well, I hadn't thought about that."

His gaze is intent on mine. "Let's be honest with each other. I'll go first. Whenever I get myself off—which by the way, lately seems to be nightly—I replay our night together in my head."

"You do?"

"Hell, yeah. Charley, you rocked my world that night." He pauses, his eyes hooded. "Do you think of me when you touch yourself?"

His words and voice are so sexy, I can't even pretend to deny anything. "Yes."

Heat floods my body and he groans. "Babe, you're turned on, aren't you?"

I nod, unable to speak.

"Me too. Phone sex is pretty much the same thing. Except we can see and hear each other."

"Bends the rule without breaking it."

"Exactly. Now, let me see you."

I pull back the phone and angle it so my torso is in view.

"Ah, your tits are huge. I've missed having my mouth on them."

I moan, my nipples tingling just from his words. With one hand, I cup my breast, rolling my nipple between my fingers.

"Take off your shirt."

I smile. "So demanding."

"Do it, Charley."

I must admit, the demanding tone nearly has me panting.

I strip down until I'm naked on top.

"I want to see you, Nate."

He angles the camera so I get a view of his naked torso and the huge bulge in his black boxer briefs.

I swallow hard. "Your body is amazing."

He rubs a hand over his eight-pack abs. "It's all yours. Tell me what you want, Firefly."

"Pull out your cock and pretend it's me gripping it."

His eyes flare hot with lust as his free hand pulls out his cock and grips the base, making him groan. "Fuck, that feels good."

Watching his hand move up and down his cock makes me wish I was there and could taste every single inch of him.

It's hot as hell watching him.

He angles the phone so our eyes meet. "I want to see your pussy."

I slide my hand slowly down between my tits, over my stomach—which has a small curve it didn't before—and push down my shorts.

His breath intakes sharply, watching my fingers run over my slick clit.

"Oh, sweet baby girl. You need me tonight, don't you?"

"Yes." I arch my back, eyes closed, chasing the pressure I crave.

"If I were with you, I'd have my cock inside your tight hole. Fuck, you feel so good wrapped around me."

I whimper, my fingers moving faster over my slick pussy.

"Open your eyes, Charley. I want to see those gorgeous blue eyes."

I open my eyes and meet his. The desire I see mirrors mine, and I know I won't last much longer.

His hand moves up and down his cock, faster as he talks. "Get your vibrator."

I'm so turned on that I don't make jokes or play coy. I want to come.

I reach into my nightstand, find the one I want, and settle back against the pillows.

"Good girl. Don't turn it on yet. Rub your nipples with it."

I drag the purple silicone across my nipples, the motion causing them to bead up and tingle.

"Nate…" I breathe out, wishing it was his mouth on me.

"That's right, Charley. Now, turn it on and rub your clit with it. Get yourself nice and slick for my cock."

My belly jumps at the low hum when I turn it on. When the vibration hits my already sensitive bundle of nerves, I moan and arch my back.

"Jesus, you look so fucking sexy." Nate's voice sounds strained, as though he's holding back.

I open my eyes and meet his. My mouth drops open in a gasp, watching his hand move up and down in a steady motion over his erection.

"Fuck yourself with your toy, baby."

I'm so wet, the vibrator slides inside me easily and I begin to move it in and out, imagining it's Nate inside me.

"Oh, God," I pant out, the walls of my pussy contracting around the vibrating toy.

"Show me how wet you are for me."

I pull it out and bring it up to the screen.

His eyes are so dark, they're almost black. "Fuck me. I wish I could taste you right now."

I put the vibrator back inside me, needing the pressure to get me off.

Even if what I really crave is on the other side of the country.

"Oh God, Nate. I miss you. I want your hands and mouth all over me. Your cock filling me up."

"Shit, Charley."

"I'm close, Nate. Ahh…"

"Yes, come for me. Come all over my cock while I fill you up with my come."

His dirty words push me over the edge, and the orgasm hits me hard. The wave of release pulls me under, his name a cry from my lips.

My name is a guttural moan from him as white ropes of cum land on his stomach.

It's the hottest thing I've ever seen.

Our labored breathing is the only sound between us for a few moments.

"That was—"

"Hot," he finishes my sentence.

"Yeah."

"I need to clean up. I'll be right back." He lays the phone down and I hear him move around. A moment or two later, he's back and I'm yawning.

"Tired?"

"Yeah, you wore me out."

He chuckles. "I'll be home in the next few days."

"Will you be here for your birthday?"

"I think so. I'll have to check my flights. Why? You got something for me?"

He bobs his eyebrows and I can't help but laugh. "You'll have to come home and find out."

"I'm on the next flight."

I roll my eyes. "Good night, Nate. See you in a few days, crazy man."

"Good night, Charley. I'll call you tomorrow."

And he does, every night without fail. We don't have phone

sex again, but his phone calls are the highlight of my day, which only confirms what I've tried to deny.

Nate Gentry is breaking down my walls, one brick at a time.

I'M HOME.

Finally.

I've been on the road two fucking weeks and I missed her.

I went my whole life not knowing who Charlotte Reynolds was, and within a few short months, not seeing her for mere weeks makes me ache.

I open the front door and I'm greeted with an upbeat pop song coming from the back of the house.

My bags hit the floor and I follow the sound to the kitchen, stopping at the sight before me.

A thin layer of white dust—I assume it's flour—covers the counters and parts of the floor. A cookbook with stains on the page lies open on the counter, and a multitude of utensils and cookware litter every flat surface.

Charley's back is to me and I lean against the wall, enjoying the scene of her shaking her ass to what I now recognize as "Flowers" coming from her phone.

Her cutoffs leave her shapely legs bare and my hands itching to stroke her skin. The oversized T-shirt slips down one shoulder as she moves them in time to the song, and her ponytail swings as she bobs her head.

Lust unfurls in my belly, making my temperature rise.

She brings the spatula, covered in what looks like chocolate icing, up to her mouth, using it as a microphone, belting out the words to the chorus.

With a spin, she turns my way and screams when she sees me, sending the spatula flying before it lands on the floor with a splat. "Holy shit, Nate!"

I can't help it. I laugh harder than I've laughed in longer than I can remember.

"Nate, it isn't funny," she whines.

I hold my stomach, pulling myself together. "Oh babe. Yes, it is. The look on your face."

"It's rude to stand there without announcing your presence."

I continue to chuckle, and her lips quirk, trying not to smile while she cleans up the spatula mess.

"By the way, I don't mind buying you flowers, and if you come to Florida with me sometime, I'll write your name in the sand. But I gotta say, talking to yourself sounds like a personal problem."

"Haha, you're funny."

Still smiling, I walk farther into the kitchen, surveying the area. "What are you doing?" I ask, then sniff the air. "Is something burning?"

"Oh shit!"

She dashes to the oven and pulls out a pan.

Dropping it on the island, she waves the smoke away, and looks down at...I don't know what.

"Damn it! I can't believe I let it burn."

I come to stand beside her, examining the project on the pan. "What is it?"

She sighs, her eyes sad. "It was your birthday dinner."

I look down at her, my lips parting. "You cooked dinner for me?"

"Well, I tried. Megan said you liked Beef Wellington so I tried..." She sighs and shakes her head. "That dish is a real bitch."

She flings an arm out. "I made an absolute mess of the kitchen and all I got for my efforts is this large piece of charcoal."

My chest swells at how good she is. "I'll let you in on a little secret, Firefly."

"What's that?"

"I do enjoy Beef Wellington, but you could have made me a PB&J and I would have loved it. You know why?"

She shakes her head, her eyes steady on mine.

"Because no one has ever made me a birthday dinner. I usually spend my birthday alone or with my teammates depending on our schedule."

"Your mom never made you a birthday dinner?"

I shake my head, but the weight in my chest whenever I talk about my parents is lighter than I remember. "Nope. That's why I don't care what you would have made me. The fact you thought to do it in the first place is enough for me."

She holds my gaze. There's kindness and understanding swirling in them. It's like a balm to my soul that I'm not sure I deserve.

Being close to her, smelling her lavender shampoo, feeling the heat of her body, has me wanting to take her upstairs and reenact our phone sex session we had in person.

A smile curves her lips. "I have an idea."

"What's that?"

"I ruined this meal, but I'm determined to do this right. We'll need to go into town for a few things, but then I know a place you're going to love."

"You don't—"

"Have to, yeah, I know. But let me do this for you, okay?"

Any trace of sadness in her eyes is gone, and the spark is back. I'd agree to anything to keep that spark there.

"Okay." I nod my head toward the other counter. "You baked a cake too?"

"Yeah, I got that part right."

My eyes meet hers. "Thank you, Charlotte."

"Of course." She tilts her head. "This feels like a time to hug."

She lifts up on her tiptoes to wrap her arms around my neck. My arms come around her waist and I pull her into me. I bury my face in her hair, soaking in her warmth and essence.

All the tension and stress from traveling and navigating our situation melts away as we stand like that for a few moments.

It's then I feel the unmistakable small bump under the loose T-shirt she's wearing.

I release my grip on her and look down between us. "Oh, wow. You've got a bump now."

"Yeah, I woke up one day last week and there it was." She looks up at me. "Want to touch it?"

I swallow hard. "Yeah, okay."

My large hands cover her entire stomach. It's warm and firm under my palms. My heart races, knowing that's *my* baby inside her.

Our gazes meet, and a flicker of something I haven't felt since I retired from the game comes to life in my gut.

A sense of being part of something bigger than me.

She wets her lips. "Um, give me about thirty minutes to clean the kitchen and change. Then we can go."

I glance around the kitchen with a wry smile. "Babe, it'll take thirty minutes, but only if we tackle this mess together."

IT'S close to an hour before we get the kitchen set to rights and head to the town grocery store.

With the warm summer wind flowing in through the windows of my Range Rover and Charley's sweet voice singing along to "American Pie," I can't recall a time I ever felt this... free.

Baseball brings me a sense of peace in a way that makes me feel like I belong. My team is my family, even if I'm not technically a part of it anymore.

But this light, carefree feeling I have sitting next to a pretty woman, who's bobbing her head to Don McLean?

It's a new feeling for me. One I want to bottle up and keep with me when I'm not near her.

But also one that sends a cold sliver of fear down my spine if I think about it too long.

For tonight, however, I push that fear aside and enjoy the company, picking up the last chorus and singing along with her.

We laugh and chat about her work and my trip until we pull into the small parking lot of Shop 'N Save.

"Okay, you stay here so I can pull off at least one surprise." She slips the strap to her purse over her shoulder. "Is there anything you don't like? Like seriously detest?"

"Nope. I pretty much eat anything."

"I'll be back." She bounds out of the truck and before she shuts the door, I call her name.

"Yeah?"

"Thanks."

"Don't thank me yet, Iceman. There's more to come." She grins and closes the door.

My nerves fire all at once as I watch her walk into the store, waving to people she knows as they walk out.

I look around at the small town, bathed in the twilight of the summer night. Charley is a part of the fabric of Madison Ridge. How do I even compete with that?

I rub a hand over my sternum when I think about what's going to happen once the baby comes and next season starts.

A few minutes later, she walks out with two bags and a basket. When she gets to my vehicle, she climbs into the backseat.

"What are you doing and what is all that stuff?"

She huffs and leans forward between the seats. "It's a surprise, Nate. Now take a right out of here and at the next stoplight, take a left."

I follow her directions and while we wait at the light, I glance in the rearview mirror. In the darkness, I can't see what she's doing but the sound of crinkling plastic mingles with the classic rock playing low.

Then I'm hit with the smell of fried chicken. And it's heavenly.

I keep quiet though, letting her have the moment.

"You're going to go about a mile until you see the sign for Midway Square Park on your left," she says after we make the turn.

I pull into the drive for the park, only to be stopped by a closed, metal gate.

"It's closed."

"I've got the keys."

I turn my head to see her grinning, a pair of keys dangling from her fingers.

Before I can ask how she managed that, she's out of the truck and, using the headlights, unlocks the gate.

She swings them open and locks them back once I've pulled through.

"You have keys to the park?" I ask, once she's back in the passenger seat.

"Nope, but my mom does. And I might have called her while I was getting ready and she may have met me in the Shop 'N Save when I got our goodies."

"You're a good person to know around here," I say, chuckling.

She sends a saucy wink my way, making my cock twitch in my shorts.

Moments later, I'm holding a basket of food and following Charley to a small building.

She unlocks the door and walks inside. Before I can follow her, her disembodied voice calls out.

"You stay there, okay?"

"Got it."

I don't know what to expect, but a few seconds and a couple of clicks later, the world around me lights up.

Memories from my childhood slam into me as I stare at the scene in front of me.

A regulation-size baseball diamond behind a chain link fence fills my vision. It's a well-tended field, clean with sharp lines and not a weed in sight. Aluminum bleachers are set up next to the dugouts on the home and visitors' sides.

And in the middle of the mound is a pitching machine.

Goose bumps slide along the back of my neck as I turn to her, standing next to me.

"How did you...?"

She just grins at me.

I'm in awe that she did all this for me. It isn't as though no one has ever celebrated my birthday, but it's usually in the form of a party that's as much for them as it is me.

But this?

This is personal and just for me.

My hands ball into fists to hold back from hauling her to me and kissing her until we both forget our names.

"Come on." She takes the basket from me and heads to the home dugout, where a couple of wood bats and other batting paraphernalia sit waiting.

"I know it isn't major league level, but I tried to make sure you had a couple of options."

I pick up one of the bats, testing the weight. It feels good in my hands, like it did the night of the home run derby.

But this time, my audience of one means more than a million strangers cheering me on.

I swallow the emotions clogging my throat as I look down at the bat in my hands. I look back at her and find her hopeful eyes watching me.

"I don't know what to say. You definitely surprised me."

Her eyes light up. "Good."

Before I can think of rules and what I should or shouldn't do, I hook a hand around the back of her neck and bring her to me.

I capture her mouth with mine, where her soft lips part for me. Her hands curl into my T-shirt, pulling me closer. My tongue strokes against hers, and she takes as much as she gives.

It's a hot, erotic kiss that makes my dick want to punch right out of my shorts.

As much as I'd love to sit on the bench and have her ride me until we both explode, dissolving all this tension between us, I can't.

Even though I know she wants me as much as I want her right now, I've already crossed another line by kissing her.

I pull away and her eyes flutter open, her mouth still parted.

She's fucking gorgeous.

Not just on the outside, but on the inside too. Charley has the biggest heart of anyone I know, even if she tries not to show it at times.

She's not just a ray of sunshine, she's the whole fucking sun, warming me from the inside out. Thawing the cold I've felt inside for too many years to count.

I kiss her forehead. "Thank you, Firefly."

"You're welcome."

A growling sound breaks the silence around us. We look at each other and laugh.

"I think Nugget's hungry," she says. "We haven't eaten in a while."

"If the kid's hungry, let's eat."

Charley thought of everything, which shouldn't surprise me given her profession. The basket is big, but how she managed to get food, bottles of water, utensils, plates, the cake she baked, and a blanket in there is beyond me.

After we eat, we lie on the blanket staring at the dark sky lit up by the field lights. It's hard to make out all the stars, but I still see more than I've seen in years.

She rolls over onto her side and lifts up on her elbow. Her dark ponytail falls over her shoulder, and even under the bright lights, she enchants me.

"Why baseball?"

"You mean why did I play baseball?"

"Yeah. I mean you're a big guy with a helluva arm. I could see you being a quarterback."

"Well, I've always liked that baseball is a mental game. I also like not getting hit by guys as big as Mack trucks."

I think back to the day my life trajectory changed. "But I didn't choose baseball so much as it chose me."

She tilts her head. "How so?"

I sigh and stack my hands behind my head, hesitating to walk down memory lane. But no one has ever asked me that question before.

"The year before my parents died, I started getting into trouble at school. Stupid shit, but enough to get me detention almost daily."

I swallow back the dread building in my throat when I think of the beatings I took when I came home with the disciplinary report. I don't want to taint Charley's goodness with that kind of shit.

"One day I came home with a bad report and my parents were so high, they just told me to get out of their sight. So, I took Megan and we went to the park. Some friends of mine were there for baseball practice, and I started tossing the ball with them, hitting some balls."

I turn on my side and mirror her pose, but I still can't look at her. I run a finger along a thread line of the blanket, my mind back on that ballfield in Nashville.

"We started going to the park every day, and I'd play with my friends until their official practice would start with their teams. Then one afternoon, my buddy's coach took notice of how well I hit the ball. I told him my parents wouldn't pay for me to play, but he somehow found a way and brought me onto the team. The rest is history."

I finally look up and find her eyes are intent on mine. Then she sits up and picks up her water bottle. "What was his name? Your coach?"

"Coach Hayes."

She lifts her bottle. "Let's toast."

I smile and lift my bottle to hers.

"To Coach Hayes," she says, her blue eyes bright. "For seeing potential in a boy who became a legendary man. On and off the field." She smiles. "Happy birthday, Nate."

"Thank you, Charlotte."

Her eyes hold mine as I tap my bottle to hers. I'm calm and cool on the outside.

But inside, my heart hammers and I'm hyperaware of her nearness. Her smile drives me wild, and I want nothing more than to get her underneath me.

Bury myself in her until I don't know where I end and she begins. Hear her cry out my name when she comes on my lips.

But I hold up my end of the bargain, even though at this point, I'm pretty sure I'm going to have permanent blue balls.

I roll to my feet and hold out a hand to help her up. "Now, let's eat some cake then fire up the pitching machine."

charley

I CAN'T THINK of a better way to spend an evening than watching Nate Gentry hit baseballs.

He makes hitting homers look easy—the way his body moves as he follows through on the swing. The play of muscles in his forearms, his calves, and the way his hips move.

It's like watching a dance full of power and raw masculinity.

The pitching machine spits out another ball and he hits it to the warning track in right field.

He smacks the top of his batting helmet and steps back into the box, gets in his stance, and waits for the ball.

One after the other, he hits most over the fence, but there are some balls littering the infield as well.

When the machine runs out of balls, he walks over to the fence where I'm standing.

I lick my lips, enjoying the view. He's hot, sweaty, and sexy as hell.

He blows out a breath. "I haven't hit that many balls in a row in a long time."

"I'm glad you enjoyed it." I hand him a bottle of water.

"Thanks." He takes a long drink before giving me a smile. "You ready to pick up some balls?"

"Oh no, sir. I've arranged for that to be taken care of as well."

He chuckles, shaking his head. "You really did think of everything."

"It's what I do."

"Ready to go home?"

We lock up and head home, butterflies filling my stomach at the seemingly innocent words that mean so much to me but shouldn't.

The ride home is quiet, and I shift in my seat. Anticipation fills the cabin of the SUV and it's driving me crazy.

I glance over at him every so often, his face and strong jaw shadowed by the dashboard lights.

What makes a man like Nate "Iceman" Gentry want to stick around in this small town with me? It seems too good to be true.

And in my experience when something is too good to be true, it usually is.

"You're quiet over there, Firefly. You okay?"

"Yeah, I'm fine. Just tired."

"Yeah, me too. The travel is starting to catch up with me." He glances over to me for a moment before looking back at the road. "I enjoyed tonight. Thank you for everything."

"It wasn't much, but it's all I could come up with on short notice."

He takes my hand in his and kisses the back of it. "It was perfect."

My breath backs up in my lungs at the touch of his lips on my skin. It doesn't matter where this man touches me. He leaves me in a puddle every time.

We pull into the driveway and make our way into the house.

In the foyer, I turn to face him, shifting my feet. "Well, I'm going to head to bed."

His hazel gaze is intent on mine as he leans against the front door, his hand rubbing his chin. "Good night, Charlotte."

Shivers run down my spine at the sound of my name. What is it about the way he says my full name that's such a turn-on?

I haven't got a clue.

Other than me being a horny bitch right now with no real outlet.

"Good night, Nate."

I scurry up the stairs, away from temptation in the form of a man so hot, he melts my brain.

But a couple of hours later, sleep eludes me. I can't stop thinking about Nate's face when he talked about his very first coach. The coach that gave him a chance and a future.

My heart aches for that little boy and all he endured at such a young age.

Other parts of me ache when I think about watching the grown man move.

Before I realize what I'm doing, I'm in the hallway, headed to Nate's room. I don't know what I'm going to say when I get there, but I just feel the need to see him, spend more time with him.

I knock but don't hear anything other than silence behind the door. I make my way downstairs and find him in the living room, stretched out on the sofa.

I expect to find him watching the ginormous TV, but instead he's reading. The man is the epitome of a hot guy reading. Any other time, I'd take a picture and post it on social media, #hotguyreading.

His long frame eats up the whole length of the couch, and his gray sweatpants do little to hide the bulge in front of them.

One large hand holds the book on his broad, muscular chest, his other arm tucked behind his head. Flat, chiseled abs lead down to the sex lines pointing to wicked promises.

I walk farther into the room. "Hey."

He drops the book down, his lips curving into a soft smile. "Hey."

I sit on the end of the oversized chaise lounge across from the sofa, my hands fidgeting in my lap.

"What's up, babe?"

Why am I so nervous? The man has seen me naked, been inside me.

"I, uh...just wanted to find out when you want to put the crib together."

"How about this weekend?"

"Yeah, sure. Okay."

He raises a brow. "Is that all you wanted to know?"

"Yes. Good night."

I stand quickly and start to leave the room, but something stops me and I turn back. "Actually, no. That's not it."

He snaps the book closed and sits up all in one fluid motion.

Jesus, he makes me sweat with every move he makes. I swallow hard and look away.

When he doesn't say anything, I bring my gaze back to him. He sits with his elbows on his knees, his eyes on mine.

"Charley, I like you. A lot. I know our relationship isn't conventional, but I like to think we're friends and we're in this thing together now for the rest of our lives. You can talk to me."

"Do you have any regrets?" I blurt out.

Okay, that's not what I expect to come out of my mouth, but the truth is, I want to know.

Nate lays the book on the coffee table and stands. His movements are slow, almost predatory as he walks toward me.

The tension in the room is so thick, I can hardly breathe.

This is how I'm going to die. Death by suffocation due to sexual frustration.

When he stops in front of me, I tilt my head back to look at him. His hand cups my chin, his thumb grazing my jaw, leaving goose bumps in its wake. "Not a single one."

My heart pounds in my ears, and it's hard to catch my breath when he touches me.

He studies my eyes. "What about you? Any regrets?"

His voice is deep and low, making sparks dance along my skin. But his gaze holds shadows. Shadows of worry and uncertainty.

Did I have regrets? Most people in my situation would probably answer "hell yes." But I can't find it in me to have any.

"No. No regrets."

He smiles, and hot, wet heat shoots straight between my legs. The man is magnificent, and while he looms over me, I don't feel intimidated at all. I feel safe.

"And if you're wondering if I'm here just for the baby, the answer is no, Charley. I'm here because of you."

His sweet words are one more chink in the armor I have around my heart.

Damn him.

In my head, I hear the last of the chains holding me back snap.

My tongue darts out to lick my dry lips. His gaze follows the action before coming back to mine. "I may have one little regret."

He narrows his eyes. "What's that?"

"Rule number three."

His eyes light up with desire, and the grin that spells trouble for me every time appears.

We're on the same page.

Thank God.

"We can always fix that," he says, shifting closer to me, his body brushing against mine. He keeps one hand under my jaw, the other dragging up my arm with a featherlight touch, lighting my body up like the Fourth of July.

With my heightened senses, I almost lose it standing so close to him.

"Give in to me, Charley," he coaxes, his voice low and raspy, his nose running along the column of my throat.

"Nate..."

He tilts his head and lowers his mouth toward mine. But he stops just short of my lips, so close his breath is hot on my face.

"Say it, Charley. Tell me what you need."

"I need you."

His lips curve in a wicked smile, making my knees buckle. "Good girl."

He lowers his mouth, and his lips seal over mine in a soft, but demanding kiss.

My mouth opens for him and his tongue slides along mine, numbing my brain to anything else.

One hand moves over my hip and grabs my ass, pulling me closer to him. I moan into his mouth, all my feelings right at the surface. My hands glide up his chest and into the hair at the back of his neck.

Crazed with lust, I want to imprint myself on him.

He pulls back and takes my hand. "Come here."

I follow behind him, giving me a front row seat to his fantastic ass.

All those years of squatting really paid off for him.

He glances over his shoulder. "Are you checking out my ass?"

I snap my gaze to him and laugh. "What can I say? Those gray sweatpants... Your ass looks exceptional in them."

He half laughs, half growls, and yanks me flush with his body. "You've got a sassy mouth, you know that? It's a fucking turn-on."

He walks me backward until the back of my calves hit the chaise lounge.

"Sit down and lean back."

I follow his instructions, holding his stare as I lean back onto my elbows, my stomach quivering in anticipation.

He drops to his knees in front of me and pulls off my leggings and underwear, tossing them behind him. His hungry eyes take in my bare pussy.

"Look at you. Such a pretty pink pussy. You ready for me?"

I cant my hips toward him, searching for release. "Yes, please."

"You're so beautiful. Already wet for me."

"I've been wet for you for a while now."

His borderline wild gaze snaps to mine. "You should've said something sooner. I'd have been happy to oblige."

"We had a rule."

"Fuck the rules." He runs a finger through my swollen folds. "My girl needs relief."

I groan at his touch and arch my back, fingers curling into the fabric of the chair. "Yessss."

The tip of his finger finds my slick opening. "Are you going to hold out again?"

I shake my head. "No. Never again." I moan and squirm, trying to get him to give me more.

He fills me with two fingers, pumping them in and out of me slowly. A delicious heat I've missed pools low in my belly. God, it feels so good to be full and yet I still need more.

"I want more," I moan.

"You'll get more, sweet girl."

His tongue flicks my clit, making me drop my head back. "Oh, shit. Yes, just like that."

Between his fingers pumping in and out of me and his mouth clasped to my clit, my orgasm builds quickly. Before long, I'm racing to the edge.

A groan from his throat vibrates against me and his fingers curl inside me, hitting that spot deep inside me no man but Nate can find. "Come for me, Charley."

"Oh my god, Nate." I grab his hair in one hand to hold him against me as the orgasm pulls me under into bliss.

As I float back down, he removes his fingers, and all I can think is how bad I want his cock where his fingers were.

He stands and unties his pants, letting them drop. My breath hitches seeing he's commando under those pants.

He's all ripped, well-conditioned muscles, broad chest, and powerful thighs. His cock juts out toward me, as if knowing I'm the intended target.

Even his dick is a thing of beauty—long, thick, and veiny in a sexy way. He grips the base and slowly tugs up and down, his eyes on mine. I lick my lips, wanting to taste every inch of him, and there are a lot of inches.

One side of his mouth quirks up. "You want some of this, Firefly?"

"Yeah, I do."

I sit up and shed my shirt and bra, now completely bare to his hot, intense stare.

"Fuck me. Your tits are beautiful."

"They're huge."

He cups one, rubbing a thumb over the sensitive nipple. I suck in a sharp breath and his eyes meet mine. "They're perfect."

I reach for his cock. "Come closer."

He steps forward and I wrap my hand around his hard, warm length.

He widens his stance, his thumbs caressing my jaw. His moans fill the room as I move my hand up and down his shaft. "Fuck, that feels good," he hisses.

Tingles flood my body as I look up at him. He's strong, yet gentle. Demanding, yet respectful.

He's magnificent.

"I want to taste you," I whisper, my hand picking up speed.

He opens his eyes and drops his head to meet my gaze. "I'm all yours, Charley."

I smile then wrap my lips around the tip, licking the precum beaded there. Damn, he tastes good. Warm and salty, with his own brand of musk, setting my pheromones on fire.

I keep my gaze on his, opening my mouth wider and taking in as much as I can. When he hits the back of my throat, I swallow and he twitches.

"Shit..." he growls out. "Damn, Charley. Your mouth is fucking amazing."

He gathers my hair in one hand and jerks his hips forward. I moan around his length as heat flares between my legs again. I redouble my efforts, wanting to give him as much pleasure as he gave me.

"Charley, baby. You need to stop." He tugs on my hair until my mouth pops off him.

I frown when he steps back and lets go of my hair. "Did I do something wrong?"

He huffs out a laugh. "Hell, no." His face sobers as he traces a finger over my cheekbone. "You're the most beautiful woman I've ever known."

His voice is a whisper, and his tone is one of awe. Those words make me breathless.

"I need to be inside you. Now."

I lie back and raise my arms above my head. "I'm all yours, Nate."

His hand wraps around his cock, pumping it.

"Stand up and turn around."

With my back to him, he moves my hair to the side and drops kisses along my shoulder blades. He moves up closer to me, his hardness pressed against my back. "Are you ready for me?"

I nod, my heart pounding in my ears.

"Good." One large hand nudges me and I bend over, my hands braced on the chair, baring my core to him.

He groans. "I have to warn you now, Charley. I don't have it in me right now to do anything but fuck you."

I press my back against him and wiggle my ass. "I need to be fucked, Nate."

"I'm going to be so deep in this pussy, you're going to feel me for days." He runs a hand down my spine, making me arch my back like a cat.

Without warning, he slaps one ass cheek. The unexpected sting causes me to yelp, and desire courses through me. He caresses the spot, soothing my hot skin, making me moan.

"Hmm...your ass. Damn, it's a work of art."

The head of his cock slides easily against my folds and I jerk at the contact. In the next breath, Nate is sheathed inside me, and I cry out as he stretches and fills me.

It's a delicious combination of pleasure and pain.

"You good?"

"I am so good," I say between pants.

Nate winds my hair around his fist, causing my head to fall back. At the same time, he pulls out and slams into me. I arch my back and push back against him, wanting more.

My whole world narrows down to Nate and me. "Yes, Nate. Fuck me."

He grips my hips with both hands and thrusts into me over and over, my orgasm building each time.

Then he changes the angle so he bottoms out with each thrust. No man has ever been able to hit my G-spot from behind.

Delirious with lust, I worry I might not survive my next orgasm.

Nate leans forward, covering my back, his cock deep in me. He reaches around and flicks my clit.

That's all it takes before I explode.

"Oh my God…yes!"

"Come on my cock, baby."

He lifts back up and grips both hips, pounding into me as I clench around him. "Fuck me, Charley. You feel amazing."

One last deep thrust and he stills, a guttural moan deep in his throat, his hips against my ass as his release spills inside me. I lower my forehead to the chair and try to catch my breath as he continues to twitch and grind against me.

His forehead drops onto the center of my back, his hands still wrapped around my hips.

We stay like that for a few moments, trying to regain our breath.

When he pulls out and steps away, I immediately miss him wrapped around me. He's back a few moments later, cleaning me gently with a warm cloth.

I'm weak in the knees, but Nate's strong arm wraps around my waist and I'm pulled up against his chest. With a tenderness that shoots right to my heart, he kisses the side of my neck.

"Feel better?" His deep voice is a rumble against my skin.

I smile and burrow against him. "Much better. Thank you."

"Anytime," he says, wrapping his other arm around me. "If you need me, I'm here."

I twist around in his arms and twine mine around his neck. "I appreciate it."

His hands roam from my waist down to my ass, where he cups my bare cheeks. "Hungry? I can make that disgusting burrito you love so much."

As much as I love my burrito concoction, I'm not hungry for food.

I grind and wiggle against his hard body, dropping a teasing kiss against his lips. "I'm starving."

Nate pulls back slightly and looks down into my eyes. A slow grin curves his lips. "Oh, you're a bad girl."

"Only for you."

His cock starts showing signs of life when it brushes up against my belly, and I grin.

"You bounce back quick."

"Only for you."

TWENTY

AFTER THE FIRST round of mind-blowing sex in the living room, we make our way to what I like to think of as *our* bedroom now, where we make up for lost time.

There's no way I can go back to being around her in the same house and not touch her.

I want to fall asleep and wake up next to her for as long as I can.

Our future is a big question mark, even though we're tied together for the rest of our lives.

For the first time in my life, I've come across a challenge I have no plan for, and I have no idea what to do about it.

All I know is I want Charley next to me.

I don't deserve her. She's too kind and full of love to be with a man who spends more time on the road than he does at home.

The fact is Charley doesn't need me; she can handle life all on her own. But I want her to want me enough to make us work.

My stomach quivers as doubt filters into my brain.

Charley sighs deeply, her head on my chest, and brings me out of my spiraling thoughts.

My breathing returns to normal as my fingers roam up and

down her arm draped across my stomach. Her skin is warm and soft and I can't stop touching it.

And the feeling in my chest when I saw her small baby belly? It's an intense level of pride I've never experienced.

She stirs, her soft tresses moving against my chest, a sleepy moan vibrating against me before she blinks open her eyes and looks up at me. A smile curves her lips. "Hi."

"Hello, Firefly."

A blush colors her cheeks and she lays her chin on my chest, outlining my tattoos with the tip of her finger. "Why do you call me Firefly?"

"When I was in Japan for a game, they had a ceremony where they released fireflies, and the way they lit up in the dark night was beautiful. They called it magic, and while they symbolize departed souls in their culture, they also symbolize love and passion."

Our eyes meet and hers sparkle in the dim light of the room. "The night of Megan's party, you reminded me of those Japanese fireflies flitting around the room. Beautiful, bright, passionate. You were like watching magic."

Her breath hitches and then she ducks her head. "Wow," she mumbles into my chest.

I lift her chin with a finger so I can see her eyes. "Don't play shy now, Firefly."

Her blue eyes blink. "I'm not shy. Well, not usually. I just still can't believe it."

"What can't you believe?"

Her gaze drops to my chest, and she draws a figure eight on it. My skin pebbles beneath her touch.

"Charley, you can tell me," I say when she continues to stay silent.

She blows out a breath and finally raises her gaze back to mine.

"You're not just some guy. You're Nate Gentry, future Hall of Fame baseball player. People all over the world know who you are. You're on the cover of magazines and people want your auto-graph. You could have any woman you wanted." She pauses a moment. "And you chose me."

The expression on her face is like a kick to the gut. She has no clue how beautiful she is, how she sees me for me, and makes me feel like a man that does more than entertain the masses.

I would choose her every time over any model or actress I've ever met.

"And you're carrying my baby."

"Exactly!" she says, eyes widening. Then she looks away again. "It's wild and like a fairy tale. I'm this small-town girl, hardly been anywhere or done much of anything. I'm twenty-six years old and managed to waste a lot of time."

She stares into space for a moment before looking back at me. "And yet, here I am. In your bed, with your baby growing inside me. I guess I'm waiting for the other shoe to drop."

There's a painful tightness in my throat knowing she doesn't see herself the way I do. The way she makes everyone around her feel welcome and special.

I want to make it better for her, show her she's everything a man could dream of and more.

I shift our bodies until she's underneath me. Holding my weight off her so I don't crush the precious cargo inside her, I lift up on my elbows and brush the hair away from her face.

I need to see her eyes, know she's listening to me.

"Don't get caught up in that gorgeous head of yours. Look at me."

Her eyes meet mine, and the uncertainty in her blue depths wakes up my protective instincts.

"Yes, strangers know who I am, but I'm not a person to them. I'm a commodity, nothing more. They don't want to know any more about me than my stats. It's one part of me. A big part of me, but just one part. Okay?"

She nods again and opens her mouth. I hold up a finger. "I'm not done."

Her mouth closes and I continue so I can make her understand. "I'm just a man. A man who is falling hard for a blue-eyed, small-town woman I can't stop thinking about."

I trace her cheekbone with a knuckle. "A woman I want to know better because the truth is, she's going to be the mother of my child, which makes her the most important person in the world to me."

I grin. "She's also the sexiest woman I've ever been with."

She rolls her eyes, but stays quiet, so I continue. "She doesn't believe me, but that means I'm going to have to show her all the ways she makes me feel with just her smile."

I tilt my pelvis and grind my length against her, where she's slick and ready for me. Those blue eyes that snared me from the first time I met her flare with desire.

I lean forward and drop kisses along her neck, making my way up to her ear, where my tongue flicks the soft and delicate lobe.

"I'm here and I'm not going anywhere, Firefly. Understand?" I whisper in her ear, just before I kiss under it.

"Yes," she whispers back and lifts her chin, giving me more room to roam her neck. She starts to writhe under me—moving against me, seeking what she's looking for—and I'm more than happy to oblige her.

I shift and line up against her opening. Our eyes lock as I push the tip of my cock inside her. It's pure fucking torture for both of us. "It's just you and me, Charley."

A myriad of emotions plays in her eyes. "Just you and me."

Her hands roam over my back and down to my ass, where she grabs and tries to pull me farther in. It takes everything in me, but I resist.

"Patience, baby. You'll get all of me."

She has my heart and soul. Things I never planned to give anyone, ever.

But somehow, this petite, sassy, dark-haired beauty cast a spell on me, and I have no desire to break free.

As I sink farther into her wet heat, her pussy flutters around my length, and I bury my face in her neck, inhaling her scent. "Mine."

My whisper is more like a growl as her nails score down my back. She pulls her knees up beside my ribs, changing the angle to where my eyes roll back in my head. "Yes, I'm yours."

The words come out in a throaty, possessive tone I haven't heard from her before, and I'm lost.

I slam the rest of the way in and she cries out, her core clenching around my hardness.

She's like heaven, hell, and coming home all rolled into one. I'll never be able to get enough of her.

An animalistic urge whips through me as I thrust into her over and over.

I rise up and lift one of her legs to my shoulder, grabbing her hips. I'm so deep, and from the change in pitch of her moans, I hit the spot that makes her crazy.

I piston my hips, a crazed man on a mission to possess. In my head, one word repeats over and over.

Mine.

Her hands grip the sheet beneath us, her tits bouncing with each thrust into her. Nothing has ever felt this good before.

Hell, it even eclipses the feeling I had when I hit a grand slam in the World Series that won us the title.

Fuck, I'm in so much trouble.

It's the last coherent thought I have before Charley screams out my name. Her pussy is a vise grip around my dick as she comes, drawing my release out of me. Her pussy milks me for every last drop as I spill into her.

Sweet Jesus.

Her leg slides off my shoulder, and I collapse on the bed beside her. "You okay?" I ask between pants.

She nods, her chest heaving. "Better than okay."

"Me too. I forgot my name there for a minute."

She laughs. "Me too."

We lay there for several minutes until a growl comes from Charley's stomach. I chuckle and roll to my side, laying a hand on the small swell of her belly. "Nugget's hungry?"

"Well, we have expended a lot of energy," she says with a wry grin.

"Then let's feed mama before she gets too cranky."

―――――――

CHARLEY SITS at the kitchen island, polishing off the last of her second bacon, egg, peanut butter, and relish burrito.

Watching her eat, in my old Bull Sharks T-shirt and nothing else, and knowing it fuels our baby is sexy as hell.

Even if it is the world's most disgusting concoction of food.

She pops the last bite into her mouth and moans before taking a gulp of milk. "It's so good."

I wrinkle my nose, my arms crossed over my chest.

"I know you find it disgusting but I do appreciate you making it for me."

"No problem."

I clean up the kitchen and she watches me, her face thoughtful.

"You know, there's a couple things we haven't talked about yet."

I lean against the counter. "Like what?"

"Do we want to find out the gender when we have the ultrasound?"

I think about it for a moment. "I say in the spirit of the situation, no. Let it be a surprise."

She grins. "Good, I thought the same thing."

"What else?"

"What about names? You have any family names you want to use?"

"No."

My stomach hardens as anger whips through me. There's no

way I'd name my child after the people who were supposed to love me but couldn't be bothered with my presence.

And let me know what a burden I was every single day.

Her eyes widen at my sharp tone. "I'm sorry, Nate. I know you and Megan were young when your parents died."

When she continues to look at me as though waiting for me to fill in the blanks, I sigh, a sour taste in my mouth.

I did say she'd get all of me, didn't I?

"How much has Megan mentioned about our parents?"

"Not much. Just that she was five when they died and y'all were sent to live with your aunt and uncle. But she doesn't remember much about your mom and dad." She focuses her gaze on me. "What she mostly remembers is you taking care of her."

I blow out a breath. This is the part I didn't want to talk about, the part that makes me feel inadequate. What I fight against all the time. I rub a hand over the center of my chest as memories assault my brain.

"Our parents were addicts. They were both in the music business, but I think they enjoyed the perks more than they did the music. They rubbed elbows with the music industry's elite. Singers, dancers, band members, producers, agents."

I sigh. "But there were all kinds of drugs and alcohol, those people in the wings willing to supply whatever they needed."

I press ahead even though my stomach is in knots. "My mother was a singer, my father a guitar player. They were both so talented. Especially my mother."

I can't help but smile a little at the hazy memory of my mother singing. "Before they got mixed up with the drugs, they were loving parents. What I can remember of it was good."

I stop, tapping into a box of memories I thought long closed. The memories I have of my parents being anything other than addicts are few and far between.

It hurts too much to think of them before they let their demons ruin our family.

"But after the drugs, they became these people I didn't know, love, or recognize. They were mean, abusive in all ways—physically, mentally, emotionally."

"Those are the hardest wounds to heal." Charley's soft voice is like a balm for my raw soul.

She threads her fingers through mine. I rub a thumb over the back of her hand, so delicate in my larger one.

"Long story short, they were too busy getting high all the time to take care of their kids. I had to grow up real quick."

I shake my head. "Megan was so little, I couldn't not take care of her."

"Oh, Nate, you were just a little kid as well."

"I was ten."

I close my eyes briefly, letting her touch soothe the dull roar of anger that always accompanies the thought of my parents.

"I was the oldest. I wanted to protect my sister. I even made up stories so she wouldn't know how fucked-up they were. But, when they died, I couldn't lie to her anymore."

My mind wanders back to the night I remember so clearly, even though it's been over twenty-five years. My mouth starts moving before I can stop it.

"My parents went to a party of some sort, a last-minute thing. They never ever missed a party. They were already high before walking out the door. So high, in fact, they forgot to call the babysitter."

My hand fists on the counter as I let the night play out in my head. "A couple of hours later, the cops showed up at our house. They were expecting to find an adult of some kind, and when they found it was just me and Megan, we were taken to the police station and sent to social services for the night until next of kin could be contacted."

I blink, weaving the pieces together in my mind. "There was an older lady with kind eyes taking care of us for the night. She's the one who told me about our parents. They'd left the party, headed to another, and on the way, missed the curve on an access road and slammed into a concrete wall head-on. Doing about sixty miles an hour. There wasn't much left apparently, but they found my dad's wallet and his ID.

"Afterward, it was a whirlwind of not knowing where we'd live and then going to live with my aunt and uncle. It was several days before they picked us up, and I remember Megan being so scared. I had to be honest with her, not about the drugs, but I couldn't lie and tell her they were just on a trip and coming back anytime. I had to tell her they died."

I look up and tears stream down Charley's face. I reach out and wipe the tears away. "Firefly, don't cry. They aren't worth the tears."

"Maybe not, but you are."

Her blue eyes are glassy and her dark hair is tousled around her face.

My heart literally skips a beat as I look at her. She's exquisite, and I want her to be all mine.

But as hard as I try not to be, I'm still a man who's emotionally damaged goods beneath the glossy exterior of fame and fortune.

However, just for now, I'll pretend I'm worthy of her. Pretend she's mine in every way.

I walk around the island and stand in front of her. Cupping her face with one hand, I lower my head and seal my lips over hers.

She opens for me and tilts her head, taking the kiss deeper. My tongue slides over hers, causing her to moan. It's a soft yet passionate kiss, one that has me harder than steel.

I pick her up off the stool, our kiss never breaking, and carry her to the sofa. When I sit down, she shifts on my lap until she's straddling me.

I run my hands along her spine, and goose bumps break out over her flesh. Her hips move, rubbing her pussy against my lap.

Lifting my hips, I shove my pants down past my erection, and when she settles back on my lap, her wet heat against my skin feels like heaven.

I lift her shirt over her head and cup her tits in my hands, thumbing her hard nipples. "Beautiful."

With a soft sigh, she rolls her hips again and I grip them, moving her back and forth against my hard length. It's hot as hell having her grind on me, the folds of her core rubbing against me.

"Oh, God. Yes…"

I move her hips faster, her wet heat coating my dick. "Your pussy is so fucking hot, babe."

On cue, she cries out, "Oh God, yes! Nate, I'm going to come."

"That's right, baby. Ride me."

She throws her head back as she rides out her orgasm, her hips slowing down to a roll.

Her breathing is harsh, and I run my hands down her back, soothing her. But a moment later, she smiles at me with kiss-swollen lips.

Her smile is the smile of a temptress.

With her dark blue stare on me, she lifts up on her knees and positions my cock against her opening. Her warmth surrounds my cock when she lowers herself all the way down to my lap.

It takes all I have not to blow right there.

"Fuck!" My fingers tighten on her hips and I hold her there, panting. "Don't move yet, baby, or this is going to be over pretty quickly."

She cups her tits, plucking at her dark nipples, soft sighs coming from her lips. Her eyes slide closed and she drops her head back, her long, dark hair cascading down behind her.

Jesus, she's a vision. Breathtaking curves everywhere I look. A vixen, a thief who stole my heart when I wasn't looking.

If I didn't feel her pussy wrapped around me and her soft skin beneath my fingers, I'd wonder if she were real.

She lifts up and slowly lowers. Over and over. All I can do is feel as her hips undulate over me, taking me in and out of her body.

My dick grows inside her heat, and the caveman inside breaks free. I lift her up off me and piston my hips up into her. Her tits bounce and she chants my name like a prayer, her hands curled into my shoulders, hanging on for dear life.

The smell of sex and the sounds of flesh meeting flesh mingle with moans filling the room. I look up and memorize the flushed skin of her body, the soft curve of her belly.

When she clenches around me, screaming my name, I finally let go. A growling sound comes from deep in my chest, and I spill my release into her.

She collapses on me, and I don't know how long we lie there, my cock still inside her, her splayed against my chest.

"Holy shit, Nate."

She leans back and snags my stare. Her lips part as though she wants to say something but decides against it.

Our eyes stay locked on one another, our stare saying all the things neither one of us can put into words without fear.

I want to promise her the world, that I'll be a regular guy who comes home every night.

But I know it's a promise I can't keep.

charley

AS THE WEEKS GO BY, the heat between Nate and me only burns hotter.

When we're in the same room, we can't keep our hands off each other, and it doesn't bother me one bit.

We stay home a lot, and it's given us time to learn more about each other outside the sheets.

The man loves thriller novels, prefers paperbacks, enjoys single malt whiskey on the rare occasions he does drink, takes his coffee black, and runs because he has a soft spot for rocky road ice cream.

He also tends to lose socks in the laundry, leaves dishes in the sink, and hogs the bed covers.

As amazing as Nate is with his hands, he's not great with putting together furniture. Especially if small screws are involved.

One Saturday morning we spent hours putting the crib together, only to find we had three pieces of wood and six screws left over.

I laughed so hard I nearly peed myself.

After muttering "fuck this" under his breath, Nate got on his phone and made some purchases.

Two days later, a moving truck shows up with the same sleigh crib and an entire nursery set, fully assembled. The movers haul away our sad attempt at being furniture builders.

Last week, Nate was able to arrange it so we had our own personal tour of the hospital's maternity wing instead of a group tour. It was eye opening for both of us.

It was a beautiful, calming, state-of-the-art center just for women, with rooms that looked nicer than some hotels I've been in.

Our guide took us to see the newborns and I was in awe.

Who knew babies were so tiny? And yet could make so much noise?

Watching them, my heart swelled with love and excitement. I can't wait to hold my own baby.

When I looked over at Nate, he was staring at one little girl near the window, who slept peacefully wrapped up like a blanket burrito.

His lips were slightly curved in a smile, but in his eyes I saw stark, raw fear. A flicker of apprehension coursed through me, but when he looked over at me, the anxiety I saw was gone as if it had never been there.

Had I imagined it?

As the day wore on and he acted like the same Nate as always, I figured I must have been projecting my worries about this whole baby thing onto him.

We're falling into a domesticated routine and I find I love it, something I swore I never would.

With each passing day, I'm starting to think Megan underestimated her brother. He's involved every step of the way, showing no signs of running.

Even though he hasn't told me his plans yet, I'm wondering if maybe he's sticking around and we'll be a family.

The third Friday in August, I wake up energized and ready to go. We have the twenty-two week ultrasound, and I can't wait to see the little nugget.

I stand in the middle of my walk-in closet, trying to figure out what to wear. I have more clothes than I know what to do with now.

Between my growing boobs and belly, a pair of pants that fit last week doesn't fit this week. When Nate saw the rubber band I used to try and extend the wear time of my pants, he swore under his breath and stomped out of the room.

The next day when I got home from work, I had stacks of boxes full of everything from bras and panties to work blouses and sundresses in various sizes and colors with a note from Sharon to let me know what I liked and didn't and she'd take care of it.

Nate and I had argued about it, with me telling him I could buy my own damn clothes and him telling me I was stubborn.

The argument ended when I landed flat on my back with Nate's head between my legs and an orgasm I felt in my toes.

I accepted the clothes.

A muscular arm slides around my waist, and a bottle of apple juice appears in front of my face. I smile and take the juice. "What's this for?"

Nate nuzzles my hair, his hand sliding under my shirt, cupping my breast. "I read somewhere apple juice can help make the baby more active. Thought it couldn't hurt to try."

My heart swells in my chest. "As much as I want you and all, we gotta go see our baby. And you need a shower. Why are you sweaty anyway?"

"Just got back from a run. What, you don't like my sweat on you?" he teases, trying to rub against me.

"Stop it!" I squeal with a giggle, squirming around to face him and slipping out of his grasp. "Go on, you animal."

He shrugs. "Okay."

He toes off his shoes and socks, a gleam in his eye. I try to look busy picking out clothes, but the cocky bastard knows I'm watching him.

My mouth goes dry and my panties become wet when he

takes his shirt off, tossing it toward the hamper. With a grin a mile wide and his gaze on mine, he drops his shorts.

He raises his arms over his head and stretches, elongating his body. Those sculpted muscles bunch and release with his movements, the tattoos on his pecs and forearms dancing along his skin.

My eyes are everywhere but keep coming back to where his erection salutes me.

He taps his chin and winks. "You got a little bit of drool right there."

Mortified, I swipe at my chin, which is dry. He laughs and I narrow my eyes.

Two can play that game.

I lift my shirt over my head, my nipples hardening when the cool air hits them. I glance up to see his grin disappear and his eyes take on a predatory gleam.

With our stares locked on one another, I push my panties and leggings down my legs, then kick them away. I sigh deeply, shrugging my shoulders, knowing it makes my breasts jiggle. "Now, what am I going to wear?"

I start to turn away with a grin, but he catches me at my waist and picks me up. I wrap my legs around his waist, laughing when he growls.

"Now you're sweaty," he says, cupping my ass. "Looks like you need a shower too."

OUR SEXY SHOWER antics only make us five minutes late to my appointment.

When they call my name, Nate and I stand together, and as we approach, the nurse looks up from my chart, the practiced smile on her face freezing. Her eyes widen and her mouth drops open.

"You're...you're Nate Gentry," she stammers out.

"Guilty as charged."

In spite of his dazzling smile, his eyes are distant. Almost bored. It's like the windows are all boarded up so no one can see in.

"Wow, I'm a huge baseball fan. My son and I just love you."

He shoves his hands into the front pockets of his jeans and gives a slight nod. "Thank you. I appreciate it."

"Oh, wow. I can't wait to tell him! You're his favorite player."

A blush colors her cheeks, and she goes from medical professional to fangirl with hearts in her eyes in two seconds flat.

I have to wonder who's the bigger fan, her or her son. My money's on her and not because Nate hit a career high, nearly record breaking seventy-one home runs in his last season of play.

He chuckles and puts his hand on the small of my back. "Well, thank you. Listen, I can sign something for him if you'd like, but how about we get my girl back into a room first?"

With the warmth of his hand on the small of my back and him calling me "his girl," I do my best not to give Nurse Fangirl a smug look.

She looks between me and him, almost as though just realizing I'm standing there. "Yes, yes, of course. My apologies. Follow me."

As we follow her back to the exam room, Nate raises a brow at me and I shrug. I'm not about to tell him, yes, I want to claw her eyes out.

In the room, he sits in a chair along the wall, crossing his arms over his chest, his broad body dwarfing the chair.

Fangirl manages to pull it together long enough to take my vitals and give me instructions on what I need to do to prepare for the ultrasound.

When she leaves, she sends a flirtatious smile Nate's way. The smile he gives her in return isn't flirty, but I still want to claw her eyes out.

Moments later, I lie on the exam table, white paper covering my lap.

"Are you nervous?"

I turn my head toward him. "Yeah, a little bit."

He places his hands on his thighs and stands, walking over to the exam table. He picks up my hand and kisses the back of it.

"Are you okay?" I ask.

"Yeah, why?"

I shrug. "It just seemed like you were...off when the nurse recognized you."

He sighs and looks down where our hands are joined. "I just want to keep you safe is all."

"I'm fine, Nate."

He nods but stays quiet.

"Listen, if there's one thing I know about Madison Ridge—and my family especially—is we take care of our own. And you're one of our own now."

He doesn't meet my gaze but nods.

"You know," he says after a moment, "I may have to change your nickname."

"What do you mean?"

"From Firefly to Wildcat. Keep your claws in around the nurse, baby. I only have eyes for you."

I stick my tongue out, and I'm relieved when he laughs, the shadows of fear in his eyes disappearing.

"We never finished talking about names," he says.

"We didn't, did we?"

"Have anything in mind?"

"If it's a boy, I'm thinking Paul. After my dad."

The smile he gives me warms me from the inside. "I like it."

"What's your middle name?"

"Thomas."

"Nathaniel Thomas. That's a great name. I love it."

"Yeah, but so is Paul."

"Well, what about Paul Thomas?"

His eyes sparkle. "Yeah, I like it."

I grin. "Good, me too. Now, if it's a girl? Lucy."

"That's cute. What do you think about Elizabeth? Maybe for the middle name?"

"Lucy Elizabeth. Kind of rolls off the tongue, doesn't it?"

"Sounds like we just named our baby." He ducks his head and kisses me softly, just as the door opens and the doctor walks in, Nurse Fangirl trailing behind her.

"Hi, there," Dr. Miller says with a smile. "How are we feeling today?"

"I'm good."

"Still experiencing nausea?"

"No, it seems to have cleared up now."

"Excellent. So, you're around twenty-two, almost twenty-three weeks along." She scrolls through the tablet in her hand before giving it to Fangirl. "Let's get started, shall we?"

Dr. Miller washes her hands, murmuring something to the nurse, who nods and makes a note.

I have to hand it to her, she's pulled herself together. She's barely looked at Nate since she returned with the doctor.

Which is good because I'd have to kick her ass.

"This might be a little cold." Dr. Miller squirts gel over my belly and rubs the probe through it. The sound of whooshing and a heartbeat fills the room. My gaze is fixed on the monitor, and my heart bumps against my ribs.

"Wow. There's our baby." Nate's awed whisper comes from beside me.

God, he's adorable. And hot. Adorably hot. It's a lethal combination.

I glance over at him to see him staring at the monitor, slack-jawed, his eyes wide. With a smile, I squeeze his hand. His gaze meets mine, and the emotions in his eyes make it hard for me to breathe.

I know one clear truth.

I'm in love with Nate Gentry.

Like one hundred percent, you jump, I jump, prime time in love with him.

I turn back to the screen, tears in my eyes, and the doctor talks about the organs growing right on schedule. The heartbeat's strong and everything looks the way it should.

I breathe out a sigh of relief and drop my head back against the padded table. Nate rubs a hand over my forehead with a soft smile.

"This little one is active. Do you guys want to know the sex? Because I can tell."

"No," we say in unison.

Dr. Miller smiles, dropping the probe into its holder before cleaning off my belly. "Okay, then. We're done here. Everything looks great, Charley. Still measuring on track, so your due date is still going to be around December 20th."

She prints out pictures and we wrap up the appointment. We stop at the front desk to schedule my next appointment, where Nate manages to fluster the office manager.

As we walk through the parking lot, I smack him in the stomach with the back of my hand, but can't help but smile. "She's old enough to be your mother."

"What'd I do? I just winked at her."

"You flashed her that trademark Nate Gentry grin." I point at him, gesturing to his face. "That grin is a lethal weapon, Gentry. That grin is how I ended up with this belly." I point at my solidly round stomach.

Nate laughs and throws an arm around my shoulders, bringing his other hand up and laying it over my belly. "I love your belly and the little nugget inside it."

At his words, my stomach flutters. He says it so casually, as though it's the kind of thing he always says to me. Without thinking about it, I lay my head on his chest as we walk to the car.

If only for a moment, I pretend Nate and I are more than friends with benefits, cohabitating for the sake of a baby.

ON OUR WAY HOME, we stop by the Chamber of Commerce to show Mom the ultrasound pictures, and once she stops crying and hugging us, she starts a list of things to do for a baby shower.

"Hey, is Megan around?" I ask her, after Nate walks outside to take a phone call.

"She should be," she says, half listening. "Last time I saw her, she had a bunch of pictures spread out in the conference room."

She adds a couple of notes to her list. "I think it'll be easier to have the shower at your house. You can relax and poor Nate won't have to carry all those gifts in and out."

I roll my eyes. "Mom, you've seen Nate, right? I think he's capable of hauling some boxes around."

She waves me away. "You're no help. Go, go. Oh, and tell Megan to come see me when you're done. We have planning to do!"

I laugh and head down the hallway from my mom's office to the large conference room.

I find Megan in there, glossy photos, some color, some black and white, scattered all over the large mahogany table.

"Hey," I say, stepping into the room, arms behind my back.

She looks up, a smile lighting up her face. "Hey! Nate with you?"

"He's outside, had to take a call."

She rubs her hands together. "Do you have pictures for me?"

I gesture to the table with my chin. "Looks like you have plenty. You don't need any from me."

She jams her hands on her hips. "Charley Reynolds, don't make me go tattle to your mom."

I laugh and cross the room to where she stands. Pulling the strip of pictures from behind my back, I hold them up for her. She squeals and snatches them away. "Oh, look! I see a little hand!" she says.

"And there's the heart," I point out on the grainy film.

"Did y'all find out the gender?"

"Nope. We agreed we wanted to be surprised."

She sighs dramatically and frowns. "But Charley! I've been eyeing this cute little dress in that shop on Center and Magnolia for weeks. How can I buy it if we don't know what you're having?"

I chuckle. "Well, you can buy it and save the receipt or wait to see what we have."

"So mean," she mutters under her breath. Then she looks at the picture again and her face brightens. "I cannot wait to meet my little niece or nephew."

She hands me back the photos, then draws me in for a hard hug. When she pulls back, tears are in her eyes. "Thank you."

Seeing her eyes well up makes me want to cry. "For what?"

"For bringing my brother back. I don't remember the last time I saw him happy about something that didn't involve baseball. It looks like he's come around on the family thing after all."

Her hazel gaze, so much like her brother's, is intent on mine. "You're the first woman he's ever been serious enough about to stick around and not let the game interfere with his life. I'm pleasantly surprised and proud of him."

I frown. "What do you mean by surprised?"

"Well, I told you about how he never wanted kids because of his career and leaving them behind. I knew where he was coming from, but I always thought he was selling himself short. Maybe now that he's retired, he's seeing things differently and he won't need the manager job."

She sighs and looks out the window. "I've always been proud of him for his career and the success he's had."

Her gaze meets mine again. "But there were times I hated the game because I thought it took him from me. He traveled all the time, or he stayed away to protect me from the media. Either way, he was gone. I'm ashamed to admit it, but there it is."

I smile, though my stomach dips at the things she says. "I understand."

She sniffs. "I'm sorry for dumping that on you."

"It's okay. But I've held you up long enough."

Before I leave, we make plans to get together soon to talk about baby things and wedding plans. When I walk outside, Nate paces the sidewalk, his phone at his ear. When he sees me, he holds up a finger, mouthing *my agent*.

"Sounds good. Email me the contract. Yep. Talk soon."

Contract.

My chest grows tight, and a wave of nausea like I haven't felt in months washes over me.

He taps the screen, disconnecting the call, and smiles.

"Good call?" I paste a smile on my face, hoping I look like a happy and supportive...girlfriend? Baby mama? What am I to him?

I hold my breath waiting for his answer. Do I really want to know about the phone call?

A call from his agent about a contract I know will change everything.

It tells me everything I need to know.

He nods slowly, looking at me. There's a flash of uncertainty in his eyes, but as soon as it's there, it's gone. His hand slides into mine. "Yeah, I think it was. You ready to go? You look pale."

"I'm just tired."

"Let's go home."

He kisses my forehead and I smile, letting him lead us to the car.

I blow out a breath and force away the tiny embers of dread burning in my chest.

nate

THE NEXT DAY dawns bright and humid.

The parade that kicks off the Summer County Fair starts in a couple of hours, and I'm looking forward to it, even if I risk recognition with all the tourists around.

I sit at the kitchen island, waiting for Charley so we can head to town early. Staring down at the phone in my hand, my thumb hovers over the email with the subject "Bull Sharks Offer" from my agent.

Lou gave me a rundown of what the email was about when he called me yesterday. But if I don't open the email, I can stay in my little bubble with Charley. Where the reality of our situation doesn't seem so complicated.

According to Lou, my old team wants me as manager of the team bad enough to give me virtually anything I want.

But the real shocker came when they said they want to retire my number. It surprises me to say the least, seeing as I haven't been retired for long, but the front office made the call.

The fact a jersey with my name and number will hang along with the greats in the stadium, number seven never to be used in the Bull Sharks organization again, is a bit surreal for me.

Never when I first started playing ball to escape my home life did I imagine I'd end up here.

It's fucking incredible.

The ceremony will be before the last home game of the season, and I want Charley to go to the game with me. I want to share the place that's been my world for the last decade-plus—and half of my life—with her. See it through her eyes.

But the thought of the media being around and sharing her with the world makes me sick to my stomach. They can be relentless, and what she dealt with the one time is nothing compared to what I've seen them do when they want a scoop. I don't want her subjected to it. Even though I can't imagine getting this honor without her there, it will be her call.

I'll have to make sure the team has tight security.

Aside from that, I don't know what my future looks like anymore. I've spent nearly my whole life playing the game. It was all I knew. I don't know anything else.

If I take the job as manager, my schedule will be the same as if I were a player. Before I met Charley and we started down this road, managing had been the next logical step for me. It was a no-brainer decision.

But all that changed when Charley told me she was pregnant.

It makes the back of my neck prickle thinking about it.

Aside from the occasional one-night stand and arm candy for a function, I haven't seriously dated much. I don't *want* to have to factor other people into my life decisions; I live my life that way on purpose.

It makes my life easy. It keeps my heart intact.

Relationships with a major league player are hard. Add in a kid, and they're even harder.

But ever since I answered her knock that night months ago, my life hasn't been the same. It was more than the fact she was pregnant.

I'd thought about her every day after our first night together.

Several times I picked up the phone to call or text her. But something stopped me every time.

Now I'm here, and a life without her sounds like a prison sentence with no possibility of parole.

But I can't imagine my life without baseball either.

I scrub a hand down my face, a headache brewing behind my eyes. I need to think of what's best for Charley and the baby.

Besides money, what do I really have to offer them?

Hell, I can't even put a fucking crib together right. I don't know a thing about being a real dad. My role models had been shit as dads. My father was no better than a sperm donor once he became an addict, and my uncle hated kids.

I have no idea what it's like to be an actual dad.

I don't even know if I can learn. And if not, I'll be no better than the men I grew up with who were no more than figureheads as father figures.

Footsteps coming down the stairs have me shutting off my phone and dropping it on the island.

Charley enters the kitchen, looking fresh as a daisy with her hair in a ponytail, a burgundy form-fitting T-shirt with the Gold Mountain logo just above one breast, and white shorts that stop midthigh. The T-shirt hugs her boobs and belly in a way that makes my heart swell—instead of other parts of my body—with pride.

Whenever I see her and that belly, I think I can do it. Be what they need.

She's mine.

Stepping onto the ballfields is the only other place I've ever had the feeling.

My stomach dips with the realization that I may already know my answer. I know I need to talk to Charley. She's always listened before, so maybe she'll listen now and we can figure this out together.

But she looks so happy, and I don't want her to lose that spark in her eye. There's still time.

"Good morning," she chirps.

"Morning, Firefly. Feeling good this morning?"

"I feel great today. It's gonna be a good day. There's the town parade and then the cookout with family and friends. You know how we Reynolds love a good grill fest."

"I get to man the grill today. My grill, my rules."

Laughing, she comes around the island and steps between my legs. "Yes, honey. You're the grill master today."

My heart turns over in my chest. I love how that sentence sounded coming out of her mouth.

Grabbing my face, she kisses me. "How are you?"

Before I can answer, she frowns, pulling back to study my eyes. "You okay?"

I smile and pull her into me, wrapping my arms around her. "I'm good, baby. Listen, I have something to ask you."

"Okay, shoot."

"You know how Lou called me yesterday?"

"Yes." Her voice betrays the slightest bit of nerves.

"The Bull Sharks contacted him, and they want to retire my number at the last home game of the season."

Her smile lights up the room and my heart. "Nate, that's amazing!"

"I want you to come with me."

"Really? You want me there?"

Could this woman tug at my heartstrings any more than she already does?

"Yes, I can't imagine you not being there. It won't be until the beginning of October. I know it's getting late in your pregnancy, but I googled it. It says you can still travel, but we should check with Dr. Miller just to be safe. They're sending the team jet, so it will be an easy trip."

"Wow, I've never been on a private jet before. And of course, I'll clear it with the doctor." She bounces on her toes and hugs me. "I'm so happy for you."

When she pulls back, I look into her eyes shining with happiness.

For me.

And there it is, that hitch in my breath whenever I see her, when she tells me about her day or asks about mine. Her laugh, her smile that lights up her whole face, the way she tilts her head when she eats those terrible burritos I make for her.

I'm head over heels, weak in the knees, in love with my baby mama.

I've spent decades running from love, and just when I thought I had it beat, I'm hit with a fastball that takes me down.

And I don't know if I'll get back up.

———

THE PARADE BRINGS out the crowds. It's hot, sticky, and tourists and locals alike flood the town.

After the last float trails by, we mingle for a bit, talking to people in town. By now, they're used to me even if I don't get into town a lot.

The ladies rub Charley's belly—something she tolerates—and the men shake my hand and slap my back, congratulating me.

Pride swells my chest and, for the most part, overshadows my earlier doubts.

We're heading to the car when Charley freezes in her tracks. "Uh-oh," she mutters.

I stop next to her, my hand squeezing hers, my gaze running all over her body. Panic like I've never felt before claws my throat. "What's wrong? Are you okay?"

"Incoming," she says out of the side of her mouth before pasting a smile on her face. "Hi, ladies! Don't y'all look spirited today?"

I look over as the Poker Posse approaches us. They're all dressed alike in white pants, black T-shirts with "County Fair Committee" printed across the front, silver sneakers, and straw hats. Two of them carry handheld portable fans, pointing at their faces.

"Look at you, Charley Reynolds. Having a baby." The shortest one in the front—the one I pegged as the ringleader at Megan's party—smiles at Charley.

"Yes, Ms. Faye, I am."

"Your mama is just over the moon, isn't she?"

Charley grins. "Yes, ma'am."

The other three do what they did the last time I met them. Surround me and look me over like a prized stallion.

Faye turns to me and smiles. "Hello, Nate. You ready to be a daddy?"

One of the twins leans over to the other. "I'd like to call him daddy if you know what I mean," she says, loud enough for me to overhear. They giggle behind their hands.

I widen my eyes and look over at Charley, who bites her lip, trying not to laugh.

"For God's sake, EllaMae, don't be such a hussy." The one with the perpetual frown glares at the other woman.

"Lighten up, Clarice," EllaMae says, huffing out a breath. "I'm just sayin' what we're all thinkin'."

Oh, Jesus.

My head spins and I look back at Faye. "Uh, yes, ma'am. I'm looking forward to it."

Clarice eyes Charley. "Boy or girl?"

"We decided not to find out," Charley says.

Clarice hums. "Good for you. We didn't get to find out in our day. Got any names picked out?"

"Yeah, we got a couple," Charley says.

"Oooh, you should name your child after a fruit or a direction," the other twin says. "All the celebrities are doing it."

Clarice rolls her eyes. "Have you lost your damn mind, Anna-Mae? They're not celebrities."

"Shows what you know. Nate here is a famous baseball player. He's been in the tabloids and everything."

"I'm well aware of who he is. I've watched him every year since he started playing."

It isn't the first time I've heard that kind of thing. But for some reason, knowing this cranky lady from Charley's hometown has followed my career since I was a rookie makes me stand a little taller.

"Okay, ladies," Faye says, clapping her hands. "Charley here looks like she needs to lie down. Probably feeling faint from hearing y'all bicker."

She pats Charley's arm with a liver-spotted hand. "We just wanted to come see how you're doing. Let's go, ladies."

We watch them walk away and I tilt my head. "Did she just say she wants to call me daddy?"

Charley laughs and puts an arm around my waist. "I'd be worried about her stealing you away, but I know she says that to all the boys."

"And here I thought I was special."

Her face is a bit flushed and she looks exhausted. I run a finger down one cheek. "Let's get you home."

A few hours later, I'm manning the grill and watching Charley work the cookout like a pro.

Her whole family—Mom, brothers, sisters, cousins, aunts, and uncles—is here as well as people from town that Charley knows.

Everyone knows everyone here.

I stay on the upper deck, using the fact that it's my grill and only I touch it.

But the reality is I'm reluctant to go down and mingle with her family. I don't know how to handle being around family, or how to have that easygoing camaraderie with someone you also shared childhood with, or what it's like to have a mother who still dotes on you no matter how old you are.

My mother stopped paying attention to me when I was about six years old. It's no coincidence that she and my father started using around that same time.

Rolling my neck, I try to ease the tension that matches the

anxiety in my stomach. I blow out a breath and flip a burger, tamping down the sudden sensation of dread that overcomes me.

My eyes flick back to Charley as she moves around the lower deck area. I narrow my focus on her, much like I do when facing a pitcher who knows how to strike me out.

The invisible band of panic around my chest loosens, and the headache brewing behind my eyes eases.

That's what she does to me. Brings me peace in the middle of the storm.

When my heart rate settles, my eyes rake down her body. The strapless sundress she changed into shows off her pregnant belly and enormous boobs.

I can't wait to peel her out of it later.

A few of the guys at the party notice her too. My grip on the spatula tightens.

"Easy, tiger." Aidan walks up behind me and slaps me on the shoulder. "They're just boys. Charley's known them forever and never had any interest in them."

"Hey, glad you could make it. Megan said you had to work. You headed in soon?"

He's dressed in his sheriff's uniform, a soda in his hand. "Yep. Would you mind taking Megan home later? I don't want to make her leave if she's having fun."

"Absolutely, no problem."

"Thanks."

We stand side by side quietly for a few moments, overlooking the backyard full of guests. Laughter, soft yacht-rock music, and the smell of burgers cooking mingle in the air.

"Great party, by the way. It was nice of you to invite everyone into your home. I know it can't be easy."

"No, it isn't." For many reasons. "But I'd like to get to know the people in Charley's life."

He half turns to me with a raised brow. "So, you're planning on sticking around?"

I meet his eyes, knowing what he's getting at. "I'll be around for Charley and the baby."

Aidan sets the soda on the railing with a sigh. He turns around, leaning his back against the railing, and folds his arms over his chest.

He has the intimidating cop stare thing down pat.

But I didn't become the home run king of the National League by being intimidated by a look.

He glances down. "You and I have a lot in common."

"What makes you think that?"

"We're part of the same club."

"And what club is that?"

He raises his head and looks me in the eye. "We're brothers who will do anything to ensure the happiness of our sisters. So now it's my turn to give you the talk."

He says the last word with air quotes.

I flip a burger, the juices causing a flame to flare up. "Fair enough. But before you start, grab me a beer."

He pulls a bottle out of the cooler and hands it to me. I crack it open and take a long sip. But instead of refreshing me, it only tastes sour on my tongue. "Okay, I'm ready."

Aidan holds my gaze. "You're a great guy, Nate. I like you a lot. You're about to be my brother-in-law. But fair warning. And I say this with love, I really do. Don't fuck this up. I don't know what kind of arrangement you and Charley have, and that's your business."

He pauses. "Take care of my sister. She's having your baby, who will also be my niece or nephew. And they deserve your best."

I swallow hard and look down at the beer in my hand, its cold condensation doing nothing to cool off my overheated skin. "Charley deserves the best of everything. But what if my best isn't good enough?"

He moves closer to me so I'm the only one that hears him.

"You know as well as I do, no one is good enough for our sisters. If I had to choose anyone, I'd choose you. But if you think you can't handle this, if you think your career is more important, walk away now."

My whole body tenses, and I clench my fist around the beer bottle to keep from throwing it.

"I'm not going to neglect my child," I say through gritted teeth.

"But the child isn't the only thing in play here. Is it?" He stares me down, one brow raised.

Damn, he's good at that. And he's got me dead to rights.

I open my mouth and snap it shut. Try again. "No."

"Anyone with eyes can see how you look at her. The only time I've ever seen your face relax is when you're around Charley. She and that baby are a package deal now, man. *Your* package deal. If you can't handle one, you don't get the option of opting out of the other. All I'm saying is, make smart choices. Do *not* hurt either of them."

He claps his hand on my shoulder. "We clear?"

I nod. "We're clear." I turn my head and pin him with my own intimidating stare. "Since we're having brotherly talks, let's not forget the one we had a few months ago."

He raises his hands up with a smile. "We're golden on my end."

"Keep it that way, Reynolds."

"Think about what I said, Gentry."

A look of understanding passes between us.

He finishes off his soda. "I need to find Megan before I head out. Thanks for taking her home."

"No problem." I nod, my gaze roaming the yard until I find Charley.

She's lying on a lounge chair with Amelia on one side, Megan on the other. Grace sits at Charley's feet, using her hands to tell some sort of story that makes Charley laugh. The sun shines on her dark hair, and she seems to glow from the inside out, surrounded by people who love her.

My stomach twists, thinking back to the contract sitting in my inbox.

It isn't as simple as choosing love over a game. Baseball is who I am; it's my identity. I will be a dad and Charley's man, but will it be enough without an identity of my own?

But if you think you can't handle this, if you think your career is more important, walk away now.

Aidan's words echo in my head. As much as his words piss me off, he found my weak spot and poked at it. I want to be angry at him, but I can't.

As usual, the problem is me. I don't know if I can handle both.

I'd never met anyone important enough to me to even try.

Until now.

What makes you think you deserve love, Nathaniel?

The voice that sounds like my father's—or sometimes my mother's—always makes me question my worth when it comes to love.

I never doubt my worth or ability when it comes to baseball. It's all so clear what must be done. I like knowing what to do with no confusion.

Love and family? It's messy, and I don't know how to handle messy. Love isn't something I've ever really had experience with. Even with Megan I don't think I did it right.

Charley and little Nugget deserve better than a guy whose first love is a sport.

Whose own parents didn't love him enough.

As though she knows I'm watching her, Charley raises her head and smiles, flashing me a wink. At the risk of sounding like a cheesy sap, it makes my heart skip a beat.

I grin at her, knowing how it makes her squirm.

All thoughts and doubts of the future and baseball are pushed to the back of my mind. I focus back on what's important in the here and now, pretending that she's truly mine and there's nothing standing between us.

I have a grill full of burgers, a houseful of guests, and a beautiful woman waiting on me.

charley

THE REGULAR BASEBALL season winds down, which means Nate and I head to Florida the first few days of October for the last Bull Sharks home game.

At around twenty-nine weeks pregnant and no complications, Dr. Miller gives me the go-ahead to fly.

On a beautiful fall morning, I end up sitting in a buttery soft leather seat of a chartered jet, looking out to the Atlantic below as we descend into a small regional airport just outside Jacksonville. It's a short flight and not far from where Nate lives.

Within minutes of landing, the humidity and warmer Florida air hits me in the face as we climb into Nate's huge SUV.

"We'll be at my house in about forty-five minutes," he says, merging onto I-95. "You tired?"

"A little. How much time do we have before we need to head to the stadium?"

He flicks his wrist to look at the time on his large watch. "A few hours. The game starts at seven and I need to be there by five." He lays a hand on top of my thigh. "So, plenty of time to rest and...*things*."

I laugh and rest my head against the seat. "I guess it has been at least twenty-four hours since the last time."

"I'm dying over here."

I glance over at him with a smile on my face. Strong jaw darkened by scruff, perfectly slanted nose, dark aviator shades covering his eyes, his wrist is draped across the steering wheel, controlling the powerful vehicle, his thick thighs slightly splayed in the seat.

He looks cool, confident, and sexy.

And all mine.

At least for now.

Every time I look at him, my stomach flutters. It isn't just the fact he's truly the most handsome man I've ever known. He's smart, thoughtful, and despite his accolades, he's humble.

Still, the way he looks right now makes me want to crawl over the wide console area and settle in his lap.

His fingers dance lightly up and down my inner thigh, driving me crazy. I need to think about something else before I tell him to pull over so he can fuck me.

A ringing fills the cabin, and the name Lou pops up on the dashboard screen.

"Shit, I'm sorry, babe. I need to take this."

I gesture to the screen. "Of course, go ahead."

I look out the side window and let out a slow breath, my stomach churning.

A call from Nate's agent is one way to douse the fire in my pants.

It isn't that I dislike Lou, but whenever he calls, there's the slightest shift in Nate's demeanor. Imperceptible to everyone but me.

He always says he's fine, but I see the shadows haunting his eyes.

Nate pushes a button on the steering wheel. "Hey, Lou. What's up?"

"Hey, bud. Just wanted to see if you're ready for tonight."

Nate's smile lights up his face. "More than ready." He takes my hand and gives me a wink that makes my heart flutter. "I got my girl here with me, and we're headed to Cape Sands to rest up. I'm looking forward to seeing the team again."

"Good, good. Listen, Nate, we're running out of time with the contract. They've—"

"Hey, Lou. I'm sorry, man. We'll have to talk later on this. I'll contact you tomorrow."

He hangs up before Lou responds and gives me a sheepish smile. "Sorry about that."

"It's fine."

"I don't want to talk business right now. I want to enjoy this trip."

Does he not want to talk business because I'm around? Or because he really wants to spend time with me?

I shift in my seat. The fact that I don't know the answer makes me sick to my stomach.

We lapse into silence for a while, and it makes me restless.

"So, tell me about tonight. Will I meet some of your teammates?"

He nods with a smile. "If you want, I can introduce you to the whole crew."

"Hell yeah, I want to meet them."

To my relief, the tense silence between us fades as we chat about the team, and before I know it, we're exiting off the highway and I smell the briny air that means we're close to the sea.

A sign welcomes us to Cape Sands before we cruise down Main Street. The buildings are made of stucco and brick, and palm trees line the side of the road. People mill around on the sidewalks enjoying the various shops and their offerings.

"This is what I imagine Madison Ridge would look like if it were by the ocean," I say, peering out the windshield. "Oh! What a cute inn! My aunt Lindsey would have a fit."

"The Lost Souls Inn. It's historical and apparently has a colorful history."

"Intriguing name." I turn my head toward him. "Is it haunted?"

"That's the rumor."

I take my phone out and take a picture of the Italianate-style house as we drive by slowly. "Even better."

The wide two-lane road of the small town becomes a mix of houses and high-rise condos before narrowing into a two-lane road with more private and larger homes.

Nate slows down at a wide, gated driveway at the end of the road. He hits a button on the control panel of the vehicle, and the gate opens slowly inward. All I see are low, thick trees mixed with palm trees, obscuring the view of the house and the driveway leading up to it.

I lean forward and look around. "Where's the house? I thought we were close to the ocean."

"We're actually at the tip of the barrier island."

"Oh." I pause, processing. "You own all of this land?"

"Yep. On this side anyway." He gestures to the left. "Chase Hanover owns the land over there."

"Former Admirals pitcher, Chase Hanover?"

"Yep."

"I'd like to meet him. He got a bad rap."

"Yeah, he did. He's a good guy and you'll love Eden, his fiancé."

I look around at the privacy the foliage provides. "I guess owning all the land helps keep paparazzi at bay."

He turns his head and grins. "Exactly."

Seconds later, the trees drop away and the large, modern beach house gleams in front of us. My eyes widen. "Holy shit. What a house."

He parks and leans across the console, kissing me hard and quick. "Come on, I'll show you around."

I look around at the lush landscape surrounding the large, white contemporary house. The warm breeze dances along my skin, and the sound of waves crashing fills the air.

It's paradise.

Inside, the house is just as impressive.

"Welcome to my humble abode."

I stop my midspin perusal of the high ceiling and give him the side-eye. "Yeah, it's a real dump."

He laughs and takes my hand, drawing me to the back of the house.

My jaw hits the floor at the view in front of me.

The back wall is made up of sliders opening to a wraparound deck overlooking the vast dark blue of the sea. The furniture is beige but looks comfy with pops of burnt-oranges, grays, and navy blues.

It truly belongs in a magazine.

I wander into the open kitchen, running a hand on the concrete countertop of the island. "Wow, Nate. You live here?"

"When I'm not traveling."

"It's beautiful. Pristine." I gesture to the cabinetry. "I love the walnut fronts of the cabinets. Very midcentury modern vibe."

He comes up behind me and wraps his arms around my baby belly, flattening his hands over it possessively. "You sound like a designer on one of those shows." His teeth nip at my earlobe.

I smile. "Well, my family's business is houses. And don't forget my brother was one of those hosts on TV."

"You know, I forget Del is a celebrity. He seems so normal."

I lean to the side and look up at him. "Now that I know you, I could say the same for you." I gaze at the kitchen around me. "Until I saw this house."

"Does that bother you?"

I shake my head. "No, it doesn't actually."

He twists me around in his arms and backs me up to the island. His gaze is dark and heated on mine. "You're the only woman I've brought here."

My brows meet my hairline and my heart races. "Serious?"

"Yep." He cages me between his arms, rubbing his nose

against the length of my neck. "Want to see my bedroom?" he whispers against my skin.

I close my eyes, wanting to give in to the temptation that is Nate Gentry.

But there's a niggling thought in my mind that stops me. I lean back, putting space between us. "Yes, but would you mind if I took a nap? I'm exhausted."

He blinks once, twice. "Yeah, of course. Come on, let's get you to bed."

His bedroom is a gorgeous master suite, decorated in blues and grays, giving it a soothing feel. A balcony with breathtaking views of the ocean stretching out to the horizon is the cherry on top.

He shows me the bathroom, which looks like something out of a high-end spa, then leaves me to rest. I slip off my shoes and stretch out in his giant king-sized bed.

I wasn't lying; I am exhausted. But I also need some time alone to think.

I've let my heart get too involved even when I knew better. Every day that goes by is one day closer to the unsaid expiration date of Nate and me as a couple.

He hasn't told me in so many words, but I feel a vibe that's familiar to me.

It feels like a broken heart.

A FEW HOURS LATER, I stand in front of the full-length mirror in the walk-in closet of the master suite.

Except this is no regular closet. Nope, this closet is the size of my bedroom in my little house and has a sitting area and vanity. All the places I could put my shoes...

But I have to shut that idea down real quick.

I can't think about the future too much or it'll depress me. And for tonight, I'm going to pretend like this thing between us is forever.

"Damn, babe. I'm going to have to keep the boys away from you."

I turn to find Nate leaning against the wall, one arm behind his back, his free hand rubbing his chin. I run a hand self-consciously over the curve of my belly and look down at my skinny capri jeans and purple, sleeveless silk blouse.

"I didn't know if this was casual or dressy, but being a baseball game, I figured casual would be good."

Seeing his tall form in jeans and a black polo shirt with the silver-and-purple Bull Sharks logo on it makes my stomach flip-flop.

As he approaches me, his gaze rakes me over from head to toe, and warmth pools low in my belly. He stops in front of me and pushes a lock of hair behind my ear. "You look hot, babe."

I roll my eyes but smile and rub my growing belly, happiness at his words filling my chest. "Whatever. But thank you."

"I have something for you."

"You do?"

The arm behind his back comes around and he holds up a jersey with his number—seven—and his name on the back of it.

"That's for me?"

"You like it?" There's a vulnerability in his eyes that makes my heart ache.

"I love it. Thank you."

"Will you wear it tonight?"

I snatch it from his hands with a grin. "Once I put it on, I'm never taking it off."

He returns my grin, all uncertainty in his eyes gone. "That's my girl."

I shoo him out, knowing if he sticks around while I change, we'll never get out of here in time, and I don't want to make him late.

I know I made the right call when I meet him downstairs in the foyer and his eyes flare with desire. His hands land on my hips and he pulls me into him, making sure I feel his hard length. "You feel what you do to me? Later tonight, you're going to wear nothing but my jersey while you ride my cock. Got that, baby girl?"

The growl in his voice sends a shiver down my spine, causing my nipples to pebble. All I can do is nod, lust tying my tongue in knots.

When he says those dirty things to me, he strips me bare of all my defenses. I want nothing more than for him to push me up against the wall and fuck me, consequences be damned.

We head out, taking his sleek black-on-black Tesla this time. When we get to the stadium, the guard at the gate of the players' lot greets him with a huge smile. "Mr. Gentry, it's good to see you again."

"Hey, Jimmy. Good to see you too." Nate shakes the hand the older man offers, giving him a genuine smile.

Jimmy points a dark-skinned gnarled finger my way. "Who we got here?"

Nate turns his head and smiles at me. "This is my girlfriend, Charley Reynolds."

I wave with a smile. "Hi, Jimmy. Nice to meet you."

Jimmy's smile widens and he slaps Nate on the shoulder. "Girlfriend? Well, it's about time, son." His warm, friendly, dark-brown eyes wander lower to my lap. "Looks like you made up for some lost time, no?"

Nate chuckles. "Yeah, it was a surprise, but I couldn't be happier about it." His eyes, full of affection, hold mine for a beat before he turns back to Jimmy. "How's the family?"

They chat a few minutes about Jimmy's wife—who Nate knows by name—and the grandbabies Jimmy just can't get enough of when they visit.

I tune them out as they chat, trying to wrangle the emotions filling my chest. The way Nate looked at me, to hear him call me his girlfriend...I know without a shadow of a doubt, I love this man, and not just because he gives me multiple orgasms or that he's my hot-as-hell baby daddy.

It's all those things and more. How he treats the parking guard, how he makes me burritos that make him gag, takes an interest in my work, and puts up with my hormonal bullshit. Among a million other little things.

The feelings I have for him are so big, they're overwhelming.

I rub my belly, soothing the twinges away as the men shake hands and Nate pulls forward through the gate. "Love that guy," he says with a smile, as we pull into a parking space.

"Seems like a nice man."

"He is, one of the best. But don't let him fool you with that hearty grin. He was a cop and homicide detective in Miami for forty years."

"Really?"

"Yep, retired about nine years ago."

Nate parks the car, and some of the media people have figured out he's here. They come running to the fence, calling out his name.

One of them climbs the fence and jumps out in front of us, causing me to yelp and grab Nate's arm.

But before he can raise his camera to take our picture, security guards magically appear and haul him away.

Nate's face is murderous. "Fucking paps," he mutters under his breath.

With a tight smile, he takes my hand and waves to the other reporters as we head into the stadium.

Once inside, he stops and faces me, anxiety etched on his face. "Are you okay?"

"I'm fine. He just surprised me." I cup his cheek. "Forget about him. This is a huge night for you. Don't let all that nonsense ruin it."

He takes my hand and kisses the center of my palm, his gaze holding mine. "I'm so glad you're here."

Warmth spreads through my chest and I grin. "No place else I'd rather be."

We walk down a long hallway that's quiet and dim, taking us farther into the belly of the large building.

"I feel like I'm sneaking around and shouldn't be here," I say, trailing behind him and looking around as we walk through a deserted lobby of sorts.

One wall has a large display cabinet with several trophies the team has won over the years and framed team pictures. Next to those is a wall of retired players. I stop short when I see a familiar face staring at me, with his trademark grin, framed on the wall.

I walk over to it, studying Nate's face. He's younger in the picture, but the strong jaw, hazel-green eyes, and smile that makes my ovaries explode is the same. He's wearing a cap, obscuring his thick, dark hair.

I lay my hands on my belly, absently rubbing it, and tilt my head. Will our baby have my blue eyes or Nate's hazel eyes? Will it have those high cheekbones Nate was blessed with? Will it have my nose?

"They haven't updated pictures in a while. It's from my best year, probably about four or five years ago." Nate walks up behind me and puts his hands on my shoulders.

"I was just standing here wondering...oh!" A distinct movement under my hand makes me spin around and take Nate's hands, placing them on my belly. "Feel that?"

He watches my eyes for a moment and then a grin slowly spreads across his face. "Yeah. It amazes me every time."

My heart pounds in my chest when he drops to his knees and lifts the jersey up over my bump and kisses the center of it. "Hey baby. I love you. Get ready for some excitement, but go easy on your mama, okay? She wants to see the game."

He glances up at me with a cocky smile before dropping another kiss and lowering my shirt. As he stands up, he kisses my parted lips and takes my hand. "Come on, babe. We gotta go."

For the next hour, we're surrounded by people, being escorted from place to place.

There are journalists, including one from *Sports Illustrated* who's covering the game. Nate appears comfortable with the guy, which makes me feel better.

Still, I'm nervous about being thrust into the spotlight being on the arm of a superstar, legendary baseball player.

He wraps up his conversation and puts a hand on the small of my back. "Come on, I want you to meet some people."

He leads me over to a small group of people, including two players I recognize.

And a stunning woman whose face lights up when she sees us heading their direction.

My steps falter and my breath hitches as we get closer, and my stomach burns with jealousy. But I do my best to push it aside. It's Nate's night and there's no way in hell I'm going to make him or myself look bad.

"Take it easy, Firefly," Nate says in my ear. "I told you before. There's only one woman for me, and she's wearing my jersey over that baby belly I love."

The way he knows me is a bit unnerving.

Before I can gather my thoughts, we reach the group, who greets Nate with hellos, shoulder slaps, and hugs.

He turns to me and takes my hand, bringing me into his side. "Guys, this is Charley."

No doubt about it, I'm intimidated by the four pairs of eyes looking at me. But I've never been one to back down from a challenge.

They also must be four of the best looking people I've ever seen.

I give them my brightest smile and a nod. "Hi, everyone."

He introduces me to first baseman Ian Sterling, Bull Sharks owner Derek Emerson, his sister Darcy Emerson, and pitcher Lucas Raines.

Darcy gives me a warm smile. "I'm so excited to meet you. Nate wouldn't tell us anything about you."

"Yeah, we're happy to meet the woman who finally took down Nate the Iceman Gentry," Lucas says with a laugh.

"We'd lost all hope," Ian chimes in.

Nate rolls his eyes. "Why do I bother with you people?"

They laugh and we're called to start heading to the field. Other team executives, stadium workers, and security guards escort us.

I try to appear cool, but I'm in awe of the place. It's huge from where I stand behind home plate.

The turf is impossibly green, the clay redder than it appears on TV, and the white lines so bright it's like looking straight into the stadium lights blazing above our heads.

"Wow, this is amazing. Almost spiritual." The energy is almost tangible, and my skin pebbles with goose bumps.

Nate stands next to me with a huge grin on his face, one arm around my shoulders, his gaze on the field out in front of us. "Yeah, there's nothing like it."

The woman with the earpiece from the network station gestures to Nate and Derek. "Mr. Emerson, Mr. Gentry, we're ready for you."

Nate pulls me closer and lifts my chin with a finger. "I'll be back. Don't let these guys run you off."

Lucas bobs his brows. "Better watch out, Iceman. You've got a live one here; someone might snatch her up."

"Don't I know it," Nate says. He drops a kiss on my lips, lingering a bit too long.

"Damn, man, get a room. After the game," Ian huffs out jokingly.

The beginning notes of his walk-up song play—Aerosmith's "Sweet Emotion"—and the crowd roars to a deafening sound.

With a smile, Nate walks away. I do my best not to swoon watching his commanding presence cross the field.

"Don't worry, girl, I got ya covered," Darcy says, looping her arm through mine. "We girls have to stick together around all this testosterone."

"Thank you. I appreciate that." As much as I want to hate her, I find I can't.

"Nate's the best guy I know and you're his girl. We won't let anyone near you."

Lucas leans in close to me. "He'd kill us if we didn't take care of you when he can't."

I look up to see him wink at me. Lucas is a complete hottie as well. Before Nate, this conversation would be going another way. But now? Looking at Lucas is kind of like looking at my too-handsome-for-their-own-good brothers.

"Thanks, guys."

A warmth spreads in my chest that these people, who are obviously important to Nate, already look at me as one of their own.

The music fades, and when the crowd's cheering dies down, the announcer starts to talk, reminding me it's time to call Megan. Pulling out my phone from my back pocket, I bring her up on FaceTime.

Her face fills my screen. "Has it started yet?"

I shake my head and raise my voice, hoping she can hear me over all the noise. "They just started talking. So here we go!"

I stand in front of the Bull Sharks dugout, with his former teammates and coaches, watching along with millions of others in the stadium and on television, as he is honored with his jersey and they reveal its resting place along the top of the stadium with the retired numbers from other Bull Sharks players.

He's so handsome, standing next to Derek in the middle of the field as he rattles off Nate's accomplishments while highlight clips of his career play on the big screen above the outfield.

Derek hands him the microphone and shakes Nate's hand. He says a few words, thanking the team and his fans and his sister, who promptly starts crying.

"And finally,"—Nate turns slightly toward my direction—"to my girl, Charley. You've turned my world upside down in all the best ways, and I can't imagine this moment without you. I look forward to our next adventure together, Firefly." He smiles and the noise from the crowd grows.

"Oh my God." Megan and I gasp at the same time. I lower the phone as tears fill my eyes before rolling down my cheeks.

My racing heart is a drumbeat in my chest. Elation is written all over his face, and the love I have for him overwhelms me.

When there's movement in my belly, I laugh and cover it with my hand. Even Nugget can't contain their joy. "We're proud of Daddy, aren't we, little one?"

"Charley, I can't see," Megan exclaims from my phone.

"Sorry!" I immediately lift the phone again so Megan can see her brother make his closing remarks and then throw out the first pitch.

He waves to the crowd and jogs over to where I'm standing.

"Here he comes, want to talk to him?" I ask Megan.

"Yes!"

When he gets to me, I jump in his arms and he holds me tight. Before he can say anything, Megan starts protesting from my phone squished between us. I'm half laughing, half crying when I hand him my phone. "Your sister wants to talk to you."

While he talks to Megan, all I can do is stare at him. My face hurts from smiling, and my heart feels like it's about to explode with love for him.

I love seeing him in his element, where he's on top of the world and the best hitter in the league.

Seeing the look of happiness and the way he interacts with the fans and his teammates, I inhale a quick breath as a realization strikes me.

In my heart, I know if his age and injuries hadn't stopped him, he'd be in uniform right now. In my mind, there's no doubt what he needs to do.

He has to take the manager's job.

Baseball isn't just a game to him. It's his identity, who he is.

How can I ask him to give that up?

I know he cares about me—hell, he just announced it to the world. But I can't make him choose.

He'll be an amazing dad, I have no doubt. After what he suffered with his childhood, I know he'll be in his child's life. But if he stays with me out of obligation, he'll resent me one day.

And my heart can't handle that. I'm not built that way.

Since I can't turn off my love for him, I'll do the next best thing for my heart.

If he wants to leave, I'll let him go.

TWENTY-FOUR

I UNLOCK THE FRONT DOOR, letting Charley in ahead of me. Lighting automatically comes on in the foyer, relieving the darkness around us.

Charley heads into the kitchen and I can't help but admire her ass in those jeans. And seeing my name and newly retired number seven on her body gives me another punch straight to the gut.

But something's up with her. And I can't pinpoint what it is.

I find her standing in front of the fridge, the light from inside illuminating her face.

"Hey, Firefly. You okay?"

She jumps slightly, reaching for a bottle of water before closing the door and turning to me. Even in the dim lighting of the lamp from across the room, I can tell her smile is forced.

"Yeah, I'm fine." She takes a long pull from the water bottle and doesn't elaborate anymore.

I raise a brow and cross the room to her. With a finger I lift her face to mine and search her eyes.

It's the first time I haven't been able to tell what she's thinking. She's holding back on me and I don't know why.

What happened between the time before the game to now?

"You don't seem fine. You hardly said a word in the car all the way home."

Her lips quirk into a half grin. "Well, I may have been dozing."

"Don't lie to me, Charley."

Her eyes dart away before meeting mine. "I'm not lying, Nate. I'm just tired. It's been an exciting day."

She gives me that smile that makes my heart soar before she continues speaking. "I want you to know that I think you're amazing. I'm so proud of you. I'm honored to have shared such a huge moment with you." She blows out a shaky breath, her eyes locked on mine. "You've turned my world upside down too, Nate Gentry."

It's like she reached into my chest and squeezed my heart. My throat thickens with all the emotions I want to say, but the words just won't pass my lips.

Instead, I go with something safe.

"Thanks for being here with me, Charlotte. It means everything to me that you're here."

She smiles. "I also loved meeting everyone. You guys are like brothers."

I chuckle. "Yeah, they're a pain in the ass like siblings at times."

"You love them."

I blink and my stomach quivers. "Yeah, I guess I do." I steer the conversation away from all that. "You and Darcy seemed to hit it off. I was barely able to talk to you at dinner afterward."

She chuckles. "She's pretty great actually. Reminds me of Emma in a lot of ways."

"I can't tell you how many times I heard I was a lucky bastard tonight."

I expect a smile but instead, she swallows and her eyes are intent on mine. "They all have such respect for you, Nate. I could see it in their eyes."

"I have the utmost respect for them as well. You have to respect and trust your teammates or it won't work."

Her eyes sparkle as she watches me. "It's sexy seeing you in your element."

I wrap my arms around her waist. "You like that, huh?"

"Well, you know, I have watched you on TV for years. And I may have had a tiny crush on you for a while." She holds her fingers the slightest bit apart.

My brows rise and certain parts of my body start to throb. This is news to me. "You did?"

"Oh, yeah." She gives me *that* smile and runs a hand up my chest. "Still feeling an adrenaline high?"

I search her eyes, and whatever shadows were there before have passed.

Something is bothering her, but for now, I leave it alone.

One thing I know about pregnant Charley. Once she gets sex on her brain, there's little she thinks about until she gets the relief she craves.

"Adrenaline? Oh yeah." I turn her and back her up against the island. "I'm revved up. Same buzz I used to have after a great game."

"Hmmm…" She twines her arms around my neck and moves as close to me as her growing belly will let her. God, I love her belly. "What does an elite athlete like you do to get rid of all that energy?"

I cast my eyes to the ceiling in mock thought. "There are a few things," I say, then lower my head to hers, moving my hands to her hips and then curving over her ass. Damn, that delectable ass. "But since you're here with me, we can do my favorite one."

"Oh?" she purrs. "What is it?"

"Fucking," I growl before capturing her mouth with mine. Her mouth opens immediately, welcoming my tongue to tangle with hers. Her hot body and heated response is a delicious contrast to the coolness of her mouth from the cold water she just drank.

Her fingers pull on the short hair at the nape of my neck, her fingernails scraping against my skin as I take our kiss deeper.

Lips locked together, I lift her up on the counter and start to unbutton her jersey, but my fingers are clumsy.

"Fucking buttons," I murmur against her mouth. Her laughter ends on a gasp when I nip at her neck.

"Take your shirt off," she says.

I barely get a glimpse of the sexy-ass bra she's wearing before our hands battle to pull my shirt up.

Once the fabric clears my head, our mouths fuse together again, my tongue sliding along hers. I put everything I'm feeling—love, lust, adoration—into that kiss, and her response makes my heart race.

When we come up for air, her head drops back, and I take advantage of all that perfect skin on display by kissing my way down her neck.

"Ah, yes. Nate. I love how you make me feel."

I lay her down on the island, pulling her jeans over her hips and down her legs, letting them drop to the floor.

I stop, my eyes drinking in the sight in front of me.

My lips part and my throat grows thick. She's the epitome of feminine beauty.

Nestled between the gap of my jersey, a navy blue lacy bra covers her chest, sheer enough to show her skin underneath. The matching string bikini panties sit low under the slope of her bump. I swallow hard and grab the counter when my knees buckle. I can't think clearly or escape the emotion that comes over me. I can only think of one word.

Mine.

My heart swells in my chest making it hard to breathe. She brings me to my knees—literally—with her beauty. She's a goddess, all curves and soft skin. The pregnancy has only enhanced Charley's body. The swell of her belly, the widening of her hips. Her dark nipples are larger and more sensitive.

I'm here for all of it.

"My God, you're perfect," I say, my voice cracking on the last word.

She bites her lip and arches her back, bringing her core closer to me. "Touch me. Please."

With my free hand, I roll a nipple between my fingers. "Where do you want me to touch you?"

"Everywhere."

"With my mouth or my hands?"

"Yes."

I chuckle and lean forward, and our joined hands come up beside her head. Her body heat radiates under the lace and I moan, sucking her nipple hard. She cries out in pleasure, running a hand through my hair and writhing beneath me.

I lift my head and meet her gaze, my mouth hovering over the other nipple. "You want me to touch you here?"

"Yes, please," she says, a whimper coloring the tone of her words.

"How about here?" I kiss just below her breastbone.

"Yes."

"And here?" I drop another kiss a little farther down her torso, adding a little lick at the end.

"Hmm...yes."

I release the hand I've been holding and slide both hands underneath her torso, to bring her body closer to me. "What about here?" Another kiss on the top of her belly.

She smiles. "Yes."

I move farther down. "Here?" I place an open-mouthed kiss right above her mound, then blow on the damp spot, making her skin pebble under my lips. My dick hardens as her musky scent fills my senses.

"Hmm..."

With my hands under her knees, I kneel and drape her legs over my shoulders. Her pussy glistens, ready for me. I lean in and rub my nose against her skin, avoiding her clit, relishing her scent. "I think you really want me to touch your pussy, don't you, baby?"

"Yes…" The *s* is a long hiss ending in a moan when I kiss and lick her clit. Her legs open wider and her hands grab my hair.

I continue to lick, suck, and nibble, lost in all that is Charley. Her moans and pleas make my cock press painfully against the fly of my jeans to the point I unzip them for relief.

I flick my tongue against her clit faster, knowing she's close by the way her voice changes pitch. I insert a finger into her wet heat, and her walls clamp around it. I moan, knowing she's going to feel fucking amazing when I slide into her later.

Her hips start to buck against my face and I curl my finger, hitting the sensitive spot that sets her off like a rocket every time.

"Oh my God, Nate!" Her fingers grip my skull as she clenches around my finger. I don't stop licking until she's come down and is a panting mess on the kitchen island.

I stand and when our eyes meet, I lick the finger I had inside her. "Sweet."

She shakes her head. "Wow, that was…wow."

I help her sit up and pull her against my chest. "It was just the appetizer, Firefly."

Her eyes brighten, and a grin curves her mouth. "Oh, yeah, what else you got for me, big guy?"

I bring her hand down to my throbbing cock, and she moves her palm up and down over my length, her eyes widening when she finds no barrier between our skin.

"Commando? You sneaky boy."

I widen my stance and close my eyes, lifting my chin. "Ah, fuck. That feels good, Charley."

She kisses up and down my neck, over my Adam's apple and up to my ear, where she bites the lobe, sending a bolt of lust to my dick.

As good as it feels to have her hand on me, this isn't how I'm getting off for the night.

Nope, I have plans.

I take her wrist and help her off the counter. "Come with me."

We cross the living room, and I press a button on the wall,

turning the living room lights off. I press another and with a soft whirring sound, the sliders open slowly, the cool ocean breeze greeting us.

Hand in hand, we walk out on the deck, our only light the nearly full moon in the sky above us. The closest houses are hundreds of yards away on either side, and my property is shrouded in trees for privacy.

Beyond the deck, the small backyard leads down to sand dunes, and the Atlantic looks dark and inky from where we stand. Waves crash against the sand, giving us the perfect soundtrack.

She looks around as we walk farther out on the deck, and I give her a reassuring smile. "Don't worry, no one can see us."

Her eyes meet mine for a beat. "Good. Because the air feels wonderful." She turns her gaze out to the landscape laid out in front of her. "This is beautiful. So peaceful."

"It's been the one place I've felt total peace in my life."

Until her.

I look down at her. The moonlight makes her dark hair shine, and with the look of awe in her eyes, she's honest to God the most beautiful woman I've ever seen.

She has no idea she's the most important person in my life. The fact she is scares the shit out of me.

Having Charley here, in my safe haven, is almost more than my heart can take. I don't know how she would respond if I told her I love her, and I don't want to ruin the moment.

Shoving aside all my fears, I tug her toward the L-shaped outdoor seating area, determined to show her all the things I'm afraid to say. "Sit down and lie back."

With a flirty smile on her full lips, she drops down onto the sofa and rests back on her elbows. "Is this how you want me?"

I rub a hand over my chin and nod. "Oh yeah. That's just how I want you."

"Yeah?" She raises a leg and lets it drop to the side slightly, giving me the glimpse of a view to my personal paradise. "What do you want now?"

I take a couple of steps backward and shuck my jeans, kicking them away. "Touch yourself." I grip my cock and start an up and down motion.

"Like this?" Charley runs her small, delicate fingers over her clit and she licks her lips.

I sit down in a chair and get comfortable, the blood boiling through my veins, ready to watch the show. "Oh yeah, just like that. Show me how you make yourself come when I'm not there."

"I use my vibrator."

"The batteries are dead."

Her hand never stops moving over her pussy as she tosses her head back with a throaty laugh. "Alright." She pauses for a beat. "But you have to do something for me."

I raise a brow. "What's that?"

"Stroke your cock while you watch me."

I growl and run my hand over the tip of my dick before stroking down to the base. Her chuckle is soft as she leans her head back, her body a contrast of light and shadows as she moves under the ministrations of her hand.

I lick my lips watching her fingers stroke slow and leisurely over her clit, taking her time. My cock is as hard as it's ever been.

Charley's breath grows shallow, and little moans come from her mouth. "Yes," she says under her breath, her head rolling back, eyes closed.

"That's right, sweet girl. Do you think of me when you're getting yourself off?"

"Yes, oh God, yes." Her hand begins to move a bit faster and I spread my legs.

"Hmmm…" She lifts her head and her dark blue gaze meets mine. A wicked smile curves her lips. "You think of me while you're jacking off?"

"You're the only one I've thought of since our first night together." My voice is one notch above a grunt. I move my hand faster in sync with hers.

Watching her get herself off is the hottest thing I've ever seen.

Her moans get louder and closer together, her pitch changing. Her skin flushes a gorgeous deep pink when she's turned on.

She's close, and I want to taste her on my tongue.

I vault over to where she is and move her hand, clasping my mouth to her clit. She explodes on my tongue immediately, and her cries carry through the sea air.

When she comes back down, I stand over her and grab my dick. "Remember what I told you earlier today?"

Her chest heaves and her eyes are wild, and I know she remembers.

"Come ride my cock."

Her eyes flare and when I sit down, she straddles me, lifting up on her knees.

She lines up my cock against her opening and sinks down on me until I'm fully seated inside her.

"Fuck!"

The tight heat of her body wraps around me, and as always when I'm inside her, I see nothing but her.

She opens her eyes and we lock gazes, making me want to savor the moment.

Her face is soft, her lips parted. My throat grows thick with emotion. I see the same thing I'm feeling in her eyes. I want nothing more than to stay right here in this moment with her forever.

My eyes steady on hers, I hook my hand around her neck and bring her closer, kissing her softly. "Charley," I whisper.

She skims my jaw with the tips of her fingers before pressing her palms to my face. "Nate," she whispers back.

When she begins to move, I clasp my hands on her hips, lifting her up and down.

My cock slides through her wetness with ease. I lift my hips, causing her to cry out when I find that spot deep inside her.

With her eyes locked on mine and the jersey with my name on it wrapped around her, she's all mine and I want her to know it. The speed of my hips picks up, and I pound into her from below. Sweat rolls down my neck and back but I hardly feel it.

All I feel is Charley. My woman.

Tingles shoot up my spine at the same time her fingernails dig into my arms and her pussy clenches around my length. "Nate, I'm going to come!"

"Ride my cock while I fill your pussy."

Her back arches and she screams my name, sending me over into the abyss with her. I throw my head back, and her name is a groan on my lips.

I'll never forget this moment. It feels like the closest we've ever been.

We just sit there, locked together, the sound of the ocean around us. She finally lifts her head from my shoulder, and her eyes are glassy with satisfaction.

A soft smile touches her lips. "It's official."

I push a lock of hair away from her face. "What's official?"

"You've ruined me for any other man."

A flash of jealousy surges through me thinking about my Charley with another man, but I push it away. Holding her stare, I swallow hard against the lump of emotions and words I want so badly to say but that are clogging my throat.

For the love of God, say it! Tell her you're in love with her!

I open my mouth, wanting those words to come out, and yet nothing does. She blinks away and a shiver runs through her.

The moment's over.

And I don't know how to get it back.

There's a nagging in my gut telling me I may have missed my opportunity.

I reach over and grab the outdoor fleece blanket from the back of the sofa and wrap the blanket around us, gathering her close to me.

All three of us.

That little thought jolts me out of postcoital bliss just as

Charley lets out a deep sigh against me. She drops off to sleep a few seconds later.

I carry my girl and baby upstairs to my enormous bed and tuck her in beside me. For the rest of the night, Charley sleeps, curled up beside me with the sound of the ocean in the background.

It should soothe me, but instead I lie wide awake and in a state of panic.

My mind whirls with thoughts of "what now?"

Derek approached me again about my contract before we left the game. They've given me ample time to sign and met all my demands. They want an answer within the week.

The fact I don't automatically choose Charley and the baby tells me what I've always feared about having a family with a career like mine.

Charley comes from a close family and that's what I want for my child. To never doubt they are loved.

But for me, it isn't in the cards. I'm more like my parents than I let on. I want to be different, like Megan. But I just don't know how to do it differently.

Aidan's words come back to me.

If you think you can't handle this, walk away now.

I don't know how I'll handle my high-maintenance career and a family.

I don't think I can.

I'm in love with Charley. I'd lay my life down for her and the baby she's carrying.

My baby.

But I also know someday, I'll hurt them both.

The job or the girl?

My stomach churns at the realization I already know my answer.

She deserves more than I can give her. I have to let her find someone who knows how to love, knows how to put her first without hesitation.

Even if it destroys me.

charley

THE NEXT FEW weeks fly by, and before I know it, it's Thanksgiving morning.

With our family away on their trip, Nate and I decide to invite Lucas, Ian, Darcy, and Derek to Madison Ridge.

At the last minute, Chase and his fiancee Eden joins us as well.

I go in search of Nate and find him in his office staring at the monitor in front of him, his hand covering his mouth.

"The catering staff are almost finished setting up."

He looks up from the monitor and nods. "Okay."

I smile. "Still the best idea you've ever had after my beef Wellington debacle."

He frowns. "You didn't need to do all the work anyway, Charley. You're eight months pregnant."

As if I could forget, but I don't say anything.

Ever since we returned from Florida, things have been different between us.

And not in a good way.

He walks the caterer out, handing him a large cash tip and wishing him a Happy Thanksgiving.

He shuts the door and rubs the back of his neck, not looking at me. "I'm going to get ready."

Without another word, he takes the stairs two at a time, leaving me alone.

With a sigh and an ache in my heart, I walk the opposite direction into the kitchen to check out the setup.

Everyone should be arriving any minute, so I finish up the last-minute details, like lighting the candles and opening the wine to breathe.

The water runs upstairs, and it makes me wish I was in the shower with Nate.

I miss his touch. And not just in a sexual way.

I miss him holding my hand while we watch TV. Or the way he draws circles on my skin when we cuddle.

Kissing my belly good morning.

Add to the fact that in the time since our return, Nate's gone back to Florida twice for a few days and then once to Texas for the last game of the World Series, where the Bull Sharks won.

He came home keyed up and gave me three orgasms.

But it had been the least connected sex we'd ever had.

That was two weeks ago.

When he's gone, he calls or texts multiple times a day, checking in on me and Nugget, but even those conversations seem less personal than before.

I throw myself into work at Gold Mountain, trying to wind down my schedule and get it squared away before maternity leave kicks in.

Work and thinking about all the things the baby needs have helped me from reflecting too much on the fact Nate has pulled away from me.

I'd never been more connected to a human than I had been with Nate that night at his beach house. Neither of us said those three little words out loud, but it had been in every move we'd made.

At least, I thought it had.

Now I'm just confused and scared.

Confused because I love him and I know he has feelings for me. But are they for me or because I'm carrying his baby?

Scared because a man who has become so important to me is going to leave me.

Just like they always do.

I feel foolish. I knew this is how it would go. I let his kisses—the sexy *and* the sweet ones—his kindness, and just *him* get to me. Lowered my guard. I let time lull me into thinking I had plenty of it.

But as my due date gets closer, so does the expiration date on our relationship.

I feel it in my bones.

I know he's made a choice. He hasn't told me verbally, but his actions say it loud and clear.

He's chosen baseball.

Just like I knew he would. It's what he knows and who he is.

I knew it was in the cards since I met him. He's told me he's all in, but that doesn't mean for us. It means for the baby.

He'll be around for our child. But not for me as a woman.

How we'll coparent with him living seven hours away half the year and on the road the other half is something I don't have answers to yet.

I blow out a breath. Only time will bring those answers, so for today, I'm going to enjoy the company of my guests.

Nate comes back downstairs looking unfairly sexy in a button-down with the sleeves rolled up, showing off those forearms, and jeans that hug his impressive thighs.

In spite of the fact it feels like a deep chasm exists between us, heat builds deep in my belly, a languid slow burn warming my blood.

I can't wait for my hormones to go back to some semblance of normal.

His eyes meet mine across the island. His gaze rakes over my body before meeting my eyes again. Those hazel eyes hold a swirl of emotions that make me lose my breath.

The doorbell rings and the moment is broken.

"I'll get it," he says, leaving me to get my bearings.

On the island rests large platters of food with a turkey sitting in the middle of it all, and a pang hits me in the center of my chest.

For the first time since I met Nate, I wish I were somewhere else. I miss my family. I miss my dad with a longing that hurts me physically.

Thanksgiving has always been one of my favorite holidays. Mom makes pies she never makes any other time of year. It was the one time of year my siblings came home after they'd moved out of Madison Ridge.

It was the one time I always felt complete.

Up until our trip to Florida, I thought I felt the same completeness with Nate.

But with the way we're acting like strangers, all I feel is alone.

It's a feeling I may as well get used to because if Nate made the decision I think he did, I have to keep the promise I made to myself to let him go.

For all our sakes.

There's a shifting in my belly, as though Nugget is reminding me I'll never be alone again.

I blink back tears and lay a hand on my belly. "I love you too, baby," I whisper.

"Hey, girl. How are you feeling?" Darcy walks into the kitchen and gives me a hug.

I feel silly for the jealousy I felt with her at first. We've talked several times over the last few weeks, finding we have a surprising amount of things in common.

I consider her a friend. One I'm going to hate losing.

"My balance is off. My ankles are all swollen, and I can't seem to stop eating. Insomnia is in full force as well."

She grins. "Getting you ready for those sleepless nights."

"Must be." My gaze slides into the living room, where Nate

talks with the guys, including a man who looks familiar but I've never met. "Nate's acting off."

Darcy follows my gaze and sighs. "I noticed it too."

She leans back against the counter, folding her arms over her chest. "Let me ask you something. Y'all have been getting closer, right? I mean, he invited you to Florida to share a major moment together."

I think back over the last several months and our last night we spent together in Florida. "Yeah, we have."

"And he's probably been pulling away since then?"

"Yeah, pretty much."

"Has he told you his plans yet?"

"No."

I refrain from asking her what she knows, even though it's on the tip of my tongue.

Besides, I need to hear the decision affecting my future from the man himself.

She pins me with her emerald-green stare. "To be clear, I don't know either. But I do know this. That man is head over heels in love with you, Charley. I've known Nate for a long time, seen him with women over the years. And I can tell you he's never looked at one of them the way he looks at you."

I glance over at him, and he's smiling at something Ian's saying. My heart turns over in my chest.

I want what Darcy says to be true, but his actions lately say otherwise.

I sigh. "I was warned, you know."

Her brow furrows. "Warned about what?"

"About how Nate works. His sister told me he has issues when it comes to getting too close to people. I did my best to keep him at a distance." I swallow back tears threatening to fall. "That didn't turn out so well."

Darcy's face softens. "Oh, Charley."

I shake my head. "I'll be fine. As much as I'd love to believe he loves *me*, I don't think that's the case. He respects me and there's chemistry there. But if he wants to go, I can't stop him. And because I love him and I don't want him to resent me one day, I *won't* stop him."

She opens her mouth to say more, but she's cut off by the guys filing into the kitchen.

"We eating any time soon?" Ian asks.

I paste on my hostess smile. "Yep, grab a plate."

"God, he's such an asshole," she mutters under her breath.

I chuckle. "He reminds me of my brothers."

"He's an uncouth pain in my ass."

But as he moves through the kitchen, her eyes track Ian in a way that makes me think she'd like a walk on the uncouth side.

Chase, and a beautiful blonde I assume is Eden, walk into the kitchen with Nate.

Within moment, they make their way over to me where Nate introduces me to them.

"Thanks so much for inviting us," Eden says, hugging me. "Saved me from having to cook," she adds from the corner of her mouth.

Lucas introduces me to Theo Taylor. "Thank you for letting me crash your Thanksgiving dinner," Theo says with a smile on his handsome face.

"We're glad to have everyone."

Even if it means my head is starting to spin from all the new faces around me.

I'm standing off to the side of the kitchen, letting the guests fill their plates when Nate walks up to me, his own plate in hand.

"You need to eat," he says, extending the food to me.

"I'm not going to take your food, Nate," I say, not looking at him.

"I made it for you."

I look up into his eyes, and the invisible band that's been tight around my chest loosens a little.

His stare draws me in, and the butterflies let loose in my stomach. I've missed the look he's giving me right now. I lean closer to him, letting his cologne wrap around me like a blanket.

"Thank you."

"You're welcome. Now go sit down. You should be off your feet, remember?"

I nod and take the plate, wishing he wouldn't be so caring. It only makes things harder for me.

"Before I go, I have a question."

"What's that?"

I gesture for him to lean down. "What's the deal with Darcy and Ian?"

He smiles. "I don't know, but it always feels like a storm's brewing when they're in the same room."

"She was just watching him like she wanted to jump his bones."

"Really? I've never noticed her watching him, but I have caught him checking her out more than once."

It's just a couple of sentences, but I feel closer to Nate talking about Ian and Darcy than I have in days.

Nate's phone pings from his pocket, and I catch the name on the screen when he pulls it out.

Lou.

A text from Lou can only mean one thing at this point.

I ease back from him, the band back around my chest once more.

As he reads the screen, his eyes go blank.

"Is everything okay?"

"It's fine," he says, shoving it back into his pocket.

A knot forms in my belly and tightens into a painful ball.

He's lying.

I see it in the set of his broad shoulders and the flat line of his mouth. Even Nugget knows he's lying and gives me a solid kick in the bladder.

Before the conversation can continue, I shove the plate into his hands. "I'll be right back."

I move as quickly as an eight-months-pregnant woman can move and lock myself in the downstairs bathroom. I wash my hands and stare in the mirror.

"Charley, you knew what was going to happen. Why did you bother thinking otherwise?" I ask my reflection, who has no answers for me.

Anger starts to build in my veins. I'm angry for letting myself fall for a man I knew would leave. Women raise babies by themselves all the time, and I have a huge family who will help me. I don't need Nate Gentry.

But I want him. I want forever with him.

The way he's shut down on me after sharing so much with me tells me everything I need to know.

He loves the baby, but he doesn't love me.

Hot tears slide down my cheeks, and I wipe them away with the back of my hand.

Pull it together, girl. Don't cry over him.

My heart aches with the knowledge of what I need to do.

It's a road I know like the back of my hand. It's littered with the men I've loved but always left me. My dad died when I needed him. My brothers left when I needed them.

Even Brian, my high school sweetheart, left me behind after graduation as though our four years together meant nothing.

It's time for me to get back to what I know. And what I know is I can take care of myself and my baby.

I clean up my face and take a deep inhale and exhale, rubbing a hand over my baby belly. "We're going to be okay, Nugget. Just me and you. I promise."

I take one last look in the mirror and, satisfied I don't look any worse for wear, turn off the light and open the door.

Only to run into a wall of muscle. I look up into the hazel eyes that strip me bare every time.

Except this time. I can't let him do it anymore. He's leaving. I know it in my gut.

"Charley, I—"

I lift my chin, meeting his stare. His eyes are shadowed with sadness and guilt. "Nope. We need to talk, Nate, but I'm not doing it now. Okay?"

He shoves his hands into the back pockets of his jeans and looks down at the ground. "Okay."

I brush past him, ignoring the flicks of electricity I feel whenever we touch, and head into the dining room.

Somehow, I manage to make it through the rest of dinner and dessert without losing my shit.

I focus on my guests, learning Derek has a twelve-year-old daughter who's with her mother for Thanksgiving. And Theo's sister is a physical therapist in New York City.

I let the conversations flow around me and keep my eyes averted from Nate's.

At least he does what I ask and leaves me alone the rest of the evening.

But when everyone leaves, the silence is deafening.

There's a gulf between us now, one growing larger with every moment that passes.

One I don't think we'll ever bridge.

charley

ONCE WE MAKE our way up to the bedroom, a weighted silence hangs in the air.

When he heads for the closet, taking off his shirt as he goes, I can't stand it any longer.

I cross my arms over the top of my belly. "Why did you lie to me?"

He stops, his shirt balled up in his hands. With a toss of it into the dirty clothes hamper, he turns back to me.

Bastard. It's hard to stay angry and hurt when he's standing in front of me shirtless.

He jams his hands on his hips and looks at the floor before looking back at me. "I didn't want to talk about it in front of everyone."

"Talk about what?"

He looks up and meets my stare. "The fact the press got wind of my news before we could talk."

Chills run over me and my stomach roils. "What news?"

"I signed my contract with the Bull Sharks yesterday."

Even knowing it's coming and wanting him to sign so he can be happy, the slice of pain ripping through me cuts deeper than expected.

"Were you planning to tell me about it at any point?"

"I wanted to talk about it yesterday, but it never seemed to be a good time."

I move closer to him, anger coursing through me. "A good time? You think there's a good time to tell me you're leaving? I've had a suspicion since we came home from Florida that you'd decided. I mean, I know I'm nothing more than your baby mama, but you could have said something."

His eyes are miserable as he looks at me. "You're more than just my baby mama, Charlotte. You always have been."

Tears fill my eyes and I turn away, blinking. When he calls me Charlotte, it touches something deep in me, an intimacy I can't explain. No one else calls me that, only him.

I wish it didn't but it dissipates my anger and leaves my heart raw.

The truth is I want to tell him I'm happy for him, that it's what I want for him. Because I know how much it means to him.

But now that it's reality, all I can think about is how I'm going to have to explain to my child that as much as Daddy loves him or her, it wasn't possible for him to be with us.

I spin back around. "Don't you think where you live plays a factor in our child's life, Nate?"

His lips purse. "Of course it does."

"So what's the plan? How are we going to deal with this?" My voice comes out so calm, I don't even recognize it. "Make me understand how this is going to work, Nate."

He sighs heavily, pacing the length of the room, never looking at me. His long legs eat up the space quickly, his breathing ragged.

After several moments of silence where I feel like I'm going to jump out of my skin, he stops and meets my stare.

"I...I'm fucked-up, Charley. I've learned to hide it well over the years because I'm in the public eye. But the truth is, there's a reason I keep everyone at a distance. It's so I can't abuse anyone like my parents abused me."

He sits down on the end of the bed and looks up at me. "I told you why I started playing ball. It kept me sane, centered me. I never dreamed I'd be in the majors. All I knew was when I played, I could lose myself in it. Forget for just a little while that Megan and I were nothing but a burden to our parents."

He drops his head and shakes it. "I never wanted a family because I didn't want to pass on my trauma to another person or a child. I mean, their genes are in me, Charley." He scoffs. "I don't expect you to understand it. How can you even understand it with all the family you have always showing nothing but love?"

I shake my head, my heart splintering at his admission. I want to wrap up that little boy he was once upon a time and tell him how amazing of a man he was going to be and not to be afraid of letting others in.

But that little boy is long gone, and Nate is a grown man choosing to let the wounds eat away at him.

"No, no. I get it. You like to keep everyone at arm's length. And this situation we're in now has made it difficult for you to keep yourself insulated."

His head raises up and he looks me in the eyes. "I thought I could do it. I really did. I thought I could shut out all those demons, white-knuckle my way through the trauma for you and Nugget." He shakes his head. "But it's not fair to you or our child."

I narrow my eyes. "You keep saying you'd never neglect your child, never make it feel ignored and used. But there's more than one way to make a child feel neglected. Trying to keep yourself at a distance is just as hurtful."

He shakes his head as though he doesn't believe me. "It's not the same thing. It's to protect, not harm."

I scoff. "Call it what you want, but the fact is you've hurt people. Just ask Megan."

His head snaps up, and he comes to stand in front of me. "I didn't want to subject Megan to the media, Charley. I told you that."

"Distance is distance, Nate."

He crosses his arms over his chest, his eyes flashing his own brand of anger and hurt. "You're twenty-six and barely had a stable relationship of your own, Charley." He moves closer. "Why is that? Could you be keeping your distance as well?"

Anger wars with sorrow and it feels like I'm having a heart attack. "Don't deflect, Nate. Maybe I keep my distance too, but I didn't do it with you. I let you in."

His expression is incredulous. "Let me in? You think you let me in? I told you things I've never told anyone, including Megan. And what did you tell me about you in return? Nothing."

My heart twists, knowing he's not wrong. Every muscle in my body aches, wishing he were wrong.

Still, I lift my chin. "I would have never made life-altering decisions without discussing them with you first."

I know my comment landed where it was meant to when he looks away.

I turn my back on him and walk over to the wall of windows overlooking the pool and mountains on the horizon.

God, I love this place. But it's never been mine to love.

Just like the man standing behind me.

I turn back to him, pulling my arms close to my body like a shield. "You know, I thought we had something, Nate. I know we didn't start that way. I mean, your sister is my best friend and she's marrying my brother, so I knew I'd see you again at some point. But I figured it wouldn't be often. And we could act like normal."

His gaze flicks back to mine, full of shadows.

I want to be angry with him, hate him.

But I can't. I can't unlove him.

I walk over to stand in front of him, so close I feel the heat from his bare chest.

"Then I found out I was pregnant, and the more time I spent with you, the more I fell in love with you. With *you*, the man. Not the baseball legend or my friend's brother or my baby's daddy. You."

I inhale deep and blow it out slowly. "I don't think you're fucked-up or broken. But you do. And I can't fix it for you." I raise a hand and cup his cheek. He closes his eyes and leans into it.

My chest and eyes burn, yet at the same time I feel like I'm drowning in sorrow and all the what-ifs.

I drop my hand and take a huge step away from him. "Go back home to Florida, Nate. I'm happy for you. I would never get between you and your dream so you could resent me later. Do what you need to do." I cover my bump with my hands, and I don't miss his eyes following my movements. "Nugget and I will be okay."

He swallows hard. "Hold on. I plan to be here until the baby is born. I'm going to be a part of my child's life."

I nod. "I'm not going to shut you out. I would never do that to you or our child. But I think it's best if we don't live together anymore."

"But your place—"

"Has been ready for months."

He snaps his mouth closed and looks down at the floor.

"I'll let you know when it's time. We can work out some sort of custody arrangement after the birth."

My mouth is like sawdust saying those words, but what choice do I have?

"What the fuck? A custody arrangement?"

I move around him, unable to look him in the eye, and head to get my suitcase from the closet. I open it on the bed and start throwing things into it from the dresser drawers.

"We'll need to have some arrangement if I'm here and you're in Florida. But don't worry, I'm not asking for support."

Nate steps in front of me, taking my hands in his. "Charley, stop."

I pull away. "It's best this way. You can do what you need to do and so can I."

He runs a hand through his hair and curses under his breath. "Please don't go. The nursery is here." He flings an arm out toward the door. "I'll stay in a hotel or the inn or my truck. Just don't leave."

I look down at the mess I've made in the suitcase. "I'm not staying in this huge house alone. I love it, but it's too much. And it holds too many memories."

There's no way I'd be able to look around and not remember all the places and ways he loved me. It would only break my heart a little more each day. "So, I'm going to go."

He closes the space between us and cups my face, lowering his forehead to mine. "No. Charley, please." His voice cracks.

A tear rolls down my face. "Let me go," I whisper.

Neither of us moves, but he's so close to me that like always, I can barely breathe. If I do, his cologne will wrap itself around me and I'll give in to him.

And I can't do that.

"There's more to this than just what we want. I have to think about what's going to be best for the baby. And for me, so I can be the best mother I can be for him or her."

I lean back and look up at him. Another tear escapes and rolls down my cheek. I swipe it away. "And right now? I need to get my life back together before I have this baby. It's been great here. Like a dream. But now I have to get back to reality."

We stare at each other for long moments. His hazel eyes are nearly green, and I just want to wrap myself around his big, strong body. Where I always feel safe.

But it isn't safe for me.

He blows out a breath and lowers his head back to mine. Our mouths are inches apart and I want so badly to roll up on my toes and kiss him.

But I won't, even if every fiber of my being is screaming for me not to leave him. To somehow try to fix him.

We stand like that for several seconds before he kisses my forehead.

And then he's gone. The front door opens and closes, and soon I hear him drive away.

I don't know how long I stand there, sobbing, feeling as though someone just yanked out my heart and stomped all over it.

I take a deep breath and zip up the suitcase, then throw my toiletries in a bag. On my way out, the door to the nursery catches my eye.

I walk in, and the waterworks start all over again when I see the crib.

The room came out better than I'd hoped for with the cream-colored walls and soft gray baby furniture.

I sit down in the rocking recliner in the corner, letting my eyes wander over the room I'll never get to use.

Where we tried to put the crib together, picked paint colors, and arranged the changing table.

Tiny clothes I've already ordered hang in the closet on tiny hangers. Empty hangers wait to hold more clothes I never got around to hanging.

The baby isn't even here yet and the room is full of memories.

My heart hurts at all the things I've foolishly planned. For getting caught up in it all. For letting my guard down and thinking he'd be the one man that wouldn't leave me.

But like all the times before, I love a man that can't stay.

Nate has his own wounds, and I can't get past them to make him love me back.

I let my head fall back and I rock, my hands cradling my belly, knowing this is the only time I'll ever get to rock my baby in the beautiful chair I picked out.

"It's just you and me now, Nugget. And you know what? We're going to be okay. You have aunts and uncles who love you already. We're going to be just fine, you and me."

After a few minutes, I haul myself up out of the chair, wincing at the lower back pain.

I want to be gone before Nate gets back. I close the door to the nursery and sniff back more tears.

I quickly grab my suitcase and handbag, not stopping to look at the house that had started to feel like a home to me.

And when I pull out of the driveway, vision blurry with yet more tears, I don't look back.

It's my past. All I care about now is my future.

A future without Nate Gentry.

And without my heart.

TWENTY-SEVEN

WHY THE FUCK is it so bright?

My eyes open slowly. Every blink brings a drum line with it carrying big-ass spotlights for some reason.

It takes me a minute to realize the spotlight is the sun streaming through the sliders. It's another minute before I realize I'm in my house in Florida.

Alone.

The view of the Atlantic would be gorgeous if I didn't have to see the deck furniture. All it does is remind me of Charley.

Hell, this whole fucking house reminds me of Charley now.

Why did I ever think it was a good idea to come back here and bring her with me? I can't bear to look at the kitchen counter. I haven't stepped foot on the back deck. My fucking closet—where she put the jersey on I had made for her, her face lit up like the sun—is off limits.

She's ruined my peaceful haven for me.

I'd hate her for it if I didn't love her so much.

It's been two weeks since she ended things, and all I think about is her. Everything about her.

I sit up gingerly, making sure my head doesn't roll off my

shoulders—though it might be an improvement—and let my stomach settle.

This is why I don't drink often and never to excess. Who the hell wants to feel like this?

I lean my forearms on my knees and hold my head in my hands. Why can't the ache in my chest settle as easily as my stomach?

My phone rings, and it's like someone stuck an ice pick through my brain. Fuck me, it hurts.

Everything hurts.

I lift my head, and among empty bottles of liquor, I find my phone lit up with Megan's name. I debate sending her to voicemail but at the last second decide against it.

"Hello?" My voice sounds like I swallowed rocks.

"Nate?"

"Megan?"

"You sound like shit. Open the gate."

"What gate?"

"*Your* gate, dummy."

I blink. How much did I fucking drink? "You're here?"

She sighs. "Yes, good God. Just open the damn gate, Nate."

She hangs up and I fumble my way around but manage to get the gate opened.

My feet slap against the cool hardwood, and my head pounds with each step as I make my way to the front door.

Surprise rocks me back on my heels when I open the door to find Megan, Lucas, and Darcy getting out of a car. "What are you guys doing here? Is Charley okay?" I ask, my chest tightening.

Megan marches up to me and pokes me in the chest. "We are saving you from doing something monumentally stupid."

Leaning forward, she sniffs my T-shirt, her nose wrinkling. "You stink."

She sweeps past me like she owns the place, and I turn to my other unexpected guests.

"Charley's fine." Darcy gives me the side-eye. "Physically."

She follows Megan in.

"What the hell does that mean?"

Lucas stops in front of me, his eyes narrowed. "It means you fucked up."

My easygoing friend who always has my back seems to have left the building. His broad shoulders are tight, his jaw set. He shoulder checks me as he walks by, knocking me back a couple of steps.

Fucker.

Before I can shut the door, Chase is there.

"Where did you come from and why are you here?"

He grins as he waltzes in and I don't like it. "Reinforcements."

I blow out a breath and slam the door. Nausea swirls in my stomach as I walk into the living room.

Megan stands over the coffee table, her hands on her hips. "Your cleaning lady quit?"

"I gave her some well-deserved time off."

She leans over and picks up a bottle. "I see your friend Jack stopped by."

I flop down on the coach, leaning back into the cushions. "Yep. So did Johnny, Jose, and Tito."

"No wonder you smell so bad," she says in disgust, putting the bottle back on the table.

"Damn, man, you trying to kill yourself?" Lucas asks, sitting down next to Darcy on the loveseat.

"Fuck, man. You're worse than I was," Chase says from his perch on the arm of the sofa.

I shrug, then close my eyes and lean my head back against the cushions. "So, what's the monumentally stupid thing you think I'm about to do?"

"Lose everything that's important to you."

I lift my head and glare at Megan. "Oh yeah? And what's that?"

"The only woman you've ever loved and a family you deserve."

I close my eyes and lean my head back again, but my gut twists into knots. "You don't know what you're talking about."

"Okay, whatever gets you through the day, big brother. But you can't tell me you don't love Charley or your baby."

I shove up off the sofa and pace, my skin tingling as I start to sweat. "Of course, I love her and the baby."

She tilts her head. "Then why are you here drinking yourself into oblivion while she's back in Madison Ridge?"

"She left me! And I couldn't stay in that house alone."

"And you gave her no reason to leave, right?" Lucas asks.

I run a hand through my hair and flop down on the sofa. "I know I fucked up, okay? I should have told her my decision before I signed the contract."

"What you should have done is chosen—"

"Lucas," Darcy says, elbowing him, "stick to the plan, remember?"

He sighs and rolls his lips in, staying silent.

My chuckle is humorless. "You guys have a plan? Good, get to it and leave me the hell alone."

"If you're going to act like an asshole, maybe I shouldn't have stopped Aidan from coming with us. He's ready to tear into you," Megan says, sitting next to me.

I roll my eyes. "Thanks for the support."

"Hey, he's not here, so I did you a favor. Besides, it isn't like you to be an asshole."

"It is now."

She pats my thigh. "No. It's not, but we do need to talk."

Sitting on the edge of the sofa, she faces me, her eyes so much like my own. They're so full of concern and love it's hard to look at her.

"Nate, you always protected me growing up."

"It was my job to protect you, Megan."

"Hush and let me talk, okay? You always made sure I never felt neglected or saw the bad things. You took the brunt of it all. Dad's temper and Mom's hateful words."

My gaze snaps to hers, my eyes wide. "How did you know about that?"

She looks away and shakes her head. "You protected me from it, but it doesn't mean I didn't know what was going on. I heard them yelling. I knew we were just kids that needed parents and ours weren't there."

Her gaze comes back to mine, tears shining in her eyes. "You were just a child too. But you were so brave. You made sure we always ate and I brushed my hair. I remember you pushing the chair up to the counter and standing on it to make us peanut butter-and-jelly sandwiches."

The mention of peanut butter makes me think of Charley, and the tightening in my chest makes me feel like I'm suffocating.

"I don't know how you did it, but I never went hungry and I was—am—so thankful. But Nate,"—she takes my hand in hers—"you've let our past taint your future. You have the biggest heart of any man I know. But you've kept it locked away for so many years. Even from me."

"How? I've always tried to take care of you."

She smiles. "Yeah, you have. You made sure I had money and clothes and all. But you stayed away from me for years. I saw you more on the TV than anything else."

"Megan, you know I did that to protect you from the media following me around everywhere."

"And you didn't think I could handle it? You think I cared?"

"I cared! Those people make up shit, take pictures they shouldn't. I knew that was part of the gig for me but it wasn't for you."

"I know," she says forcefully, "and I love you for that. But this is part of what I'm talking about. You keep your heart and yourself locked away from those you love, thinking we're all better off for it. But I'm here to tell you, we're not better. It's not enough just to have bits of you. We need all of you."

Her voice cracks on the last word, and tears spill onto her cheeks. I pull her into me, and her shoulders shake with sobs.

I squeeze my eyes shut, and my throat grows thick with emotion. "Megan, I'm so sorry. The last thing I ever wanted to do was hurt you. I thought I was doing the right thing."

"I know," is her muffled reply before she sits up and wipes at her tears.

"Nate," Darcy says, leaning forward, "I won't pretend to know what it was like for you growing up in your situation. But I do know this."

She pokes a nail into my knee. "I've known you a long time. I've seen you with women over the years. You always looked bored. You smile more when you're around Charley than I've seen you smile in a decade." She tilts her head. "Except at Thanksgiving when you were all up in your head trying to figure out how to screw this all up."

I frown. "Do I really never smile?"

"You're not called the Iceman for nothing."

"Look, man," Lucas begins, "you love the girl and she loves you. If you want her, fight for her. I can promise you, if you don't, you *will* regret it." He holds up a hand. "And before you ask how I know, it's because I let the one get away from me."

Darcy and I turn to him, wide-eyed. "You had the one?" she asks.

He nods and looks away. "It was a long time ago. But this isn't about me." He looks back at me. "Just know you've got a chance some of us will never have. You can't blow it on some idea you got in your head when you were a kid. You've got to take a chance."

"I only have one thing to say to you," Chase says, finally speaking.

"What's that?"

"Do you remember what you told me when I tried to let Eden get away?"

He doesn't wait for me to answer, just continues. "You told me that if you ever a woman worth fight for, you'd hold on to it with all you have."

Yeah, I had said that to him. At the time, I didn't think I'd ever find a woman worth fighting for, but I did.

And she's carrying my baby.

Megan lays her head on my chest, just like she did when we were kids. "I've done you a disservice, Nate. I should have told you years ago all I ever wanted was my big brother around. I mean, sure you had your crazy schedule to deal with, but in the off-season we could have hung out, gone on vacation together, made our own memories."

She lifts up and leans away from me, but her eyes, still shiny with tears, are hopeful. "We can't change the past, but we can make the future different. We have so much to look forward to. You're having a baby! And with a woman I love like the sister I never had. I'm getting married to an amazing man who actually loves *me* this time, not as a trophy wife. Let's change the family tree, Nate. Break the cycle of abuse."

There's the tiniest bit of lightness in my chest at her words. It makes me question the decision I made years ago to keep my heart under lock and key.

A decision that did the one thing I tried not to do.

Hurt the ones I love.

I swallow against the fear thick in my throat, trying to process all that's been thrown at me. "But what if she doesn't want me now? She's admitted she kept her distance from people, but she didn't do it with me." I sigh and look down at my hand, balled into a fist. "I've probably fucked it all up now."

Megan takes my hand. "Let me give you a little insight on Charley. Did she tell you about how her dad died?"

"She told me she was young when it happened."

"According to Aidan, Charley had their father wrapped around her finger. All the girls did, but Charley was by far the one he doted on. She was a happy accident."

She sighs. "Charley was only seven when their dad passed suddenly. It changed the way she saw things. Then Aidan went into the military, Del was in California, and Noah was dealing with his own issues at the time. All her protectors were gone.

"Aidan thinks that's when she started looking outside the family. I know there was one guy in high school who hurt her. But she got her heart broken time and again. Until one day, I think she decided it was better to never get too close."

My fists bunch and I clench my jaw so hard I worry my teeth will crack. I want to tear apart whoever the asshole is that hurt her.

Then it hits me. I'm the asshole.

Her gaze slides to mine, and I see disappointment in her hazel depths. "Of course, those times she had her heart broken are nothing like this. It was silly puppy love compared to this. If she let you in, she saw something in you that made her think you were worth taking a chance on."

My heart sinks, my head throbbing not from the residual alcohol but from the knowledge I've lost the one thing I found that filled the void in my soul.

"I'll give you another piece of unsolicited advice, Nate," Lucas says, standing. "The media will always be who they are and so will you. Meaning, you're someone they like to report on. At this point, they know who Charley is even if they don't know much about her."

"But she's safe," Megan says. "Del called in some favors."

Lucas folds his arms over his chest. "But wouldn't you rather be taking care of her yourself, instead of her brothers doing it?" He points at me. "Don't let the fucking media be a reason to stay away from what's important to you any longer."

Chase rise and stands next to Lucas. "Fuck the media, Nate. Another wise thing you said to me."

Looking from Megan to Darcy then Chase, Lucas holds out his arms. "I think we need to let Nate digest this for a little while."

The ladies rise, and my bewildered brain takes a minute to catch up to the fact they're leaving. I stand and follow them out.

"Hold on, why don't you guys stay here tonight? We can talk some more."

"We've got the jet waiting at the airport for Megan," Darcy says.

I turn to Megan, eyes wide. "Stay, Meg-Pie? I can get you a flight back tomorrow."

She wraps her arms around my waist and leans her head on my chest. I hug her and lay my cheek on her soft hair. "I'm sorry, Nate. You've got a lot of thinking to do, and it'll be better to do it alone."

I swallow hard and pull back, looking at each of them. I don't want them to leave. They're my only connection to Charley right now.

"Is she...feeling okay? It's so close to her due date. She said she'd call me, but I haven't heard from her." And it makes my soul ache. I swallow again. "I-I just want to know she's okay."

"She's fine," Megan says. "Other than Braxton-Hicks, she's had no signs of early labor or anything. I keep a close eye on her and have stayed at her place a couple of times to keep her company."

"I've been calling her daily and driving her nuts," Darcy says with a grin.

"You have?" I ask, bewildered.

"Yeah, I like her. She's sharp and funny. We have a lot in common."

I nod, wishing I could see her. Wishing I was with her at the house we'd made *our* home or she was still here. It doesn't matter where because Charley has become my home.

Chase claps me on the shoulder. "I'm right next store if you need me."

Nodding, we say our goodbyes and I shut the door behind them.

I walk back through the living room and stand in the middle of it, looking around and feeling like I'm seeing it for the first time.

I've been here alone for the last two weeks, but I didn't feel alone until now. They weren't here long, but it is a deafening quiet now that they're gone.

As my brain processes all it was hit with over the last twenty minutes, I see how disgusting I let the place get.

I clean up the coffee table and kitchen, my eyes avoiding the spot where I made Charley scream my name. When I finish, I take a shower and head into the closet to get clean clothes.

My heart races and my stomach is hollow thinking of my girl here, but I keep breathing.

I take it as a good sign.

I head back downstairs and slowly walk out onto the deck.

Memories of our last night together wash over me. I want to touch her, hold her in my arms again so badly my muscles ache from the loss.

I lean against the railing and watch the sea crash along the shore. It's a beautiful day, the December sun high in the sky, and the beach is deserted. It makes me feel even more alone.

All the words said by Megan, Darcy, Chase, and Lucas tumble through my brain.

The fact that for all my efforts, Megan hadn't been completely insulated from our parents' abuse.

Knowing Lucas—playboy extraordinaire—had met someone and lost it all, makes me want to never be that guy. The guy who only has memories to keep him warm for the rest of his life. The guy with an empty void in his chest that's never satisfied.

I saw the pain in his eyes when he spoke of the mystery woman.

And I remember how devastated Chase had been when he thought he'd lost Eden.

Seeing their anguish is like looking in a mirror.

And to know Charley—my beautiful Firefly—had her heart broken a long time ago and it changed everything for her.

Like she changed my world the second I saw her on the other side of the door, wearing a dress that brought me to my knees.

Baseball was my first love. It saved me during a time when I needed to be saved.

But every playing season ends, so a new one can begin. If you're lucky, the team is better than it was before.

I'm in a new season of life. While the game will still be a part of it, it isn't baseball I need to save me anymore. It's a five-two, blue-eyed, sassy ball of energy, carrying my baby.

And has been all along. I was just too caught up in my head to realize it.

She's my magic. My Firefly. The prize I've been chasing my whole life and never knew it.

My chest lightens, and I feel like I can finally breathe again.

I close my eyes and grin, inhaling the salt air wrapping around me and energizing me.

After a few moments, I turn and head back into the house.

It's time to step up to the plate even though it won't be easy.

I'm up against a pitcher who knows how to strike me out while looking.

But this time, I plan to swing for the fences.

charley

I STAND at the door to Mom's house, trying to decide if I really want to walk inside and open a can of worms.

It's been two weeks since I walked out of the house Nate and I shared. I've been the hot mess express ever since.

The tears finally stopped about three days ago, and my eyes are starting to lose their puffiness. On the outside, I look like I'm getting my shit together.

On the inside?

I'm a raging storm of emotions decimating everything in its path.

Yesterday, I managed to go a full five minutes without thinking about Nate. The distraction came in the form of false contractions, where I try to breathe through the panic that inevitably floods my system like a dam just broke.

About the time the waterworks stopped, I came to a realization.

I need to talk to my mom about my dad.

My fear of losing someone I love managed to run off a man that, while not perfect, was perfect for me.

The thought that I'm stuck in a cycle of loving and losing men in my life makes me sad not only for me, but for my child. I'd never want to pass down my fucked-up thinking to my baby.

Nate's words come back to me.

You must go with what your gut tells you.

My gut is telling me that Mom has answers. To what, I'm still figuring that out.

I blow out a breath, willing the anxiety to ease up, and walk inside. "Mom?"

She comes out of the kitchen, wiping her hands on a towel as she strides toward me. Her beautiful face breaks into a smile, and the warmth in the curve of her lips settles me.

"Charley, this is a happy surprise."

We hug and she pulls back, studying me with one raised brow. "That's a serious look on your face, Charley."

My eyes fill with tears, and my mom, being who she is, doesn't prod, just puts her arm around my shoulders and guides me to the kitchen.

"I put water on for tea. Want some?"

"Yeah, that sounds nice."

And it was.

Sitting at the island of my mom's sunny kitchen, watching her make tea and plate my favorite butter cookies, gives me the feeling of being wrapped in a cozy blanket.

She brings the mugs over, sitting next to me, and slides one to me. "So, what's going on, baby?"

The tone in her voice tells me she knows I'm not here for a casual visit.

I sip my tea and run a fingertip around the rim. She stays quiet, waiting me out. That patience she has, I can only pray I grow into for the sake of my child.

When my courage finally takes hold, the words spill from my lips. "I feel like I'm forgetting Dad. I remember snatches of time with him, but as the days go on..."

With a pause, I swallow the ball of emotions in my throat, tears slipping down my cheeks. My voice is wobbly. "I feel like I lose a little more of him every day. I can't remember his voice like I used to. And at this point, I don't know if what I remember of how he looked is my memory or the pictures I've seen."

Mom lays a hand on mine but stays quiet as the tears come faster.

"I hate that he's not here to share life with you. I hate that he won't be here to see his first grandchild and kiss their boo-boos better. I hate he missed out on most of my childhood. All of the father-daughter dances we didn't get to attend. I hate he won't be the one walking me down the aisle someday."

I meet her eyes. "And I hate that I can't let myself fully be with a man I love because I'm afraid I'll get my heart broken again. I'm not sure I can handle that again."

My hand fists the fabric over my heart, and her image becomes clouded with tears. "It hurts, Mom."

The words are a strangled whisper as I break down in sobs.

Weight like a lead ball sits on my chest, while simultaneously there's a tearing in my soul that leaves me desperate and aching.

Mom wraps me in her arms and we cling to each other, crying over the what-ifs and could have beens. Things we wished for, dreamed for, but will never have the way we want them.

Tangible, physical, whole.

Alive.

They're forever locked in our minds and hearts to visit when we need them.

For the first time in a long time, comfort and safety in my childhood home surrounds me while Mom holds me.

It's a cleansing I didn't know I needed.

When my sobs subside to sniffles, Mom leans back and blots her eyes with a tissue. Her smile is watery as she pushes a strand of hair behind my ear, but her voice is strong, steady.

"Charley, you need to know that I wouldn't change a single thing about my time with your dad. I'm glad I didn't know our life together would end tragically and too soon. Could I have missed the pain? Sure. But I also would have missed out on an entire season of my life. The season where we created a family out of a deep, once in a lifetime love.

"I know your dad dying at such a young age has led you to believe you have to keep your heart intact by any means necessary. You think it protects you from never feeling hurt, abandoned, or less deserving of love. But nothing could be further from the truth. You deserve all that and more. And there's no protecting yourself from those things. If we could, we wouldn't be human."

Her hand cups my cheek and I lean into it. "If your dad were here physically, he'd tell you how proud he is of you and how he loves you more than he could ever express."

My bottom lip trembles and my chest feels heavy. "How do you know that?"

The smile she gives me rivals the sun, and the air around her practically glows. "Your dad's always with me. I can't see him, can't feel his touch, but his presence is here. Every day."

She clasps my hands in hers. "Life is better off letting it play out the way it sees fit, instead of some sort of reality you think it's supposed to be."

Her gaze wanders down to my burgeoning bump, where the beginning of the next Reynolds generation grows, then meets mine again. "If you could dictate how your life would play out, do you believe you'd be where you are now?"

Since I've carried a piece of Nate and me around for nine months, I can't imagine not having this baby. The thought stops my heart cold, and the aching in the pit of my stomach that threatens to overwhelm me returns with a vengeance.

"No, I don't think I would." I rub my hand over my belly protectively, as though to keep Nugget from hearing this conversation. "Because I pictured a big wedding, a solid career, and then having two point three kids."

One side of my mouth quirks up. "Of course, in that scenario, at my age right now, I'm married to a man who's working his way up the corporate ladder and comes home every night. I'd be building my own career." I pause. "And that sounds boring as hell."

She chuckles. "Instead, you fell for a man that sets your soul on fire but is complicated. Both with his heart and his career."

Sitting back in the chair, I blow out a breath. "Complicated doesn't even begin to cover our situation. Besides the job situation and living in different states, there's the fact that he has family trauma. Trauma I can't fix for him."

My heart clenches in my chest, even while a new emotion seeps in.

Anger.

"He talked about how he didn't do family—whatever that means—and yet, he kept telling me he was all in. But when the time came for him to be all in with me, he pushed me away instead. Unilaterally made a decision that affects not just him, but Nugget and me as well."

Mom eyes me over the rim of her mug. "And you didn't do any pushing of your own, right?"

Leave it to Stella to take the wind right out of my sails. I sigh, knowing she's right.

Again.

"Yeah, I know I did. And now I know why. I'm still angry he didn't talk to me about his contract before he signed. But…yeah. I know now I wasn't forthcoming with him in the ways he was with me."

"You had your reasons, Charley. It doesn't make it right, on either side, but love has a way of making us lose sight of good judgment sometimes."

"That's the understatement of the century."

To my dismay, my eyes fill with tears again.

Son of a bitch, I can't wait until my hormones go back to normal.

She smiles and kisses the back of each hand with a smacking sound, like she used to do when I was a kid to make me giggle.

My mom still knows how to make me smile through tears.

"Life's about taking chances, Charley. Letting go and trusting the journey of life. You'll end up exactly where you are meant to be when you're meant to be there."

She slides the plate of cookies toward me. "Now, help me eat these cookies."

I spend the rest of the afternoon with her, talking all things baby. By the time I leave with a container full of cookies, a peace has settled over me.

Sometimes a girl just needs her mama.

Later that night, I lie staring at the ceiling, thinking back over her words.

The future between Nate and me is foggy at best. Where we end up is anyone's guess.

But I've always said my mom is rarely wrong. No doubt this time will be any different.

Maybe life is best left to chance.

TWENTY-NINE

ROSEMONT HILLS.

A pretty name for a place that's all about death.

Behind the black wrought iron gates, my parents lie in their graves, topped with a large granite headstone, bearing the birth and death dates.

As well as those bullshit things everyone says like, "loving mother" and "devoted father."

Not that I know this for myself; Megan told me. I haven't been to my parents' graves since the day we laid them in the ground.

When people from the industry showed up for them and cried for the loss, I'd heard the comments like, "I didn't even know they had kids" said in hushed tones.

Somehow, even the most heartless of bastards are revered in death as though their dying washed away all the shitty things they'd done in life.

I step out of the rented SUV and into the cold air of Nashville. It's as biting and bitter as the resentment that festers in my gut.

The dreary gray skies match my mood. Standing on the beach in Cape Sands, I had all the confidence of the man I'd become on the baseball diamond. Of the home run king that left the best pitchers in all of baseball with sweat running down their spines.

Now that I'm here, standing hundreds of yards from where my parents are taking their dirt naps, I'm thrown back to being the ten-year-old boy who knew his parents didn't love him as much as they loved the feeling a white line of powder gave them.

Why did I think coming here would be a good idea?

Charley's face invades my mind just like it has since she left. While she and my unborn child are the biggest reasons I'm here, I'm also here for me.

After my friends came by, I did a lot of soul searching and plotting on how I'm going to convince Charley that when I say I'm all in, I mean it in every way possible.

Facing my past is the only way I'm ever going to have what I always wanted from my parents and was too blind to see it otherwise—love and acceptance.

Putting my past behind me is the first step in picking up the sharp, broken pieces I'd swept under the rug for decades.

My baby deserves a dad who will never withhold his feelings. A dad who will love and take care of them, even when they have children of their own.

Charley deserves a man that will appreciate everything about a woman. A man who wonders why the hell she picked him to share her mind, body, and soul. A man that knows she's a precious gift to be treasured.

Megan deserves a brother who will be there for her in ways that have nothing to do with my bank account. A brother who looks at her and sees the woman she's become and not some child who needs to be shielded from the world.

A gust of wind blows around me, making the dead leaves rattle on the pavement as though telling me to stop stalling and get on with it.

Renewed resolve moves me, one foot in front of the other, walking along the path between the graves. It's a meticulously kept cemetery, the yellowed sod trim and free of debris.

A mix of flower bouquets, some bright and new, some faded

with time, lie on various headstones, showing that whoever occupies that area six feet under has someone who loves them.

I keep walking, somehow knowing where I'll find their final resting place, in spite of the fact I haven't been here in twenty-five years.

It's as though the wind at my back is leading me.

A chill runs down my spine and the hair on the back of my neck rises. The quiet, sprawling field around me isn't a peaceful quiet anymore.

"Just get this over with, Gentry," I mutter under my breath.

I find the double headstone with my parents' names in elegant, clean letters. Shoving my hands into the pocket of my jeans, I stand there, reading their names and the date they died over and over, my gaze snagging on the fact their death date is the same.

What had I expected to feel? I'm sure the numbness in my chest isn't what I'm supposed to feel.

But at the moment, it's all I have.

It seems I come by my nickname Iceman naturally.

A part of my mind wonders who paid for the funeral and the burial plots. Even before my parents fell into the addiction trap, they weren't the type to plan ahead for death. They were more live for the moment sort of people.

Looking back with the wisdom of an adult, it isn't all that much of a surprise they let the life of sex, drugs, and rock and roll destroy them.

I sit on the granite bench next to their graves. The stone is cold and hard, an ironic metaphor given the situation.

For the first time in more years than I can remember, I let the memories of my childhood play in my mind.

Memory lane is officially open.

The bitterness I carried in here with me dissipates some when I think back to my first memories.

"I'm sure you expected me to come visit before now."

There's no answer, no rebuttal. Nothing but the wind.

Goose bumps pop on my skin, the eerie quiet heavy in the winter air.

"The fact is I had no desire to be here for you guys. Why should I? The last few years of your life, you weren't there for us."

A ball of emotion is lodged in my throat, and as hard as I try, I can't swallow it away.

"We were just kids. I was only ten years old when you ran your car head-on into that wall. At least when you were alive we had the hope you'd both get better. But you performed the coup de grâce by taking that hope away from us too, then left us to Aunt Cathy and Uncle Jim, who you knew didn't like kids. I had to learn how to be an adult before I barely had the chance to be a kid. And Megan..." I shake my head. "Well, she's amazing, and you know what? I did that."

Tears blur my vision as I stab my finger into my chest hard a couple of times just to make sure I can still feel.

Long, cold skeletal fingers of betrayal have a solid grip on me.

When the wind kicks up again, I close my eyes and lift my chin, the cold air drifting across my face.

Out of nowhere, a distinct memory hits me, and my eyes pop open. The force of it slams into my mind, taking my breath away and leaving my heart pounding so hard, a heart attack seems imminent.

What a headline that would make.

Former Bull Sharks catcher Nate Gentry found dead in a cemetery next to his parents' headstones.

FUCK THAT, I'm not going out like that.

But the long buried memory has to play out. It's why I'm here. To face the past.

And this memory feels important, like it was a catalyst to something I should know.

I stare at their graves, but I don't see them. My mind has

rewound, over thirty years in the past where I'm crammed in the backseat of dad's old Mustang. Even at only five years old, I was tall for my age and never had enough room for my legs.

I LOOK *out the small side window in the backseat and stare at the moon. It's a big white ball in the sky that moves along with us.*

It's because those space men are inside and moving it so they can follow us.

I wonder if their controllers look like the ones that Wes and I use when we play video games.

How cool would it be to control the moon? Maybe I'll be a space man so I could see how they do it.

"Daddy, where are we going?" I ask, the moon completely forgotten.

"The hospital. We need to pick up your mom and your new little sister."

I frown. I didn't want a little sister. Wes had one, and she did nothing but bother us while we tried to play Mario Brothers.

Dad cheers at something said on the radio.

"Yes! Won the first game of the season. Nate, my boy, I think the Braves have a good chance at the series this year."

I don't know what any of it means, but it makes Dad happy and that makes me happy too.

He continues. "You know, I used to play baseball in high school. I was pretty good too. My coach said I was the one to watch in college. But it wasn't meant to be for me."

"Is that when you started playing gee-tar, Daddy?"

"Yeah." He pauses and turns the steering wheel. "It was always my dream to play at Fenway."

"What's a Fenway?"

He laughs. "It's not a thing, buddy. It's the oldest baseball stadium in America." He looks over his shoulder with a smile. "Would you like to join little league next season, bud? I could coach you."

"Yes!" I raise my fist in the air, bouncing in my seat. Wes plays ball,

and this way we could play together longer. Plus it means I'll get to
spend more time with Daddy and less time with the stinky baby.

   Wes had told me about how babies stink when they poop.

   "Daddy, if I play, will I get that big thing for my hand?"

   "A glove?"

   "Yes! I want one like Wes has. Can we get one like his?"

   "Sure, buddy. Whatever you want."

I BLINK and a wave of dizziness hits me.

   Holy shit.

   How had I forgotten that my dad played baseball and never
got to live out his dream?

   Or that my mom never left the bed, crying all the time after
Megan was born?

   The years up until they died were a blur of yelling and crying,
plus a parade of babysitters for us and musicians, singers, and
drug dealers for my parents.

   More snatches of time play in my head. This time after we'd
moved in with Cathy and Jim.

   "There are only three ways an addict ends up, Cathy. Clean, in
prison, or dead. I'm sorry your brother chose the latter, but we both know
it was only a matter of time before he relapsed."

   She sniffles. "I knew what would happen as soon as she ended up
with those painkillers after the baby. They've been his vice ever since he
blew out his knee playing baseball. And they always led him down the
slippery slope to the hard stuff."

   I didn't hear anything more after that, and until this moment, I
had forgotten hearing the conversation at all.

   The wind blows through my hair, and nausea churns in my
belly. Anguish battles with grief and disappointment.

   Cathy and Jim had been the only family we had left—Mom
had been an only child—and now they were gone as well.

   It meant I'd never know for sure the story of my parents.

But if I sat back and looked at it through the lenses of an adult and not a terrified little boy, the puzzle pieces came together.

Could it be that it wasn't that my parents hadn't loved me, but in their own way, *couldn't* love me?

If demons plagued them, had they only been capable of taking care of themselves?

The fog in my head I've lived with for twenty-five years starts to lift, little by little.

Could I forgive them for neglecting me and Megan?

Could I forgive them for cutting my childhood short?

For leading me to believe that love, family, and all that went with it wasn't an option for me?

And that had turned me into a workaholic? I'd used my career as a crutch because baseball was an easy mistress to satisfy.

I need to try.

If I forgive them, it doesn't give them absolution.

But it would give me freedom. Freedom from my past and a situation I had zero control over but that I'd let run my life all the same.

My gaze runs over their names and dates again, but this time they look different.

Blowing out a breath, I lean my elbows on my knees. "I can't say that this is going to be an easy thing for me. I wish I knew for sure what happened to you both, so I can make it make sense. But that isn't an option, is it?"

I pause as though waiting for them to answer, but again, it's just the wind.

"I want to forgive you guys. Once upon a time, you were good parents, and maybe you really did want to be a loving mother and devoted father. That's what I want to think anyway. What I do know is that it's exhausting carrying around this anger and regret. Which means, I'll come visit more often. Though it won't be for a few months."

"I met a woman. One who makes me feel everything, and up until now, I've only let her see the parts of me that aren't broken.

But now I want her to see every wound, every flaw. Because I know she'll love me anyway." A grin curves my lips. "And she's having my baby. Your grandchild."

The loss of them hits hard, and alone on the bench, I let the tears fall.

I sit for another hour and ramble. It's surprisingly easy to talk about my life the way I would if they were still here. If life had played out another way.

It hadn't though, but I'm no longer willing to let the what-ifs dictate my life.

I feel lighter than I ever remember being and walk out of Rosemont Hills a different man.

It represents my past, broken and sad as it may be, and while it is a part of me, it will no longer define me or dictate my future.

Charley and our baby are my future.

Now it's time for me to step up and hit that grand slam.

charley

"THERE. DONE."

I shut down my laptop for the day, my last day before maternity leave kicks in.

Standing, I grab my lower back which seems to protest twenty-four seven these days.

A sudden pain in my chest grips me. "Nugget, you can stop kicking my ribs any time now."

As though protesting, the baby gets one last solid thump in before settling down. "Always gotta have the last word already. You're definitely a Reynolds."

I turn at the soft rapping of knuckles on my door and smile when I see Emma. "Hey. I just finished up and was going to come look for you."

"Hey," she says, with a smile, walking farther into my office. "Get everything wrapped up?"

"Yep." I put a hand on a stack of file folders. "These are the upcoming events while I'm out. I've scanned all the paperwork to the share drive, and all the budgeting is on there as well. But these files have the initial questionnaire and a printout of the summary and timeline of each event."

She nods. "Got it. Efficient as always, Charley. Thank you."

"You're welcome." I sigh and look around. "I guess that's it."

"Before you go,"—Emma walks back to the door and gives the "come here" gesture to someone before turning back to me— "you've got some visitors."

My heart beats hard against my chest, wondering if one of them is Nate.

I want it to be and yet I don't. I'm not strong enough to face him, but I also miss the hell out of him.

So when Darcy walks through the door with Megan behind her, I'm devastated, relieved, and shocked.

"Darcy? What are you doing here?"

She smiles and comes around the desk to hug me. "I had some time off and wanted to see how you were doing. And since you can't travel, here I am."

She pulls back and looks down at my belly. "You look like you're about to pop."

"Yeah, I seem to have exploded in the last three weeks."

"How are you feeling?"

"Mostly just tired. My back aches like a bitch. And I have to pee every five minutes. At my last appointment, the doctor said it could be any day now." I gesture to the chairs, as I sit down gingerly. "Y'all have a seat."

Darcy and Megan take the seats in front of my desk, while Emma remains standing. I glance around the room, puzzled.

Why do I feel an intervention is about to take place?

"I can tell by the look on your face you don't buy I'm just here to visit," Darcy says, leaning back in her chair.

I tilt my head. "As much as I love seeing you, why are you here?"

Megan speaks up. "What's stopping you from being with Nate? Is it because you think all men leave you? I know you love him."

I rear back, anger coursing through me. "Of course I love him, but he pushed me away, Megan."

She nods. "Oh, I know he did. But I also know you, Charley.

Between what you and Aidan have told me, you did your fair share of pushing away too. Or at least keeping him at arm's length."

I keep my face passive, not wanting to acknowledge what she's saying. And trying desperately to keep my blood pressure down and not lose my shit with my best friend.

"I know he's your brother and you love him, but you don't get to bring my past up, Megan. You don't know what you're talking about. You weren't there."

"No, but Aidan was."

"And so was I," Emma says.

My eyes bulge as I look back and forth between them, my heart pounding. "No. This is not on me." My words are laced with all the hurt and anger coursing through me. "Nate made a major decision without even factoring me or the baby into it."

I hold up a hand, still seething. "And I know you warned me, Megan. And I did a shitty job heeding your warning. But I thought at the very least, he'd give me a heads-up before making a decision that impacts our future."

My voice cracks on the last word. Megan reaches out and takes my hand. "I know he did, and he really screwed up. Trust me, he's suffering."

I swipe at a tear. "You saw him?"

"Yeah, that's where I went last week."

"H-how is he?"

I hate my voice wobbles. I hate I even asked.

"Miserable. Grumpy. He asked about you. Wants to know how you're feeling."

I sniff and lift my chin. "Well, I hope you told him I'm perfectly fine. Feeling just fine."

Emma crosses her arms over her chest. "Charley, did I ever tell you about how things went down between Shane and me?"

I shake my head.

"I don't know how much you remember about my mom and dad, but my childhood wasn't stellar. Your mom and dad were more like my parents than my own. But even with all their love and support, I ended up becoming an addict like my dad. Just a different vice."

She's quiet a moment before continuing. "I thought it would be easier if I kept everyone at arm's length, never letting anyone in." She shrugged. "I mean, our situations aren't the same. But trauma is still trauma."

Looking down, she shakes her head. "It took me losing everything before I realized if I was ever going to move forward in any part of my life, I was going to need to let my past go."

"How did you do it?"

"It wasn't easy, I'm not going to lie. My sobriety was tested. My reputation was questioned. My heart was broken."

She raises her eyes to mine and smiles. "I threw Shane out of my house and out of my life. But he wouldn't let me get away so easily."

Intrigued, I tilt my head. "What'd he do?"

Her laughter fills my office. "He tore up my resignation letter, told me he couldn't live without me, and without getting mired in details, made me a deal I couldn't refuse. So I didn't. He loved me despite all my flaws. And in the end, it was all I needed to know."

I sit back in my chair. I thought I had let my guard down with Nate. But the truth is, I didn't let him in all the way. I made sure to learn about him and what made him tick, but I never reciprocated the way he did.

And I made sure I left him before he could leave me. I trusted him and yet I stuck to the pattern I'd set up for myself a long time ago.

And I'm in the same place I'm always in.

Alone.

Except this time I don't want to be.

I drop my head into my hands. "Oh my God. I totally screwed this all up."

"Well, in fairness," Megan says, "it's not all on you. Nate did his fair share of screwing this all up too. But I think you guys can get through it."

"How?" I cry, lifting up and looking at her. "He's in Florida, and I'm here." I swipe at another tear that rolls down my cheek.

"Charley," Darcy says, scooting to the edge of her chair, "what if there was a way I could help?"

I furrow my brow. "What do you mean? You plan to move the team to Madison Ridge? Make Nate's contract null and void?"

A smile plays on her lips. "What if I offered you a job?"

Is she crazy? My eyes widen and I tilt my head at her, trying to convey the message, "My boss is standing right there!" with my eyes.

Darcy laughs and I shoot a look at Emma, who is…smiling?

"Has my pregnant brain finally rendered me stupid?"

"No, I'm serious. I'm reorganizing the marketing and communications group. It's created some new positions, and one of those is manager of events. And I want that to be you."

My jaw drops. "Me? You want me?"

"I do."

"Why? I mean, I'm flattered but I just started doing this a few months ago."

"I know, but Emma and I chatted for a bit earlier and she spoke highly of you."

"What?" I didn't know whether to feel flattered or not.

Darcy chuckles. "I'm not trying to poach you. Emma told me about your work a few months ago before I met you."

I point back and forth between her and Emma. "Y'all know each other?"

"Sure," Emma says, "we met years ago at a marketing convention and hit it off. Talked off and on since."

Darcy's eyes sparkle. "Imagine my surprise when I found out Nate's girlfriend and this up-and-coming go-getter working for my friend are one and the same."

"Huh. Small world," I murmur.

It seems no matter how I look at it, Nate and I are connected.

Hope rises in my chest. Is that my sign I should go for it?

Shed my old ways and start a new chapter in life? Not just with the baby but with my heart too?

But what if Nate decides I'm not worth the trouble? How will I be able to work for the same organization as him?

A stabbing pain makes me inhale sharply, and the thought of seeing him and not being with him makes me ache.

But there's no way of getting around seeing him, regardless of our relationship status. It's time to face my fears instead of running from them.

It will be scary starting over with just me and the baby, but I want to show my child they can do anything if they commit to it.

And I'm committed to being a new Charley Reynolds.

I look over at Emma, whose eyes are shining, but her mouth is curved in a smile. "Emma...I—"

"Need to take the job. Yes, I know."

"That's not...but..."

Emma crosses to me and squats down, taking my hands in hers. "Charley, I love you. I want you to be happy. If I were in your shoes and had the opportunity to be with the love of my life? I would take it and run. No questions asked."

"You would?"

"Absolutely." She glances down at my belly. "Especially if I were about to have his baby and wanted nothing more than to share the experience with him."

"But I just started for you. You took a chance on me. What are you going to do for these events?" I gasp. "Oh my God, your wedding!"

She pushes a lock of hair out of my face. "You can still help me plan the wedding. That's why we FaceTime and Zoom. As far as the rest of it, that's for Shane and me to handle. And yeah, I did take a chance on you, and you exceeded our expectations. You've learned so much in such a short time. You're going to do amazing things with Darcy and the Bull Sharks."

I stare at my wonderful cousin. I can never repay her for the chance she gave me. Guilt and shame try to worm their way in, but the look on Emma's face is nothing but joy.

We stand, and I give her the biggest hug I can with a nine-months-pregnant belly. "Thank you," I whisper into her hair.

"Make me proud, lady."

I pull back and turn to Darcy. "I accept your offer."

Darcy claps and jumps up to hug me. "Welcome to the Bull Sharks family."

I smile, but there's a pain in my chest because I want to call Nate. Tell him the great news and see if we can talk. Work things out.

We have too much at stake to throw it away over fears. Deep-seated fears, but fears, nonetheless.

I'd rather conquer them with him than without him.

I just hope he feels the same way.

Emma's phone pings and she looks at the screen. She bites her lip and glances toward Megan and Darcy.

"Charley," Emma says, putting away her phone, "before you leave, I need you to take a look at one last thing for me for one of the upcoming events."

"Sure."

I hug Megan and Darcy goodbye with promises to call and get together before Darcy leaves tomorrow.

"We need to go outside, so grab your coat," Emma says.

"Okay."

We bundle up and head out into the darkness. The sun has set, and the night is still and cold. I follow Emma around to the back of the building.

"Didn't you tell me one of the couples met here and the gazebo holds a special place for them?" she asks.

I purse my lips, trying to think about the upcoming events.

And try not to think about how close that sounds to the night I met Nate.

I shake my head. "I'm sorry, Em. Must be the pregnancy brain because I can't remember which couple that is."

Well, I can, but that's not the answer to her question.

"That's okay," she says with a grin. "But I was wondering if you think she might like this."

She opens the door to an electrical box and flips a switch.

The gazebo lights up and I gasp.

Several mason jars sit along the rail and bench, lights inside them twinkling. More lights hang from the roof line in long strings. They dance in the wind.

All the lights look like…fireflies.

Tears fill my eyes at the beauty of it all.

But the lights dim in comparison to the beauty standing in the middle of the gazebo. My jaw drops.

"Oh my God. He's here."

Goose bumps slide along my skin, and adrenaline rushes through me when I see him.

Nate Gentry makes my knees weak no matter how he looks, but Nate Gentry in his charcoal-gray game day suit is a force to be reckoned with.

And I'm powerless against the surge of love I feel for him with my entire being.

"Your future's waiting, Charley," Emma says. "Go get him."

THIRTY-ONE

MY BREATH HITCHES when I see Charley.

She's never looked more beautiful, and I missed her so fucking much.

Her belly is huge, and pride swells in my chest.

Those gorgeous blue eyes I get lost in are wide as she walks toward me, surrounded by lights.

Before she can take the step up into the gazebo, I'm there holding out my hand to help her up.

When her fingers clasp around mine, the spark I feel every time shoots up my arm.

I want to pull her into my chest and never let her go. But I don't want to scare her off.

One step at a time, Gentry.

Her perfume floats in the breeze, and I take a moment just to look at her.

The lights cast a warm glow across her face, and her white sweater makes her dark hair look almost black.

She's stunning, and I hope in the next few minutes, she'll be all mine.

Nervous doesn't begin to describe how I feel.

"Hey, Charley. Are you feeling okay?"

Her hands automatically go to her belly, rubbing it. "Yeah. Tired, but that's to be expected."

"No issues?"

"No. I'm good for a woman about to give birth any day now."

I swallow hard as she looks at the mason jars sitting on the railing around us. "What is all this?"

I rub the back of my neck. "Well, the idea was to have fireflies in the jars but then I found out it's too cold for them right now and they wouldn't light up anyway. So, I did what I thought was the next best thing."

She rolls in her lips and her eyes shine, taking in the scene around her. Then she straightens her spine and meets my stare.

"What are you doing here?"

"I love you, Charley," I blurt out.

Way to go slow, man.

I look down and huff out a laugh. "I meant to be a little smoother than that."

When I glance up, utter shock is painted across her face.

My mouth goes dry, and before I lose my nerve, I need to get the words out.

"Charlotte, I fell in love with you that very first night. And not because we had mind-blowing sex, but because you brought out a side to me I haven't felt in more years than I can count. You treated me like Nate Gentry the man, not Nate Gentry the commodity.

"And the more time I spent with you, the more I wanted to be a better man. When you told me you were pregnant, I was shocked, no doubt. But I've loved that baby since I knew it existed."

"Nate..." Her whisper is soft in the air, but I hold up a hand.

"Wait, let me get this out. Please."

She nods and I let out a deep breath, settling my nerves. Nerves that are far worse than my first at bat in the majors.

"Baseball has been my first love nearly my whole life, but over the last few weeks I've learned that while the game saved me when I needed saving, it's a fickle mistress who wants all my time and energy."

I meet her eyes. "I told you before, it's a part of me, but it's just a part. It's not the whole me. And I no longer need it."

"What changed?"

"I lived life without you. And it was fucking miserable." I glance out into the surrounding darkness that reminds me how my soul felt the last few weeks. "I drank too much and began to see my father every time I looked in the mirror. I didn't want to turn into him and subject my child to that."

I smile, bringing my gaze back to her. "Then, some wise people I know came to visit and essentially told me to get my head out of my ass before I lost the best thing that ever happened to me." I blow out a breath, my stomach quivering. "I also visited my parents' graves for the first time."

Her eyes shine with unshed tears, but she tilts her head, doubt shadowing her eyes. Doubt I put there with my dumbass actions. "But you still signed the contract and didn't even tell me."

I blow out a breath, shame coursing through me. "I know. I'm so sorry. I should have talked to you. All I can tell you is I was scared."

"Scared? Of what?"

"What being part of a relationship felt like. But most of all, I was scared of how much I love you."

Her chin lifts. "Me or the baby?"

I take a step toward her, my heart leaping with hope when she doesn't take a step away.

"Both of you. But right now, this is just about you and me, Firefly."

She inhales sharply at the nickname I gave her and looks away. "How do I know you won't shut me out again the next time you get scared? Things are about to get real terrifying, Nate."

She isn't going to make this easy for me and I expect no less.

That's my girl.

"I know. And I know my recent actions haven't done anything

to make you trust me, but I swear to you, I'm all in, Charley. Terrified or not, I'm all in."

She bites her lip as a tear slips down her cheek. I move in closer because I'm desperate to be near her.

"An apology seems so inconsequential for how much I hurt you. But all I can do is show you how much I love you every day for the rest of my life, and I'll never leave you again. If you'll let me."

I close the distance between us and cradle her face in my hands. "My whole life, all I've done is survive. Going through the motions. The money, baseball, the career, it means nothing without you."

Her eyes search mine. "But how are we going to make it work? You'll be traveling all the time."

"My manager's contract is null and void."

Her jaw drops. "What? Nate, no. I know you're not ready to leave baseball behind. I saw it in your eyes at the ceremony."

"I said my manager's contract is voided. But I have a new contract. I'm going to be working in the front office for the Bull Sharks starting in the spring. And my home office base is here in Madison Ridge."

"Here? In Madison Ridge?" The end of her sentence ends on a high pitch.

"I told them the only way I'd take the job is if I could do something where I could do most of my work here. We have a family to raise, and I'm not doing it from the road. I will have to go to Florida occasionally, but maybe you and Nugget could come with me."

"Nate, I won't—"

I lay a finger on her lips. "You're my life now, Charlotte Reynolds. You've given me love I didn't think I deserved, a family I thought I was too broken for, and a life that's more than a series of long road trips and nine innings. Baseball is still going to be a part of my life. But in a smaller capacity."

She frowns at me.

"Why are you frowning?"

"Nate, you can't move here."

I rear back. "Why not? I thought that's what you wanted so we could be together."

"Of course, I want to be with you. I love you. But you can't move here because after this baby is born and I get the all clear, I'm moving to Cape Sands."

Confusion whips through me. But one thing she said makes it through the fog. I blink once. Twice. "You love me?"

She smiles and lays her hands on my chest. My heart pounds under her touch. "Yes, I love you. Haven't you been listening to me? By the way, I was scared too. I'm sorry I didn't let you in. It just felt like if I loved you the way I wanted to, you'd leave me. I thought I could just let you go when you got too close."

With a head shake and a smile, she moves her hands up and grips the lapels of my jacket, pulling me as close as her belly will allow. "But you aren't so easy to shake, Nate Gentry. And I'd rather take the risk than be alone and wonder what if."

I drop my forehead to hers, gripping her hips. "I left because you asked me to, Charley, but also because I thought you deserved better than the broken version of me. Leaving you was the last thing I wanted to do."

"I want all versions of you, Nate. The broken, the put together, the baseball legend, the guy who likes rocky road ice cream. They all make up the man I fell in love with. And I'll only be happy if you're with me."

She takes my face in her hands. "Also, I want you to know that I can handle the issues with the press. Don't ever try to leave me thinking you're protecting me from that."

"I'm never leaving you, Firefly."

"Good."

Her grin sets me on fire and my heart swells.

I can't wait any longer.

My lips crush to hers, and with a moan, she kisses me back

with as much passion as she did the first time we kissed in this very spot.

A thought breaks through the haze. "Hold on. Did you say you're moving to Cape Sands?"

Her smile lights up my insides. "Yep."

"How?"

"I'll get a moving truck and—"

I kiss her hard. "God, I've missed your sassy mouth."

With a laugh, she wraps her arms around my waist and looks up at me, love shining in her blue depths. "Darcy offered me a job. She's reorganizing the sales and marketing department and has a job for an event director."

A warmth spreads through my heart. "And you accepted?"

"I did." Her face grows serious. "I came to the same conclusion you did. That the best thing in my life was about to slip through my fingers. I was going to fight for us. But even if I'd lost you, our baby needs to be near his or her father. I would never take that opportunity away from you. No matter how we turned out."

Just when I didn't think I could love this woman any more, she proves me wrong.

I have a feeling she'll be proving me wrong for the rest of my life.

"I love the fuck out of you, Charley."

"I love you too, Nate. So much it scares me."

"Wanna be scared together for the rest of our lives?"

"Sounds perfect."

I lean forward to kiss her, when a look of pain crosses her face and she doubles over. Panic claws at my throat as she grabs my arm in a tight grasp. "Charley, are you okay?"

"I-I'm not sure." She breathes out through her mouth and then straightens slowly. "I think I'm in labor."

"Are you sure?"

She nods and then her eyes are wide on mine.

"What happened?"

"My water just broke."

"How do you know?"

"Because my pants are wet."

I earned the nickname Iceman in baseball because no one intimidated me. I faced down one hundred mile per hour balls both behind the plate and at the plate.

But that man is nowhere to be found when faced with Charley telling me her water broke.

"Holy shit. Okay, let's go."

I'm shaking like a leaf but pick up Charley in a bridal carry.

"Nate, put me down. You'll ruin your suit!"

"I'll buy another damn suit."

She looks up at me, her arms draped around my neck, and the world goes calm around me.

In her eyes, I see our future. One full of laughter, love, and family. It's everything I've always wanted and never thought I'd have.

"Ready to go have our baby, Firefly?"

She nods with a tremulous smile, and it's like she's reached in and squeezed my heart. "As long as you're with me, I'm ready for anything."

The woman is pure magic.

And all mine.

epilogue 1

CHARLEY

Three months later

I TUG on the hem of my suit jacket and run a hand over my ponytail, smoothing out the flyaways.

It's my first day on the job as Events Manager for the Florida Bull Sharks and the first time I'll be away from my baby girl since she was born.

Between the two, my stomach is a jumble of nerves that has me on the verge of being sick.

Fortunately, Nate doesn't start in the front office for another two weeks, so he'll get to play Mr. Mom until then. After that, the new nanny will be here to take care of Lucy.

It took a few weeks to find the right fit for a nanny. Some were too old, some were too young—and did nothing but make "fuck me" eyes at Nate—and some of them made me think of drill sergeants.

Then one day, the service sent over Julian's resume. He had an impeccable record, a degree in education, and recently moved to Cape Sands with his husband.

He's also six-three and looks like he should be a bouncer in a club rather than a man dealing with kids.

Nate and I thought we were being pranked until he picked up a crying Lucy and started singing a lullaby. She immediately went quiet and stared at Julian with wide eyes.

We hired him on the spot.

I nod at my reflection, grab my bag, and head downstairs, searching for the loves of my life. I still have forty-five minutes before I need to leave, and I want to soak in all the baby snuggles I can.

Some days, I can't believe this is my life.

"Nate? Where are you?"

No response.

I follow the faint sounds of a morning show into the living room and stop in front of the sofa.

My heart flips in my chest and my ovaries explode.

Nate's stretched out, fast asleep, and wearing nothing but gray sweatpants and a burp cloth draped over one shoulder.

In the middle of his chest, directly over his heart, lies our baby girl, Lucy. Her little legs are pulled up to her chest, causing her diaper-clad butt to stick out. Her little hand curls into a tiny fist against Nate's broad chest.

She sleeping as soundly as her daddy, her mouth forming an O.

Tears make my vision blurry. I haven't even left yet and the pull in my gut is almost unbearable.

I'm going to miss the hell out of both of them.

After my water broke in the gazebo, Lucy showed up eight hours later. Nate was by my side the entire time. He fed me ice chips and didn't complain when I crushed his hand during contractions.

And I fell in love with him all over again when he cried holding a five-minute-old Lucy.

That girl already has her daddy wrapped around her tiny finger.

As soon as we were able, Lucy and I moved to Cape Sands permanently, living with Nate in his beautiful seaside home.

I miss Madison Ridge more than I thought I would, but I talk to someone in my family almost daily, and Darcy has become a great friend to me.

I'm excited about my job and starting a new chapter in my life.

I gingerly pick up Lucy off Nate's chest, and when I rub circles on the smooth skin of her back, she curls into my shoulder with a soft sigh. I inhale her fresh baby scent before placing her in the bassinet set up in the living room.

A pair of arms wrap around my waist.

"Hey, Firefly."

Nate's deep, sleep-laden voice in my ear sets off a host of sparks, all landing right between my legs.

"Hello, handsome."

He rests his chin on my shoulder, looking down at Lucy. "God, she is just so beautiful. Just like her mother."

I grin and tilt my head, giving him better access to my neck, where he drops kisses on it.

"Hey, come with me for a minute," he says, stepping away from me.

"But–"

"She'll be fine."

He grabs the baby monitor and my hand, pulling me into his office down the hall. Closing the door behind him, he leans against it, his eyes taking a slow, heated tour of my body.

"You look sexy as fuck in that suit, babe." He tosses the baby monitor onto a nearby chair.

"Thank you." The look of desire in his eyes makes my skin flush under the suit.

"I keep thinking about what you're wearing under your little skirt, and it's driving me crazy."

His gray sweatpants don't hide the massive hard-on he's sporting as he stalks toward me, all broad shoulders and muscles.

There's a gleam in his eye, like a predator after its prey.

I'm happy to be devoured by him anytime.

I've been insecure about my body since having Lucy. I haven't lost all the baby weight yet, but since we'd gotten the green light at my six-week checkup, Nate can't keep his hands off me.

I step back until my ass hits the desk. "Well, it should give you something to think about all day."

His grin is wicked as he shakes his head. "Oh no, baby. You're going to show me before you leave."

"No way. You're not messing with my hair, Gentry."

He stops in front of me, close enough my chest brushes against his when I breathe, but he doesn't touch me.

His smoldering hazel eyes hold me captive.

"Turn around, Charley."

"Nate, I—"

"Turn around, Charlotte."

A shiver runs down my spine at his demanding tone.

It's hot as hell.

I follow his directions, feeling his intense gaze on my back.

His hand lands in the middle of my shoulder blades and bends me over his desk, before hiking up my skirt around my hips, baring my ass to him.

My core clenches in anticipation of having Nate inside me.

He whistles low as his hands squeeze me. "God, I love this ass. If it's possible, it's even more perfect than before the baby."

A sharp slap makes me gasp, then moan, pushing back against him.

"You want my cock, Firefly? Want me to come in your tight pussy?"

"Yes..." I drop my forehead to the desk. The need to be fucked by the man who owns my soul slices through me.

He reaches around and, with amazing accuracy, zeros in on my clit. His magic fingers work me into a panting, frenzied mess.

Pulling my thong aside, he rubs the head of his dick along my slit.

"Oh yeah, you're wet and ready. I'm going to fuck you so hard wearing this suit you're going to think of me every time you sit down."

"Please..." Like every time, he has me near delirious with need for him.

He leans over me, caging me between his broad naked chest and the desk, dropping kisses on the back of my neck. Warmth surges through me, and without warning, he thrusts into me, filling and stretching me, before pulling out and slamming back in.

I cry out his name, begging for more.

"This isn't going to take long, baby."

He grips my hips and sets a punishing pace. Each stroke is deeper than the last and as always, no matter what position, Nate manages to find the spot that sets me off.

"I feel you clenching around me, baby. You're going to make me come."

"Yes, come for me, Nate."

A few more thrusts and we're both flying off the cliff together, breathless and sated.

Moments later, we're cleaned up and I'm straightening my skirt.

He wraps his arms around my waist. "The plan was to bring you in here to talk once Lucy fell asleep. But then you came down in that outfit and fried my brain."

"It's a suit!"

He shrugs. "I love you and you turn me on—what can I say?"

I laugh, rolling up on my toes to kiss him. "I love you more."

"Not possible."

A cry comes from the baby monitor on the couch. I clap. "Oh good, she's up. I want some baby snuggles before I leave."

I head out to the living room and lift Lucy out of the bassinet. Her crying turns to little mewls that pull at my heartstrings.

"Hello, my sweet baby." I kiss her soft hair, swaying back and forth with her in my arms.

She smells like baby powder and fresh baby laundry detergent. I love her so much; I just want to hold her all the time so I never miss a moment.

Honestly, I never thought this would be me. Before, having kids was such a far-off notion for me, I wasn't sure I'd have them.

While it wasn't in my master plan to get pregnant from a one-night stand, I wouldn't change a thing.

"Let's go find Daddy," I say, kissing her forehead.

"He's right here."

I turn around and Nate's behind me, holding up a small gift bag.

"What's this?"

"Open it."

"Now?"

"Preferably."

"Okay…" I tilt my head, studying him as I hand over Lucy and take the bag. He clears his throat and a muscle in his cheek tics.

Is he nervous?

Inside the bag is a square iconic turquoise box.

Oh my God…

My breath catches as I pull it out, my heart pounding in my ears. "Nate…" I whisper.

When I open the box, I can hardly breathe.

Nestled inside, a diamond solitaire sits between two of the bluest sapphires I've ever seen in my life.

I look up to find Nate, holding our baby girl, on his knee, his hazel eyes intent on mine.

"I know it's not a conventional solitaire, but nothing about you and me has been conventional."

I chuckle, tears making my vision blur. "That's true."

"Plus, the sapphires reminded me of your beautiful blue eyes."

"Oh, Nate." I clasp a hand over my mouth, staring at the ring, my heart racing.

He looks at Lucy and back at me. "And this isn't the way I'd planned to propose, but honestly I can't think of anything better than having her with us." He grins that panty-melting grin he saves just for me. "Truth be told, I couldn't wait any longer."

I swipe at a tear. "Oh, Nate. It's perfect."

"I haven't even gotten started. But here we go." He clears his throat, the grin disappears from his face, and he looks me in the eye.

"Charlotte Reynolds, when I opened the door that night, I took one look at you and knew it was game over. And not because you looked smokin' hot in that dress."

He grins and I laugh. "Seriously though, somehow I knew you were meant to be mine. It was magic." His lips curve up on one side. "And I'm not really a guy who believes in magic when it comes to love. I never thought I'd be the guy who found his person.

"But here I am. A man, standing in front of the woman I'd lay down my life for, holding the child we created together, asking her to be his wife. I'm not nearly good enough for you, but I'll spend the rest of my life showing you no one will love you more than I love you."

He shifts Lucy in his arms and takes the ring from the box. He holds my stare when he says the next words.

"Marry me, Firefly. Make my heart whole. Because my life just isn't complete if you're not in it."

Happy tears fall down my cheeks. "Yes, yes, yes."

I hold up my hand and the sun catches the light of the diamond as he slides the ring on my finger. It fits perfectly.

He slides a hand behind my neck and pulls me to him. Our kiss is sweet and lingers until Lucy starts to fuss.

We laugh, and Nate wraps his strong arms around me and draws me in, the three of us together.

We may have had an unexpected beginning, but now we're in this love forever.

Thank you so much for reading **UNEXPECTED FOREVER**! Want

more Nate & Charley? Scan the QR Code below to subscribe to my mailing list or tap here and you'll receive access to the bonus scene!

Already a subscriber? Check out the latest newsletter for the link to the bonus content!

UF Bonus code

epilogue 2

CHASE

I DON'T WANT to be staring at Eden Mitchell right now. It fucks with my head whenever I see her.

Just when I finally feel like I'm starting to put my life back together and find my little bit of peace here in Cape Sands, Eden Mitchell shows up.

How the hell did she find me anyway?

"Hello, Chase."

Her voice is controlled, cultured in a way it wasn't a few years ago. It's sexy as hell and rubs me the wrong way.

She's changed her hair since I last saw her. It's longer, brushing past her shoulders. Where it once reminded me of dark, smooth caramel, now it reminds me of honey.

And her eyes?

Fuck, those eyes have always been my undoing. All the greens and blues that swirl in them. Depending on her mood, some colors are more prominent than others.

Right now, they're a dark blue and wary.

Shake it off, Hanover. You sound like a damn pussy waxing poetic over her eyes and comparing her hair to food.

"What do you want, Eden?"

"I want to talk to you."

"What could we possibly have to talk about?" I narrow my eyes and cross my arms over my chest. "Did Liz send you out here?"

For the last few weeks, my agent has been trying to get me on the phone for more than five minutes.

And while she's the best agent in the business, I'm going to fire her ass as soon as possible if she helped Eden find me.

It would be just like her to do that as a way to get me to call her.

"No. But I do have some business I'd like to discuss with you."

"Business, huh?" The muscle in my cheek tics, and my jaw clenches. If I don't let up, I'll break a tooth.

Nate clears his throat and starts to back away. "You know what? I'm starving. I think I'll head back to see...yeah..."

I don't respond, unsure of what will spew out of my mouth that I'll be sorry for later.

Nate drives off a few moments later, and there's nothing but sounds of the wind and seagulls between us.

"I don't care what business you want to discuss, Eden. I can't help you. There's your answer. Now get the hell off my property."

"I'm not leaving, Chase. Not until you hear me out." She straightens her spine and drops her hands to her hips. "You owe me at least that much."

My gaze flits down to her chest where her blouse stretches across her breasts that move up and down with her breaths. Breasts that I...

No, damn it!

I focus on her words and let the angry part of me lead the way.

My eyes snap back to hers. "Owe you? I don't owe anyone anything, Eden. You'd do best to remember that."

That isn't entirely true.

We've done our fair share of hurting each other, and my actions are no small part of that.

I should try to hear her out, but I know what will happen if she's around me for too long.

She's my fucking kryptonite, and I'm no superhero.

Her eyes flash green fire, and the defiant look in them makes the blood rush to my dick.

Fucking A.

"I'd do best to remember that? Who the fuck do you think you're talking to, Hanover? I'm not some minion on your team or one of your little groupies."

My palms itch to touch her.

I scoff. "I remember once upon a time when you loved being my personal groupie, Sunshine."

Silence hangs heavy between us.

It's a shitty thing to say, no matter how I feel about her now. And I don't mean it in the way it came out.

I hate how the nickname I'd given her in college slips off my tongue, and I want to take that back too.

Nicknames like that signal affection, and I don't have the capacity to give any woman—but especially this one—that sort of thing.

I put my hands on my hips and look down for a moment. After a couple of deep breaths, I lift my head to meet her angry gaze. "Eden, level with me. What do you want?"

She continues to stare at me for a moment before clearing her throat. "My company was hired by a group to plan and coordinate a charity ball. Big names, high rollers. But my A-list keynote speaker is now…indisposed."

"And you want me to be your keynote speaker."

"Yes."

"No."

I walk toward the ladder and bend down to gather my tools.

She's hot on my heels. "What do you mean, no?"

I raise up and look her in the eye. "As in the opposite of yes."

"But you barely listened to me."

I place the drill in the tool bag and hoist it up.

Pain radiates down my arm, but I keep the wince off my face. I'd overdone it today and my shoulder is protesting.

Loudly.

"Sure I did. You lost your keynote speaker and you want me to take his place. Bail you out. I said no." I raise a brow and smirk. "I think it's pretty simple. But then, you always were the queen of complicated."

Damn, she really can bring out the asshole in me. But I need to push her away, send her back to New York. Get her the fuck off my island.

Four years isn't long enough to get her out of my system since I can't continue to look at her and not want to touch her.

She's my own personal heaven and hell all rolled into one.

Why the hell does she want me to be her speaker anyway? I'm a bad bet and we both know it.

I walk past her toward my truck, pushing away the stab in my chest when hurt flashes through her eyes just before anger settles back in.

And fuck, if she doesn't smell the same as she always had, a heady mix of vanilla and amber. Rich with just a touch of sweetness.

I don't even want to think about if she tastes the same.

"Chase." Eden follows me to the back of the truck, where I lift the tool bag over the side and drop it in with a loud clatter.

"What?" I ask, turning back to her. I roll my shoulders in an effort to keep the pain in my right one from taking me out.

"The least you could do is hear me out. Let me tell you the whole story." The sun shines onto her hair, lighting up the blonde-colored strands. "I don't like mixing business and personal—"

"Then don't."

She sighs heavily and looks away for a moment, before bringing her gaze back to mine. "I'd owe you big. Please. Just listen to what I have to say?"

"What more could you have to say? You asked; I said no."

She rubs her forehead, and that vertical line between her eyes tells me she's mentally counting to ten.

"Let me just give you all the details before you totally shut me down. I promise I won't take much of your time."

I search her eyes for anything that signals she's putting me on. But all I find is determination with a side helping of desperation.

Shit.

I never could say no to this woman, not since the day I met her. That's part of my problem when it comes to her.

I twirl my keys on my index finger, looking away. There's no way in hell I'm ever going back to the city that's ground zero to the demise of my career and personal life.

But listening to why she's here seems to be the only way to get her back over the bridge and out of my life.

"If I listen, will that get you on a plane back to New York any faster?"

Quiet for a moment, she finally says with a nod, "Yes."

"Okay, fine." I jerk open the driver's side door and slide in. "Meet me at my house at three. I'll hear you out, but my answer won't change."

I slam the door to put some steel between us.

She moves closer to the open window. The breeze catches at that moment, and her unique scent tickles my senses.

"Thank you, Chase." When I start the engine and drop it into gear, her eyes widen. "Wait, where's your house?"

I smirk. "You have a way of finding out things, Eden. I'm sure you'll figure it out. I gotta go."

With my chin, I nod in the direction of her SUV. "You might want to go ahead and move that monstrosity of a vehicle off the curb. I don't want to have to help you out if you get stuck in the sand."

She rolls her eyes and makes a noise that resembles a growl but walks away without another word.

In the side mirror, I watch her stalk back to her vehicle.

My gaze stays on her ass and legs that look a million miles long in those sexy-as-fuck heels. I lean my head back and close my eyes.

I'm in so much fucking trouble.
Again.

WHAT CAN you expect from Mine Forever?
- Second chance
- Lovers to enemies to lovers
- One bed
- Possessive hero
- Small town sports
- It's always been you
- College sweethearts
- Pierced MMC
- Forced proximity - trapped in a hurricane
- All. The. Spice! 🌶️🌶️🌶️

PRE-ORDER MINE FOREVER - Coming September 25, 2024!

Thank you so much for reading **UNEXPECTED FOREVER**! Want more Nate & Charley? Scan the QR Code below to subscribe to my mailing list or tap here and you'll receive access to the bonus scene!

Already a subscriber? Check out the latest newsletter for the link to the bonus content!

UF Bonus code

up next

Want to know Chase and Eden's story?
Check out Mine Forever!

Two broken hearts that never mended. An impossible favor. And a hurricane that forces us to share a bed.

I had it all – a legendary baseball career, sponsorships, all the women I could want.

But the only one I wanted was Eden Mitchell, the woman who gave me her heart years ago until I broke it.

It was only a matter of time before my house of cards came tumbling down in a public scandal that ruined my career for good.

I had no choice but to return to my hometown of Cape Sands.

Then Eden finds me, asking for my help to save her business.

I've never been able to deny her, especially when she begs, but it means traveling to the scene of my demise.

Hard pass.

She doesn't know the whole truth about my downfall, and I don't want her to know.

But when a hurricane traps us in my house, with only one bed, we can't keep our hands off each other.

I want to win her heart again. And going back to my past is the best way to do it.

My head says hell no, but my body and heart say to make her mine forever.

What can you expect from Mine Forever?
- Second chance
- Lovers to enemies to lovers
- One bed
- Possessive hero
- Small town sports
- College Sweethearts
- Pierced MMC
- Forced Proximity - trapped in a hurricane
- All the Spice! 🌶🌶🌶

get a sneak peek of all things eliza!

If you'd like exclusive content, first look at cover reveals, bonus material and other announcements first, join my weekly newsletter, The Sneak Peake!

Want to stay up to date on all things Eliza? Then get exclusive access to ARC's, giveaways, and all the book fun in a drama free zone, by joining my reader group, Eliza Peake's Posse. We have a fun group going and growing all the time!

acknowledgments

Whew. I gave my heart and soul to this book. I've been with Nate and Charley for a long time now and I thought this might be the book that broke me. Turns out life broke me. But I came back and it might be a year late, but Nate and Charley are out in the wild!

There are a ton of people to thank for helping me get this book out into the world. I'll do my best to remember them all, but I'm sure I'll forget someone and if I do, please know it wasn't intentional.

To the Ann's at Happily Editing Ann's, Julianne Fangmann at Heart to Cover, Wander Aguiar, Katie Phillips, Tiffany Hernandez, Rachel Hill, the Small Town Steam Group, Amanda Anderson, Melanie Harlow and the Harlot Authors group, Richelle Emory, Jackie Walker, Melissa Ivers, Lilian Harris, Loren Beeson, Kassie Geist, Mary Carson, Emily Silver, the Peake Posse, my ARC team, bookstagrammers and bloggers who took a chance on me, and to my readers all over the world! You all had a profound impact on me at some point in this journey!

To Mr. P and Nat for supporting and being patient with me when I have deadlines, talk your ears off about things you don't understand, and promoting me everywhere you go. Including the Starbucks drive thru line and the doctor's office.

And to God, for blessing me with all of the people in my life supporting me and for bringing my dream to life.

XOXO
Eliza

about the author

Hey y'all! I'm Eliza and I write steamy, all the feels romance full of heart, heat, and humor. My heroes are swoony alphas, my heroines are strong and audacious, and family is at the center of it all.

I'm a proud mom and a Southern girl who can bless a heart with the best of them. I live with my very own book boyfriend, a snoring dog, and a sassy cat.

In my downtime, I read all the panty-melting romances I can get my hands on, drink coffee by day, wine by night, and indulge my woo-woo side as often as possible. I'm also hopelessly addicted to tacos.

I dream of retiring to the beach someday where I'll continue writing sexy romance stories to my heart's content and taking sunrise and sunset walks in the sand, thinking of my next book!

Join my newsletter, The Sneak Peake, to get updates on all sorts of shenanigans, exclusive content, and news on books and appearances at http://elizapeake.com/subscribe/